UNCOMPLICATED CHOICES

CARA DEE

unc♡mplicated choices

Edited by Silently Correcting Your Grammar, LLC.
Formatting by Eliza Rae Services.
Proofreading by Rachel Lawrence.

DEDICATION

To all the wicked princes and badass princesses.

CAMASSIA COVE

Camassia Cove is a town in northern Washington created to be the home of some exciting love stories. Each novel taking place here is a standalone, and they will vary in genre and pairing. What they all have in common is the town in which they live. Some are friends and family. Others are complete strangers. Some have vastly different backgrounds. Some grew up together. It's a small world, and many characters will cross over and pay a visit or two in several books. But, again, each novel stands on its own, and spoilers will be avoided as much as possible.

Uncomplicated Choices is a novel taking place in Camassia Cove. If you're interested in keeping up with the characters, the town, the timeline, and future novels, check out Camassia Cove's own page at Cara's website.

www.caradeewrites.com

CASEY TEAGUE

I t always came up, somehow. It was always a deal breaker, somehow.

Did you leave Detroit for school?

What did you do before coming to Washington?

This time, because my date and I met at the studio, we reached that point when she asked, "So how did you come to meet the rock legend Lincoln Hayes?"

Rock legend is his Christian name, by the way.

I wiped my mouth and took a sip of my beer. "We were incarcerated together."

And it was *okay* for a former rock star to have been to prison. For reasons even Lincoln was baffled by—and admittedly pissy about—famous people could do no wrong. His ten years in prison had given him an extra *edge*. These days, as a well-known producer and family man, his slate was clean.

Mine wasn't.

"Oh...wow." Allison set down her wineglass, unsure of what to say.

I smiled stiffly. I was used to this. Dating *sucked*.

One might think I'd have a bigger pool to swim in since I was attracted to people, not genders, but that only applied if you weren't an ex-con. Or a single father. Actually, if I wanted to get laid, I just needed to snap my fingers. Plenty of women thought the prison history was hot—for a night or two. And men didn't care I was a father—for a night or two.

Relationships were another story.

"Can..." She hesitated. "Can I ask what you were in for?"

"Larceny." You could say I despised this topic. "I got mixed up with the wrong crowd and did some stupid shit." Like steal jewelry, expensive equipment people tended to keep in garages and tool sheds, computers...

"But you're not involved with those people now," she said with a placating smile.

I would've been relieved if I didn't know the signs by now. Allison was moving past it too quickly; we would go through the remainder of the date with shallow conversation, and then I'd never hear from her again.

Thank fuck she didn't actually work with Lincoln in his studio. She was the assistant of a client of his, and Seattle was a big city, one I didn't even visit that often. I belonged a couple hours north of here.

I was back in Camassia Cove the next morning, and I headed up to the northern district of Ponderosa to have brunch with the family and pick up my girl. Driving through Downtown, I got closer and closer to the hillside neighborhood and all its mansions.

Lincoln and his wife Adeline had their big house some-where in the middle, and once I entered their premises, I noticed the driveway was strangely empty of cars. Sunday brunch was a thing here. Maybe the others hadn't arrived yet.

I stepped out of my truck and glanced up at the three-story home. Four, if one included the underground basement. Their estate may very well be one of the most expensive in the district, and given my degree in landscape engineering, it was a life-long project and passion of mine to work on. What was once a lifeless, grossly modern structure in metallic tones that stretched along the hillside, rather wide and narrow, now displayed a vibrant, homey design and looked like it belonged here. I'd had new oak paneling ordered to cover up the lifelessness, and the balconies that traveled the length of the house on each floor had a wall of flat stone and boxwood now as opposed to the glass that was there before.

Ponderosa was sort of my favorite district for that reason. It took creativity and a solution-oriented mind to build in the mountains. Lincoln and Ade's house in particular sat on one of the steeper hillsides. There was no backyard. Instead, they'd hired me shortly after my graduation to turn their roof into a green haven. It was where they had their garden, pool, and barbecue area.

Jogging up the pathway to get out of the rain that was starting, I switched off my phone before opening the door. Their property was gated, so the door was rarely locked. It'd taken me a while to lose the Detroit mentality. One simply did not leave a house vulnerable, even in the nicer parts of town. I'd grown up with *nice*. And that came with tight security and alarm systems.

"Ade, our favorite stray is home!" Lincoln was coming up the stairs as I took off my shoes. Judging by the sweaty state of his sweats and T-shirt, I'd say he'd been working out. The basement was one part gym and one part recording studio. "Did you crash at our place in the city?"

I nodded, and he gave my neck a gentle squeeze. "The only ones getting lucky there are you and Ade, though."

He chuckled and winced. "Another date crashed and burned? What was it this time?"

"Same old. Women are usually all right with children. Prison, not so much."

He shook his head, and we headed toward the kitchen. "Maybe it's time to go with Ade's suggestion. There's no reason you gotta tell them about that on the first date. Wait a while, at least 'til there's an attachment. It's less likely they'll judge you for it if they know you better."

"I don't mention it to get it out of the way," I replied. "But like yesterday, she asked how you and I met...? I can't go around that. I won't lie."

"Makes sense." He opened the fridge and took a bottle of water. The large kitchen table was already filled with food, though Ade was nowhere to be found. I couldn't hear the girls, either.

"Where is everyone?" I asked.

"Probably still on the roof." Lincoln tossed the kitchen a wry smirk. "The wife's gotten it into her head that our kitchen needs to look more *French*." Well, that was the main inspiration for this area. It was cozy and rustic, despite the bigger size. "She and the princesses are bringing down some herbs to hang up there." He pointed at the grid above the kitchen island where pots and pans hung. "I think she's just missing work."

The travesty. Must be hard to be on vacation. Christ, it was a few weeks, not a year. That woman needed to learn how to relax. She was always on the go.

That said, I had to admire her dedication. She worked with men and women who were escaping abuse, and she'd opened a residential center a few years ago that had only grown since then. These days, she worked alongside everyone from psychiatrists to education counselors.

"I struggle to feel bad for her."

Lincoln laughed. "Right? I keep telling her..." He trailed off with a shake of his head, and then we made ourselves useful by bringing the rest of the food to the table. Pancakes, scrambled eggs, crispy bacon, and sausage links were staying warm in the oven, so I went for that. "Pop's out fishing, so he's not coming. Madigan's hungover. Ellis will be here."

"All right." That was a man I didn't see often. "How's he doing?" Ellis was Lincoln's cousin, and last I heard, he was on the verge of divorce. He and his wife were separated but were going to counseling or something.

Lincoln shrugged. "He says he's fine. I think it's bullshit."

Fair enough.

Right around the time brunch was ready, the doorbell went off, and little feet were stomping down the stairs. Lincoln went to get the door for Ellis, and I braced myself for my little hurricane.

"Daddy!" There she was. I smiled widely, and Haley barreled into me with more force than a four-year-old should possess. "Best sleepover ever!"

I laughed and picked her up for a hard squeeze. "You say that every time, baby." Possibly because Ade and Lincoln spoiled her *rotten*. "Let me look at you." Getting down on one knee, I brushed a lock behind her ear and gave her rosy cheeks a playful pinch. "Did you go to the beach?" I noticed she'd gotten some color.

She nodded, bright blue eyes going wide, and held up two dirt-covered fingers. "We had ice cream *two* times."

I faked a gasp. "That's *nuts*. Did you thank your aunt and uncle properly?"

"Yeah, like dis." She demonstrated a curtsy that was too fucking cute.

"Hi, Uncle Casey." Lyn ran over next, her hands as dirty as Haley's.

"Princess Nova-Lyn." I winked. "How about you two go wash up so we can eat?"

Thick as thieves as they were, they darted out of the kitchen to go wash their hands. We all dreaded the day next year when Lyn started first grade and the girls would be separated during school hours. They couldn't act more like sisters.

Focus was on the girls while we ate. It was information overload on everything they'd done, movies they'd watched, and what they wanted to do for their next sleepover.

When they declared they were done and asked to play, I crushed their little dreams by saying, "I'm sure you've made a mess in Lyn's room, so I suggest you put all the toys away."

Automatically, they turned to Lincoln at the head of the table.

Lyn pulled out her best pout. "Do we gots to clean, Daddy?"

"Well, yeah." He stole a smooch from her before she backed off with a scowl. "And next time Uncle Casey tells you something, you listen. That clear?"

Both girls got huffy but nodded sullenly in understanding, then went upstairs.

"With that out of the way..." Adeline glanced between Ellis and me. "Who goes first?"

"Not it," I said quickly.

"Goddammit," Ellis muttered.

Lincoln snorted a chuckle and refilled his coffee mug.

No one needed to hear more of my depressing dating blunders. That was why I blogged.

"I'm not sure I have anything interesting to share," Ellis said.

"You let me decide that." Ade patted Ellis's hand and smiled sweetly. "Go on. How's everything?"

She was relentless, not to mention quick to defend herself by saying if she didn't know what was going on in our lives, she couldn't help. Never mind that Ellis was a year older than Ade at...thirty-seven, I was pretty sure; Adeline was everyone's mother and meddler.

"Isn't that obvious?" Lincoln drawled and lifted his coffee mug. "Wife is giving him lemons."

I choked on a laugh and instantly felt horrible for finding that hilarious. Lincoln smirked at me, until he met the death stare of Adeline. She could be scary.

"Right. Sorry." Lincoln cleared his throat and got serious.

Ade gave him a little more heat, then returned her attention to Ellis.

"I think there may be some progress," he responded pensively, choosing his words carefully. "Our therapist is encouraging us to try dating each other."

Lincoln frowned. "You're gonna ask your wife of eleven years out on a date?"

"What's wrong with that?" Adeline lifted a brow. "You and I go on dates all the time."

"Right, and we love each other," Lincoln pointed out. "They don't."

Ellis cleared his throat, uncomfortable. I felt for him. "Perhaps we can find our way back to that."

I had my own issues, so I couldn't contribute. If he figured out a way to make it work, I could only hope he divulged the secret. *Why* he struggled was another mystery. The gene pool from which he and Lincoln came must've been made of liquid sex. They shared the same brown hair and striking gray-blue eyes, were equally tall at six foot three—maybe even four—and had the same broad shoulders and chiseled jaws.

Lincoln was ten years older and sported ink everywhere instead of the suit Ellis chose, but those were the only differences in style. Add successful career and the fact that Ellis was incredibly kind and compassionate, and I was at a loss. I had no idea what issues his wife had with him. He wasn't even one of those types who was married to their jobs.

Adeline was supportive and encouraging, hoping this dating thing would work. Lincoln thought it was a lost cause but kept most of that to himself. Instead, he dropped out of the conversation and grabbed another bagel.

"You wanna sync schedules for next week?" he asked me.

"Sure." I nodded and pulled out my phone. Summer break meant the girls were home, and they wanted to spend as much time as they could with each other. "Will you be in Seattle?"

"No more than usual." He scrolled through his planner on his phone. "I have a meeting with a client and his wife on Friday, and I wanna bring Ade. Mind taking Lyn then? It's here in town, so we can pick her up afterward."

I nodded slowly, rearranging a couple appointments. "No worries. I get off at four, and I gotta meet with the electrician..." I hummed then shook my head. It wouldn't be any problem. I could squeeze it in. "She might as well stay the night. We'll have a movie marathon."

We went back and forth for a while and managed to organize everything from work, summer activities for the girls, *and* some precious kid-free time. It was one of the things I loved most about being so close with Lincoln and Adeline. We made a lot of our plans as a unit.

When we were done, I pocketed my phone and finished my coffee.

"How's work?" Lincoln asked.

I cocked my head, suspicious. "It's...good." We were on the phone about this just a week ago, and my work was a topic he struggled with. He zoned out when I prattled about geology and ecology. If I threw out irrigation, he returned with irritation. He gave it an honest try last week because my company had grown. I'd hired my three first employees, so it was kind of a big deal. "Why do you ask?"

He got defensive. "I can't show interest in your job?"

That amused me. "Not really, no. You know the latest. More landscaping, less engineering, but no complaints." I had a passion for both; it'd just been a while since I put my geek on and used math and science to pretend I was a superhero who could bend the elements.

"He's buttering you up," Adeline chimed in.

So I was right to be suspicious. Interesting. "What for?"

She and Lincoln went into a brief stare-down battle to determine who was going to be the messenger.

I narrowed my eyes.

"Fine." Ade rolled her eyes, then faced me. "Since your new house won't be ready until the end of August, Lincoln and I were thinking about taking the girls to Disneyland."

I didn't know I required lube to accept that news. It wouldn't be the first time they included Haley in their impromptu vacation plans. "That's very sweet of you. You know the drill." I paid for Haley, end of story. I assumed they'd take a weekend before the next semester—

"Given your mellow reaction, I'm gonna guess we're not thinking about the same Disneyland," Lincoln said. "It's not even my fault this time."

"Thank you for throwing me under the bus," Ade laughed.

Lincoln winked at her. "My pleasure."

With a shake of her head, Adeline refocused on me. "I'm

actually surprised Adrian hasn't told you." Wonderful. Confuse me further, please. Adrian was a friend we had in common. He volunteered at a community center for kids and joined forces with Ade often enough.

"We're meeting up next week," I said. "Should I ask him instead?" Because, Christ, they were taking forever.

"We're starting a pen-pal exchange this fall as part of our education program," Ade explained. "The school we're doing the collab with invited Adrian and me to visit. And, well, you know..." She got fidgety. "The school is in France."

I stared blankly, and I was afraid my mind couldn't process that last little tidbit.

"We figured, might as well extend the trip and make it a vacation," Lincoln supplied.

I nodded. "Yeah. No. I... What you're saying is, you're taking the girls to Disneyland in *Paris*—halfway across the *world*, for...how long?"

"Three weeks," he said.

"That's..." I was speechless. "Why do you wanna kidnap my daughter for that long? I've never spent more than a couple days away from her." This wasn't going to work. "What the fuck is wrong with Anaheim?" I exclaimed. "I can even swing Orlando, but fucking *France*?"

Ade knitted her brows. "We didn't exactly pick schools based on proximity to Disney resorts."

"I don't see the big deal, Kid—"

I cut Lincoln off. "You freaked out last year when you went a week without Lyn, so fuck you and your big deal."

Ellis looked away to hide his amusement, and I glared at him, having all but forgotten he was still here.

He thought this was funny, huh?

"Jesus, with the melodrama," Ade sighed. "Listen to me, Casey. Think about Haley. Either she can leave her house, go on a fun vacation to Paris with us, then come home to a brand-new home, *or*...she can get shuffled around—leave the only home she knows, then stay here while you wait for the house to be ready, *then* move in to the new place and be surrounded by boxes and mayhem."

Pot, meet kettle. She was turning a move into some traumatic event. "I'll file one under *spoiled* and one under *shit happens*. Kids move all the time," I told her.

Lincoln rolled his eyes. "For fuck's sake. You know this is gonna go down. But tell you what, next year, you can take them for three weeks."

I'd rather not. They were a handful. That was why I liked these weekend sleepovers and such. A weekend was perfect. Long enough to unwind when I was without Haley, not long enough to lose my mind when I was the one who had the girls.

"How about we negotiate?" Adeline suggested. "I'm sure we can come to an understanding."

Well, I was fucked. A negotiation with her never turned out well for the other party.

here is he?

W I checked my watch, then took a swig of my beer. Adrian was late, so there was little I could do but people watch. The restaurant's dining area was full, consisting mainly of couples on dates.

You lovey-dovey motherfuckers.

It was a nice place, but Adrian and I met up here for the wings and we stayed at the bar.

Okay, maybe *that* particular couple wasn't too lovey-dovey. It was Ellis and his wife.

We exchanged a nod, and that was it.

"Dammit, I didn't know I was gonna be this late." Adrian appeared from the minor crowd waiting for a table at the hostess's desk. "Did you order without me?"

"Yeah, the wings are more irresistible than you, sorry." The wings were late too, though.

Adrian chuckled and sat down on the stool next to mine. "I recommend eating them off of someone."

"Can we not go there?" I didn't need to know about his spectacular love life. I got it, everyone was happy but me. *Whoa, you bitter fuck. Tone it down.* "I'm gonna make a very subtle change of subject. How's Thea?"

His daughter. Safe topic.

"Amazing." His eyes got that warm glow at the mention of her. It was sweet. "We're taking her to Disneyland in Paris. She's over the moon."

Oh, joy. I scratched my jaw and wondered where the hell my wings were. "Adeline told me. They wanna take Haley with them."

"Isn't that a good thing?" He turned to the bartender and ordered a beer and his own serving of those delectable wings.

I had dirty thoughts about licking the glaze off my fingers.

That was my love life in a nutshell.

"That's up for debate." I drained the last of my beer and ordered a second. "I agreed to allow her to go, but let the record show I'm reluctant about it."

Adeline and me...there was no contest. She won every fucking time.

"I'll tell a notary," he chuckled. "First time you'll be away from her?"

I nodded.

"Why don't you come with us?" he wondered.

"I have work." It was summer in Camassia Cove. Our second busiest season. Only spring offered more jobs. That said, I wasn't gonna be out much in August. I rented a warehouse for all equipment, and since it wasn't just me anymore, I needed to keep crap more organized. While two of my guys were out working, Beth—my office manager—and I were gonna make room for an office and make plans for a better website.

"Before I forget—" Adrian committed a crime when he used a

napkin to wipe the buffalo sauce off his fingers, but I let it slide because I was a good friend. "A coworker of mine asked for your number. I was uncomfortable handing out your digits, so he offered his instead." He handed me a slip of paper with a phone number.

"So it begins." I eyed the name above the number, recognizing it. *Toby*. Must've been from the Christmas party last year, in which case this guy really needed to contain his enthusiasm to meet me. For chrissakes, it'd only been seven months. "I can see it now. I'll be the old fucker who goes on blind dates with every friend of a friend he knows."

"For the love of—you're *thirty*, Casey. I won't dignify that with a response."

"...he said in response," I quipped. "Honestly, though. He waited seven months?" That was long enough to forget everything but traits that really stood out. Like a big forehead. I also recalled a nice ass, so life wasn't over.

"He mentioned seeing you in the area."

"Whoop-de-doo, thanks." I pocketed the number. "You know, I really miss your dry comments on my blog posts. They've gone AWOL since you started making kissy faces with your man."

To be a jerk, Adrian puckered his lips at me.

"He's nicer than you," I told him.

He laughed. "Oh boy, you need to get laid."

I wasn't going to argue that.

Our wings were long gone, and Adrian looked like he was ready to go get some. I did the nice thing and told him to get lost. Maybe I was too bitter for my own good, though that didn't mean I wanted my friends to swim in my puddle of misery.

"You should come over for dinner soon." He stood up and put on his light windbreaker. Summer didn't automatically mean heat in this state. "Bring Haley."

"It's a playdate," I replied with a nod. "Give your hottie an ass grab from me."

"I'll do no such thing."

Testy. I'd known him a few years, and he never struck me as possessive until lately. Lucky bastard.

Was there anything better than having a partner who just walked up and took you because they had to fucking have you?

Oh, someone was gonna blog tonight. I had some venting to do.

Another beer first, though.

Since it was just me again, I swiveled in my seat to face the dining area. People watching was more fun after a couple beers. A beautiful woman made eyes at me, and I gave her a faint smirk—until I peered around a plant that was in the way and noticed she wasn't here alone. Seriously, woman? Greedy.

Taking a long swig of my beer, I glanced over at Ellis, surprised to find him alone. His wife's jacket and purse were gone, as was her plate. Had she left? Ellis looked irritated.

That made me wanna check in on him.

Down, boy. Heel. Stay put. Not your business.

I was a disobedient mutt. I took my beer and walked over to their table by the window.

"Are you okay?"

He looked up and quickly schooled his features. "Casey. Yes, sure—I'm fine." He managed a polite smile. Impressive, though he needed to work on the lying.

"Mind if I crash your party?" I wondered.

"Er...sure, if you want. Have a seat."

I wasn't wanted. Didn't take a genius to see through him, but if I could put a genuine smile on his face, I'd consider this night a success. "First dates, huh?" I sat down and stole a piece of bread from the basket.

"Indeed. I suppose they're not easier even if you know the

person well." He gave up on his meal and wiped his mouth with a napkin. "Were you here on a date, too?"

"Nah, just a buddy. We come here for the wings. They're seriously awesome."

"Noted." A trickle of mirth gleamed in his eyes.

Hardly what I'd call a genuine smile.

"Could be worse." I threw that out there to get a conversation started. "I'm guessing your wife didn't ask if you've done time in prison."

"Ha. No, I guess not." He furrowed his brow. "People really ask that?"

I lifted a shoulder. "Someway, somehow, we end up there. I have a lot working against me."

Finally, I caught a sliver of curiosity. "Such as?"

"Well, there's the prison sentence. Women tend to go for guys they eventually wanna take home to their parents. Then there's Haley. Natural guy repellent, that one." I paused, thinking. "Oh, our family. There's nothing like complicating a person's *life* before appetizers are served when you're asked the simple question of what your parents do."

"Hmm. Fair enough. I assume that leads to your saying you don't speak to your parents."

"Something like that, and that's just the beginning of follow-up questions most people don't understand—or care about on a first date."

Ellis saw a challenge there. "Humor me. Is it so difficult to explain our family dynamic? I think it's fairly accurate to refer to Lincoln and Adeline as your pseudo parents, despite the insignificant age difference between you and her. Jesse and Abel would be your brothers in that regard, no?"

I withheld my wince. "Given my history with Lincoln before he and Ade got together, I'm not sure it's wise to go there. Shit happens in prison."

So did blow jobs, and Lincoln had been my cellmate. I'd been mildly terrified of Adeline's reaction, but I'd worried for nothing. She'd reacted playfully, once joking, "Shame I couldn't watch."

To be fair, I'd never gotten that far into *The Story of Us* with someone I dated. Not many knew. I guess it was easier to discuss with Ellis because he was part of the family.

"You mean you and he...?" His eyebrows went up. "Ah." Next, he grew uncomfortable. See? It was a first date all over again.

This shit could not be covered without discomfort. Barely anyone in my family was related. Adeline adopted two brothers —Jesse and Abel—while Lincoln was locked away. Two brothers whose father had worked with Lincoln's band... It was a complicated story; that wasn't even all of them, yet it was the sort of thing dates asked about. They had no clue they were walking straight into a minefield.

"I try to tone it down," I said. "I usually say my family's a band of misfits. If they ask further, that's when they're screwed."

Ellis let out a chuckle and reached for his wine. "Band of misfits. I suppose that works. I, for one, am grateful for everyone."

Shit, so was I. It went beyond family—a few people's sexual history notwithstanding. We were all *friends*. Jesse and I were almost the same age, and we were close for a while. Now he lived in Los Angeles, though. Abel was gone for the most part, too. Professional hockey players didn't see home often. He'd come home briefly this summer but was now at some training camp in Canada.

"Why don't you come around more often, then?" I wondered.

I was granted a smile, except it was too dry for my tastes.

"I don't like to share my issues."

I scratched my neck, embarrassed. "Meanwhile, I blurt them out to anyone who's willing to listen. *Oy*. Point taken."

"That's not what I meant at all, Casey," he told me. "To be perfectly honest, I envy Lincoln and Adeline. It can be tough to be around."

I could relate to that, and dammit, I was done talking about myself. Time to be straightforward. "Listen, princess. You can always hang out with me. Nothing to envy, and I tell decent jokes. The reason I sat down here now was to make you smile, so lemme get started."

He made a noise. "Did you just call me princess?"

Did I? *Listen...princess.* Yes. Yes, I did. *"Maybe."* But that was neither here nor there. "Now, focus. How does one go about making you smile?"

That halted him. He blanched, only to frown and empty his wineglass in one gulp. Then he adjusted his tie and looked out the window. "I don't think anyone has ever asked me that."

I didn't know how to respond. Maybe my question wasn't common? It didn't seem like a very strange question, however. Before I tried to make someone smile, I had to know how.

"What if I forgot?" he pondered.

I sat back and watched him, his eyes meeting mine. Forgetting how to smile or what it was that gave you said smile would be a fucking shame. And I was talking about the smiles you felt everywhere, the ones that ran deeper. Not the polite, brief moments of shallow amusement. Anyone could pull that off.

"We should work on that," I told him.

"*We?*" He had one of those shallow moments right now. His mouth twisted up until the moment passed.

"Who's better suited for the job? I'm the class clown."

"Question is why." Now he was messing with me. "You know, this is Psychology 101. The class clown tends to have something to cover up."

Let's not go there.

I grinned, ignoring the sharp tug in my chest. "Did you learn that in marketing school?"

"Marketing school," he echoed with a chuckle. "I'll have you know I minored in psychology. You're quite useless in advertising without it."

I couldn't imagine. I was horrible at selling. He did it for a living. Or...well, he had minions who did it. His ad agency moved in to a new building a couple years ago because the old one was too small. Now he had a whole minion factory.

Speaking of minions, I should probably pick up Haley soon. Keith, Lincoln's dad, requested an evening with her and Lyn because he had fish to gut and needed two tiny human slaves.

We'd ended up with daughters who loved anything that was *yucky*.

"Do you ever feel like you want to leave everything behind?"

Ellis's somber voice snapped me back to the present, and I leaned forward again, arms resting on the table. He didn't look well—in that happy sense, so to speak. The man was gorgeous, but that went without saying. He was a Hayes. He was a very *unhappy* Hayes.

"Can't say I do." I struggled with what to say. "I need our misfits too much. I mean...I get tired, but—" I cut myself off before I could start rambling. It wasn't about me. "Ellis, how can I help?"

He shook his head. "I appreciate the offer, but there's nothing you can do. I think I need to get away for a bit and clear my head."

Made sense. We all had our methods for that. "I hope it works. If I wasn't such a people whore, maybe I would enjoy it, too."

"You have a very...colorful vocabulary."

I widened my eyes at his smirk. "I blame the internet. You learn the worst shit on there. It broke my halo."

That earned me another chuckle. "You could avoid it."

"God, no. My blog has an astounding twelve thousand followers, all of whom I suspect are as jaded as I am. It's also where I do my shopping, and my name on Facebook is pretty darn funny. The internet needs me."

"Jesus. Isn't Casey your name on Facebook?"

"No." There was nothing creative about that. "You should join. We can be BFFs."

"What is your name, then?" Was he getting frustrated with me? That was cute.

"It's complicated," I replied.

"What's so complicated about—"

"No, no. That's my name. *It's complicated.*"

Ellis gave me a look that said my Facebook name suited me. I smiled.

"You're certainly something." He stared at me until my smile broke his resolve to look all huffy. "What do you blog about?"

"Dating and parenthood, mostly. Sometimes, I take selfies and post food porn."

Very interesting stuff.

I wanted to talk more about him, though. During our very short non-date, he'd learned a lot about me because of my big mouth. I'd learned virtually nothing new about him.

"I'm adding elusive to the list of your traits," I informed him. "Not counting your lengthy rambling about minoring in psychology, of course."

"Of course." He grinned faintly and gave me his umpteenth head shake. "I'm hardly elusive. Maybe there isn't much to know."

Why did I doubt that so fucking much?

3

I'm a Talker

I talk when I'm nervous, when I'm happy, when I'm pissed, and a lot when I'm drunk. Therefore, I'm an open book. It's both good and bad. You know the saying, "If you don't ask, you won't know the answer," right? Right. Chances are, you'll know way before you even thought of asking. Sorry about that.

Growing up, my parents rarely talked. I wouldn't say I was caught in the middle or anything, but I heard both sides because they had no issues talking to others. Mother would gossip to her friends, and my father would vent to his golf buddy as his only child trailed behind as the lucky, lucky caddy. More often than not, I wanted to scream at them. Just talk, dammit! Communication brings us closer.

Unfortunately, I may be overeager in my sharing sometimes. Re: dating. I keep thinking, if I put all cards on the table from the beginning, we might save time and move on quicker if we're not a good match. And I guess...in my haste, I sometimes forget to listen. I set the pace so fast to get past the obstacle that is The First Fucking Date.

Maybe I need to shut up and listen some more. Maybe

someone will call me elusive and want more. Or...something-something witty, just bring us closer.

—Casey

"**D**addy?"

I hummed, scrolling through the comments on my latest post. "Yeah, princess?"

"Ugh! I tolded you! It's prince now!"

Shit. I tucked away my phone and left the kitchen table. Haley and Lyn were turning my little kitchen into a war zone, but I had to hand it to them. They did it in style. As a "please don't forget me while you're in France" gift, I'd told the girls to pick out a Disney costume online that I'd buy for them. They went with matching Prince Eric costumes, which arrived today, just in time for a final hurrah with Daddy slash uncle.

"Apologies, Prince Haley." I bowed to show my respect. "May I inform Your Royal Highness that a bag of flour has exploded in your face?"

"You talk silly!" Lyn laughed.

"He's always silly," Haley giggled. In an attempt to reach out and hug my arm, she almost fell off the chair she was standing on. As their butler, I was quick to steady her. I took my job seriously. "Oops."

"As long as it's you saying it and not a doctor, I'm good." I kissed her flour-dusted cheek. "Are these works of art ready to go in the oven?"

They nodded furiously, and I told them to prepare for bath time so I could get the cinnamon rolls *ready*-ready for the oven. They were buttery, cinnamony, and sugary, but the glaze had been dumped in the middle of the pan. Poor outsider rolls wanted to get glazed, too.

So do I, for the record.

"Girls, give me a peep so I know you haven't gone under!" I called from the kitchen.

The rolls were done, and the scent made my mouth water as I took them out of the oven.

I got a giggled double "Peep!" from Haley and Lyn, which was always a relief.

"It's only a bathtub, Uncle Casey!" Lyn felt the need to point out.

"You can drown on land, hon." I let the pan sit on the stove to cool some, and then I went to the bathroom and took a seat on the closed toilet lid.

Lyn was full of skepticism and suds. She was rocking the best bubble beard. "That's not true."

"Is, too." I retrieved my phone again to have something to do. "Drowning isn't about your body being underwater. It's about your lungs *filling* with water. So technically, you can drown in a puddle. All you have to do is inhale it—breathe it in."

Well, Lyn's mind was blown.

Haley didn't quite get it yet.

"Make sure to tell Mommy and Daddy that I teach you all kinds of good stuff," I told Lyn, and she grinned and nodded. "Next week: why exercise is bad for you."

My joke died. All they heard was "next week," and so they squealed out, "Disneyland!"

Haters.

I returned my attention to my phone instead. Most of the comments on my posts were positive, if not all about others who could relate. The anon trolls existed too, though they were luckily few and far in between. There were the hobby shrinks who had solutions to everything. There was the group of women and men letting me know they would date me. Thanks, guys. Some other anonymous comments...

Anonymous replied: As someone who was called elusive recently, I can say it's overrated. Keep talking. It's very refreshing. ∴

I mean... But no. In the seven seas of millions of blogs, one didn't simply stumble upon mine. The odds of winning the lottery were better. That comment couldn't belong to Elusive Ellis.

The weekend passed too quickly, and when Monday rolled around, I took the day off to be a good father and uncle—and a horrible friend.

I arrived with Haley and Lyn at Lincoln's doorstep in the early afternoon. I had Haley's luggage because their hands were full. I'd found these cute, thirty-five-ounce duffel bags at the store—on sale, so I couldn't resist—in pink, transparent plastic.

Lincoln opened the door, his forehead creasing at the sight of the girls. Or rather, the duffels. And because the bags were see-through, he could see I'd filled them to the brim with candy.

"Hi, Daddy!" Lyn grinned. "Look what we got!"

"Uh...hey, baby girl." Lincoln lifted his gaze from a six-year-old to a thirty-year-old. "The red-eye with two kids on a sugar high. Thank you."

"Finally, some recognition. You're *welcome.*" I handed over Haley's luggage to him and entered the house. "You haven't asked me to water any plants and bring in the mail. Should I be offended?"

"The cleaning service will do that." Lincoln set down Haley's bag next to three other bags in the hallway. "Seriously, Kid. They'll inhale that shit before we even get to Seattle."

That was the point. Kinda hard to get it past security. "I hope they don't throw up on the plane."

Unfortunately, nothing could ruin Lincoln's travel mood. If there was one thing that rivaled his passion for music, it was whisking away his family on trips. He smirked and shook his head, then focused on the girls. He dutifully complimented their costumes that they demanded to travel in, and he took the "We're princes now" talk like a champ.

"Auntie Ade!" Haley ran over to the stairs as Adeline descended. "Daddy gave us vacation candy!"

"Oh, wow. Yeah, I'd say he gave you a *lot*." She sent me a playful scowl before kneeling down at Haley's level. "You know the rule here, though. We eat our veggies before we get to the candy. And luckily for us, we have time to eat something before we go. Isn't that awesome?"

Oh God, she was a skilled manipulator. Haley and Lyn actually cheered.

Now they'd be full of *veggies* on the way to the airport.

"Fuck, I love you, tiny dancer." Lincoln smiled at Adeline.

She blew him a kiss, and when she passed me on the way to the kitchen, she whispered, "Checkmate."

Witch.

While she whipped up some leftover Alfredo with pasta and zoodles, I did everything in the book to keep from thinking about being away from Haley for three weeks. Lincoln asked about the house, so that worked as a decent distraction for a bit.

"Everything packed up yet?" he wondered. "You haven't asked us to help out. Should we be offended?"

"You're hilarious," I deadpanned. "No, I got an extra week, so I haven't even started." I was handing over the keys in six days. Then I had two weeks of crashing here while our shit was at my work. Why waste the storage space?

Our new house was bigger. No more sleeping on a pullout for me. I'd have my own bedroom.

"You know all this could've been avoided if you'd just let me buy you a house after college."

I only gave him a look. After my parents disowned me because their sweet, quiet geek had turned into a criminal, I spent my prison sentence getting a rude fucking awakening. Immediately after, Lincoln took over. He and Adeline put me through college and gave me a home, but I put my foot down after that. He made it possible for me to bounce back, and since then, I'd made my own way. Slowly but surely.

Welp. I'd made it all day without shedding a tear, but I wasn't going to lie. When I went to bed that night, my eyes watered. Had I packed everything for her? What if she got homesick? It was one thing that I hadn't been away from her that long before; a whole other that she hadn't been away from *me.* She didn't cope the way adults did, such as get hammered and have one-night stands you regretted the morning after.

It was only a matter of time.

"Blah. Cover up the mush." I threw aside the covers and sat up, reaching for my phone. In times like these, when I felt weak, I could count on humor. With my app ready, I wrote a short blog post.

No one would know I felt like crying.

It's Been Too Long, My Dear

Do you still remember me? The memory of your sweet giggles grows fainter and fainter in my mind. Soon, I fear I'll forget your voice. This journey without you has been torture. Do you miss me like I miss you? I doubt that's possible. The most vivid memory I have would be of your bright smile as you hugged me so tight, then your soft voice saying "I'll miss you, Daddy!" It's been too long, my dear. It's been... God, eleven hours and counting.

#DaughterOnVacationWithoutMe

—Casey

Not five minutes had passed before the first handful of comments appeared, and I cocked my head at the anonymous one.

Anonymous replied: The love you have for her is extraordinary. ∴

That weird sign afterward... A colon and a period. I'd received a comment like that before. Whoever it was, they subscribed to my posts. Probably. Unless they'd happened to check out the blog right after I updated.

"We're here, Daddy! Gotta go, love you, bye!"

"Gee," I muttered, trapping the phone between my shoulder and cheek. I guess she wasn't missing me much. I figured after three days she'd be going bananas. Then again, they'd spent the first two days in a rural part of France where they visited that school. Now, as I was on my way to work, they were arriving for their evening check-in at some fancy Disneyland hotel.

"You there, Kid?" Lincoln's voice filtered through the phone.

"Yup. How's everything?" I made a turn onto a dirt road in the forest district of Westslope where Henry was waiting for me. He was old-school, not much of a conversationalist, but he was a hell of a landscape designer. Born with green thumbs and a passion for hydrogeology.

"I'm tired as fuck," Lincoln yawned. "What're you up to—I got that, love. You take the girls."

"Just got to work," I answered, killing the engine. "Nothing's new here—oh, other than I got the park project." I was admittedly stoked as hell about that.

"That's fucking awesome. When does it start?"

"Presenting the 3D model in October," I answered. "You guys should go get settled in. We can talk later."

"Yeah, okay. Proud of you, though—*what?*" Now he was shouting. Ade spoke in the background. "Uh, okay. I'm supposed to tell you your blog post on—Jesus, whatever-the-fuck—she likes it. No, baby girl, go with Mommy. She'll help you." He blew out a heavy breath, and I chuckled. "What is it about that goddamn blogging of yours? I keep hearing about it. Ellis asked for the address just the other day." *Oh, really.* "I thought it was single-life ranting."

"You make it sound so cool," I said flatly. "Time to go, Daddy rock star. Buy yourself a crown. I'm gonna tell a client he should have an irrigation system for his little fish farm."

"That word," he bitched and hung up.

Irrigation, meet irritation.

I grinned and stared at my screen. So Ellis had gone behind my back to find out my blog address. He was elusive. Albeit poor at covering up his tracks.

I was gonna have fun with this.

4

I didn't particularly want to go home after work, so I took myself out for dinner. I picked up a grilled salmon sandwich, some fries, and a Pepsi, then drove down to the marina. Finding a sunny spot, I unzipped my coveralls and tied the arms around my waist. It was T-shirt weather today, much appreciated.

"Don't you fucking dare." I eyed a seagull skipping past my bench, obviously in the mood for my sandwich. "Can't handle the competition by the fishing boats, huh? Loser."

Keeping my fries close and my Pepsi closer, I bit into my sandwich and pulled out my work phone. My agenda was twofold: mess with Ellis, and text the guy who'd asked for my number through Adrian.

Ellis came first.

Hi. :.

I snickered. I wasn't sure he had my personal cell, but I knew for certain he didn't have my work number. There was no reason for him to.

The other guy was next.

Hey, this is Casey. You asked Adrian about me.

Ellis responded quickly.

Who is this?

I chewed around a mouthful of food, debating with myself. I wasn't going to drag this out because when push came to shove, I wanted to get to know him better. But first...

I'm me. Call me elusive, but I prefer to go nameless. :.

Checking the time, I reckoned he'd be on his way home from work soon, and—shit. I jumped a little, surprised to see his number lighting up on the screen. Who *called* these days? This was a texting world.

"Hello?" I took a quick sip of my pop.

"Casey." Damn. Why did his voice and the way he said my name bring such a smile to my face? It was his rueful amusement, the warmth of his voice, and the fact that he was fucking caught.

"Who's Casey?" I chuckled.

He sighed. "All right, you got me. Who ratted me out? Lincoln or Adeline?"

"I can't snitch. It wouldn't be right. Besides, I have to give you some shit."

"What on earth for? Last time I checked, reading someone's blog wasn't a criminal offense."

"You should check again." I stuck a couple fries into my mouth. "I haven't even read your charges yet, though. It's not the blog."

"Then what is it?"

Wasn't it obvious? "Come on, Ellis. You can't skip out on family dinners and be all secretive about yourself, then read my personal stuff on the sly and not expect me to object."

There was a pause, and I was pretty sure I heard the telltale beep of a car alarm being switched off. Next came the opening and closing of a car door. "Fair, I suppose. Should I get myself a lawyer, then?"

"Or you can come to the marina and buy me dessert." I figured that was a good deal. "My dinner's almost gone."

He went quiet again. I wasn't going to budge. I agreed with Lincoln; Ellis wasn't doing all right, and as his family—pseudo or not—wasn't it our duty to dig our claws into him and make him come out of hiding?

"Just dessert?"

I smashed my lips together. Had this man been single and into other men, it would've been the *perfect* opening for a dirty pun. "No, Elusive Ellis," I replied slowly, "your participation in some chatting is required. I'm on the boardwalk, and you have ten minutes, sir."

Ten minutes later, he was walking toward me. Fresh out of work, he still managed to look drop-dead gorgeous. He made suits sexier.

"You are a demanding young man, aren't you?" He sat down next to me on the bench and squinted a little for the sun. "What kind of dessert do you want?"

I held out a box of Tic-Tacs. "You're too late. I satisfied my sweet tooth already."

"I wouldn't call that dessert." With a shake of his head, he surveyed the marina and peered over at the boats. "Which one is Lincoln's—ah, never mind." Yeah, Lincoln's yacht was hard to miss.

Supposedly called a baby in the yacht world, it was nevertheless an impressive sixty feet long, had two decks, a kitchen, two dining areas, three bathrooms, three bedrooms, and two sundecks. Along the side of the white, sleek, floating castle,

"Tiny Dancer" was written in an elegant font, and the boat stuck out like a sore thumb among modest sailboats, fishing boats, and bow riders.

It was a new purchase.

Adeline had nearly lost her shit, first in the angry way because of the price tag, then in the melty way because her rock star named a boat after her.

I emptied the other half of my Tic-Tacs into my mouth. "Any plans this weekend?"

"I'm a married man. I never have plans."

"Wow," I mouthed to myself, a couple mints falling out. The seagull had now been served dinner. "Be sure to let *happily* married men know that."

"Good point." He dipped his chin.

"And I thought you were separated."

"I am, technically. Marilyn's staying with her sister."

I'd never understood separations. Sure, if the next step was divorce, it made sense. Ellis and his wife went to couple's therapy, though. "What are your restrictions as a separated man?" I wondered. The man didn't even wear a ring anymore. "I mean, can I take you out and get you laid? Or maybe it's just like marriage, but without the sex."

Ellis turned to me with a frown. "There's supposed to be sex in marriage?" He was kind of funny, in that highly depressing way. "No, she made it clear that she wanted to see what's out there." He was unimpressed by that.

I nodded slowly. "Well, I'm sold. I can't wait to get married." Dammit, this wasn't the time to crack jokes. I rubbed the back of my neck. "Can I ask something?"

He made a vague *go-ahead* gesture.

I cleared my throat. "The counseling and the dinner dates... Are you making a genuine effort to reconcile with your wife, or are you going through the motions?"

Ellis averted his eyes and frowned at the ground as he loosened his tie. "I think... I think in order to answer that, I need alcohol."

If a few beers were what it took for him to open up, then beer we were going to have. "Wanna go over there?" I nodded at the row of low buildings that was parallel with the parking lot before the boardwalk began. The dinner rush hadn't started yet, so we could get a table outside at one of the small seafood restaurants.

"Hell, why not," he replied. With *such* enthusiasm.

I threw away my trash from my early-bird dinner on the way, and then we found ourselves at a little round table with two menus. The sun was dipping lower, giving the sky an orange, pinkish glow. We ordered a pitcher of beer and a snack plate with fried halibut pops, chips, potato skins, and lime aioli. I didn't think he'd had dinner yet, so he better eat most of it.

"I like this," I confessed. "Seeing you more often, I mean. Meeting up like this for drinks."

The crease between his brows smoothed out marginally, and he managed a faint smile. "Your honesty is something else, Casey. You *speak* so easily."

"Because I'm a talker," I said with a smirk.

"It's more than that." He shook his head. "You'd be surprised how difficult the simple truths can become."

I understood him, but for me it was different. It was a coping mechanism of sorts. Blurt out what was on my mind right away, and if it wasn't appreciated, they could move on. Eventually, people did leave, and I just wanted to make sure I got an honest word in edgewise before we parted ways. That way, I would always know I'd shown nothing but myself.

As painful as it was, I wanted to be rejected for me, not due to some ridiculous miscommunication or misunderstanding that would haunt me forever.

"But then, you hide other things." He smirked, and then our beer arrived.

The snacks were gonna be another ten minutes, not that I cared. I wanted to know what Ellis meant by that. I hid things? *I think not.* I hid nothing.

"Anyway, I was going to explain myself," he went on, much to my frustration. I didn't hide anything! "To make you understand the effort versus going through the motions, I have to go back a bit. You know how we hear people say marriage is hard?"

I furrowed my brow and nodded once. *I don't hide anything.*

"It hasn't been for me," he admitted. "It's been effortless since day one, and it's hit me lately that it's because we never aimed particularly high. We slipped into the safe lane and found the illusion of happiness in contentment and stability. Our careers are demanding enough. We didn't need our marriage to be a struggle, too."

I pinched my lips, thinking of couples who struggled, yet were happier. Lincoln and Ade could have fights that were one wrong word away from turning violent. They fought as passionately as they loved because the end goal was always the same—to fix the issue and grow stronger.

"Going through the motions is what you do when you aim for easy," Ellis said. "So, yes, it's what I'm doing now too, and it's because I can't make up my mind." He took a sip of his beer and brushed his thumb across his upper lip. "I know exactly what to do if I want our marriage to go back to normal. I make some empty promises of better things to come—that ultimately won't —and she will do the same. Then we'll put this therapy nonsense behind us, and we'll continue leading separate lives together."

That fucking hurt. It sounded all too much like my parents. "Why would anyone *want* that?"

He averted his eyes, finding something to do by aligning his glass atop the coaster. "It's easy. It puts the relationship on the back burner so you can focus on what you're passionate about. And it's not half bad to have someone to come home to, even if you don't really speak."

I could only shake my head. This went so far beyond cynical.

When our snacks arrived, I munched on some chips and chugged my beer while my mind spun. Did I know the issue between Ellis and Marilyn? I wasn't sure; it had to be more than what Adeline had told me. Which was essentially that they'd drifted apart and prioritized differently. Differently enough that they'd begun arguing more, and one fight led to another, then boom, "What are we even married for?" According to Adeline, it was Ellis who'd said that.

"Ade may have told me you brought up the talk of divorce," I said.

He nodded with a dip of his chin. "It was a moment of realization, I suppose. I genuinely didn't understand why we put up with each other." And then he did, when it hit him it was because they aimed for easy. "I suggested the counseling, as well. Seemed like the right thing to do."

Seemed like the right thing to do.

Yeah, definitely going through the motions.

"And she agreed," I stated.

"On one condition," he laughed quietly. "That she gets to try out the single life."

I didn't answer. It was getting too frustrating. Who in their right mind agreed to fix a broken marriage while also insisting they go out and *get some*? Ellis wasn't much better. He knew what he was choosing between, an uphill battle that might be so rewarding he would find life-long joy...and settling for *easy*. And he couldn't make up his mind?

"So you're passionate about your job," I said. "I thought you weren't one of those who worked all hours of the day."

"I don't." He tilted his head at me, a little confused. "I love my company very much, but I have other interests, too."

They had to be some awesome interests if they ranked higher than his wife. "Like what?"

"Er, well...I enjoy reading—"

"Oh, come on, Ellis." I stared incredulously at him. "If you'd rather get lost in a book—which in this case might be what we call *escapism*—there's not a chance in hell you should stay married."

"I haven't argued that, have I?" he shot back. "It's about priorities."

"You don't prioritize happiness?"

He got stuck on that one.

Ellis didn't strike me as a cautious or fearful man. How could he be when he'd gone all in to build his own agency? He made a living off of taking risks and predicting what would trend and sell. It took a certain level of assertiveness to be able to tell a representative from another company that Ellis and his team could market their brand. No...if anything, it felt like Ellis had forgotten what happiness was altogether.

"Look," I said, easing off on the pedal. "It's not my business to tell you what to do, and I'm the last guy to give advice on relationships."

"But?" He lifted a brow.

"But I hope you won't wake up one day and regret a big part of your life."

Where was my party mood?

I had a date tonight. It was Friday; the workweek was over,

and I should be in my usual high spirits. I couldn't blame it on Haley being gone. While I missed her, it wasn't the end of the world anymore. She was having the time of her life, creating memories with people we loved, and I was happy for her.

Sure, it felt wonderful when I spoke to her yesterday and she exclaimed she missed me *so much*, though my butthurt had healed. Next summer would be my turn. I'd snatch up the girls and take them to Narnia or something.

I'd gotten a lot done yesterday and today too, so that couldn't be what stole my Friday happiness. This morning, I drove the last of my crap to work, and then I handed the keys over. I was officially homeless. Which... I glanced around the hallway, and okay, it was entirely wrong to joke about being homeless when I was spending the rest of the month in an estate worth a couple million.

Patting the pockets of my jeans, I made sure I had my keys, wallet, and phone while I inspected myself in the mirror. A hand went through my hair. It took effort to give it that freshly fucked kind of look. I blinked and squinted at my reflection. *Look alive.* It was a little chilly tonight, so I changed my mind about the button-down and ran upstairs to my old room to grab a tee and a fitted sweater instead. Then I was ready to leave Lincoln and Ade's place.

Since I banked on drinking tonight, I passed my truck. The walk down the hillside to Downtown only took ten minutes or so, and at least it wasn't raining anymore.

I checked my blog and read a few dozen comments on the way, and I had to admit I was disappointed that Ellis hadn't responded to this post. I was getting used to seeing his comments. They were often on the sweet side, in that supportive, grown-up way. Then again, today's post was mostly snark. I'd posted a couple memes in an update about first-world problems on dating both men and women. Because if there was one thing I'd learned quickly, it was to expect different outcomes depending on the gender.

Not much to comment on, and to be honest, I kind of regretted the post. I'd had something more meaningful in mind, but I'd chickened out. I had no desire to start a gender debate today, no matter how much it bugged me. So I'd turned to humor.

At a quarter to eight, I reached the marina and strolled over to a little place I knew was sort of the only gay-friendly restaurant in Downtown. Cedar Valley was otherwise the best neighborhood for my brand of heathens.

The marina was buzzing with the Friday crowd, and the inside of Quinn's Fish Camp was just as lively. Given it'd been a minute since I'd seen my date—seven freaking months—I'd asked him to tell me the color of his shirt. And no guy in a purple shirt sat at the bar. I did, however, spot Madigan and Jameson.

The latter was a more recent addition in my life. He ran a tattoo business with Madigan in the Valley.

"Fancy running into you guys here." I clapped them on the shoulders and squeezed myself in the middle of them. "Oh, look, it's a Casey sandwich in the making."

Madigan laughed. "Hey, punk. What're you doing here?"

"I think the better question is, what are you two doing here?" As far as I knew, they rarely left the Valley. Downtown was my domain. I turned around to lean back against the bar so I could keep an eye on who was entering the place.

"Chasing skirts?" Jameson inched back long enough to give me a once-over. "You'd look good in one."

I chuckled. "Aren't you sweet."

He winked and took a swig of his beer.

Natural flirt, that one. Sexy, too.

So was Madigan, but I had a bone to pick with him. He could be eye candy another time.

"Ade's pissed at you," I told him. "I'm not happy with you either, but I'm sticking to the miffed category."

He frowned. "I haven't seen you in weeks. I fail to see what I've done wrong."

"That's the point, you cretin." I rolled my eyes. "Abel spent all of two weeks at home, and you couldn't be bothered to drag your ass over for dinner even once?"

Madigan was part of our band of misfits. Back in the day, his older brother was the drummer in Lincoln's band, and Madigan took a job early on as crewmember. That was how he got to know both Lincoln and Ade. When the band broke up and Lincoln went to prison, Madigan and Adeline grew closer.

"I've been busy as fuck," Madigan defended. He got touchy. No clue why. Considering how close he and Abel used to be, it was a mystery to me. Madigan was older, a few years short of forty, and despite the age difference, he and Abel came to life in a whole new way whenever they were in the same room.

Or, that's how it used to be, anyway. They'd seen less and less of each other since Abel was drafted by the NHL. Madigan even missed Abel's twentieth birthday earlier this year.

"Did you fight?" I asked. Because the more I thought about it, the weirder it got. Did they see each other over the holidays? I wasn't sure... Actually—now I remembered. Madigan introduced a boyfriend to the family. First and last time we saw the guy. But yeah, Madigan and Abel saw one another then.

"No, we didn't fucking fight. Enough with the third degree, kid."

I sent him a look of warning. Kid was Lincoln's name for me; I could accept that one. Not from others, though. I didn't like it.

In response, he grabbed my jaw and planted a loud kiss on my cheek.

I snorted and wiped my cheek, and as my gaze flicked to the door, I saw a guy with a dark purple shirt walk in. *Well, damn.* It must've been some other guy who had a big forehead at Adrian's holiday party, because this guy was cute and had a normal-sized forehead.

"Looks like my date is here," I said. "Bye, bitches."

5

Toby was my age, yet acted like a teenager on crack. I wasn't used to being the mellow one. I tended to attract assertive men, often a bit older, and women who were either equally assertive or drawn to jokesters.

Was this how others saw me on dates? As a teenage crackhead?

I had the strangest urge to call Ellis and apologize. He was the last one who'd been exposed to my upbeat manners.

You're a dick.

Probably.

I was being too hard on Toby, and I didn't know why. He was handsome, and we clearly had a lot in common, namely a personality. He was a substitute teacher and liked kids. Blond, blue eyes a little darker than my own, nice build. On the short side. And being five-eleven myself, that was saying a lot. Being the tall one wasn't anything I could take for granted, either. Around men, anyway.

Ellis is taller than you.

Yes, he was, and why was I thinking of him?

I shook my head and refocused on the fellow *talker* I was on a date with. What was he saying? Something about the yearly festival that was coming up. Once a harvest celebration, now a tourist attraction that drew in hordes of people from all over.

"Will you be there?" he wondered.

I nodded and shifted in my seat. "Yeah, I think so." We'd scored a table in the back, and if I turned away from the bar a little, maybe it wouldn't be so tempting to return to Madigan and Jameson. They were currently cracking jokes with the owner, Darius Quinn. Three men's laughter rang out above the already noisy din, and I pushed down the envy.

I liked to crack jokes, too...

"You have a daughter, right?" Toby inquired. "I'm guessing she loves the festival."

Jesus, I really sucked. The guy was making an effort.

"I do." I cleared my throat. It was time to pay attention and give this a go. "She's in Paris now though, so she'll miss it this year."

"Oh, wow. Paris. How exciting." Toby smiled. "Is she there with her mother, or...?"

That would be my least favorite topic, so it was time to use Lincoln as a diversion. "Ah, no. My family. Have you heard of Lincoln Hayes? Our daughters are more like sisters than anything."

"Damn. Who hasn't heard of him?" Mission accomplished. Toby didn't have Haley's mother in mind anymore. "Shit, so you know a rock legend," he chuckled and shook his head. "Didn't he kill someone?"

When he put it like that, Lincoln sounded like a cold-blooded murderer. Christ. "It was manslaughter. It's a long story, but he's not a bad guy." Far from it, thinking of the circumstances. Time for another topic change. "I take it you like rock music?"

I know. I know. Lame.

"That was brutal." I returned to the bar and found an empty stool next to Jameson. I was quick to order two shots and a beer. They were lit, so I had to catch up.

"It *looked* brutal," Jameson noted.

"I blew it." I wasn't going to pretend it was Toby. I was off my game tonight. "Thanks." I accepted the drinks and requested to start a tab, and then I downed the first shot. "He was cute though, wasn't he?"

It wasn't over yet. Toby and I had made loose plans to meet up at the festival before he'd left. Apparently, he was getting up early tomorrow morning, which...didn't make much sense. It was Saturday tomorrow, and he was a teacher. Well—substitute, so maybe he had a second job.

"Fuckable, I guess." Jameson shrugged and emptied his beer. "At this point, I think I'd hit anything with a heartbeat."

I laughed under my breath. "Been a while?"

"I passed a *while* last year." He belched into his fist, then excused himself to go take a piss.

That left Madigan and me. And the other stragglers. Or maybe it wasn't late enough for anyone to be stragglers. I checked my watch and blinked. Lord, it wasn't even ten! The only reason the crowd wasn't as big anymore was because the dinner guests had left, and now we were waiting for the drunks to show up. Woohoo, party people.

"Am I getting old?" I asked. Maybe finding out it was early shook me up a bit.

"Oh, fuck you." Madigan huffed a laugh and held up two fingers at the bartender. "If you're feeling old, it's got nothing to do with age."

Either way, it was a weird night. Throwing back the other shot, I ordered two more and set my phone on the bartop—oh, a message. I dug those. I unlocked the phone and felt a bolt of excitement when I saw the text was from Ellis.

I forgot to tell you earlier this week. I'm enjoying getting to know you better, too. Hope you have a good weekend. —Ellis

Someone was practicing openness. I grinned and took a healthy swallow of my beer.

"You know who's hotter than hell?" I turned to Madigan, who offered an expectant stare. "Ellis," I said. And maybe I was starting to feel the effects of the alcohol. My chest felt warmer, my tongue looser, and my spirits higher. "Ellis Hayes has got to be one of the sexiest men on this planet."

Madigan laughed, half surprised and a whole lot of amused. "You're just now noticing that he's handsome? He's only been in the family longer than you and I have."

"He's more than handsome," I insisted.

He lifted a shoulder and smirked. "Okay, I get it, you think he's fine as fuck. Are you carrying a hard-on for a straight man, Case?"

Motherfucker, was I? Oh, who was I kidding? I most likely was. It would explain the excitement. There might even be the beginning of a minor crush, but those were harmless. "Wouldn't be the first time." I became infatuated easily, so I wasn't worried. They rarely ran deep.

Jameson returned and asked what we were talking about, which brought us to a mildly intoxicated toast about being infatuated with sex. It seemed I wasn't the only one struggling with the dating scene. We were all in the same boat. Casual flings held no appeal any longer, and that *sucked* when the sexual frustration built up.

Around midnight, we were all lit, and a rush of a younger crowd cranking up the volume in the bar made us leave the center of attention and seek out a table. It was darker here; the music was slightly louder too, but fewer people around helped.

"I'm not sure you have the right to bitch about it," Madigan told Jameson. "You're not even trying to meet someone. You're holed up in that cabin of yours with Alex."

That would be Jameson's older brother. They'd ended a couple disastrous relationships around the same time. As a way of moving forward and healing, the two brothers had bought a piece of land up in Westslope, the town's forest district that was perfect for hermits and woodsy folk. I didn't know many people in Westslope, though I worked there often enough.

"That's the fucking point of being in hiding, idiot," Jameson exclaimed, nearly tipping over the bowl of peanuts with his gesturing. "Why do you think I'm taking fewer clients at the shop?"

"Clearly not to focus more on your writing, which I *knew* was a goddamn excuse." Madigan narrowed his eyes accusingly, and I was cracking up. We were a whiny, bitchy trio. Why Jameson was avoiding their tattoo shop was confusing, however, and I guessed it showed. Madigan explained it to me. "Our apprentice follows Jamie around like a horny little puppy."

"And he's—fuck, sexy as hell," Jameson groaned. "But I won't go there. I don't shit where I eat."

I hummed, something jogging a memory. For some reason, I thought of Adrian. Hadn't he mentioned a little brother who was an apprentice there?

"As if that's not enough," Madigan continued, "our boy here's just realized his ex's daughter's all grown up."

"*Dude.*" I punched Jameson's arm, and he flinched and cursed.

He shot Madigan a quick glare. "That *boy* is older than both of you, and I can drop you on the floor like a sack of—"

"Keep talking dirty, pet." Madigan was in the mood to challenge.

"Pet," Jameson snorted. "Keep your kinky shit to yourself."

"Says the guy who's perving on his former stepdaughter," I laughed.

Jameson swung his gaze to me, and then he leaned close and spoke in my ear. "I can shut you up too, but I'd use my cock."

Gulp.

If that didn't silence me, I wasn't sure what would. Heat rose to my face, and I shifted in my seat. Don't think about it. Don't go there. If only I were obedient. So...what would happen if I did throw in another dig? Would he really do...that? No, he was joking.

"Wow, I'm officially drunk." I hiccupped and cursed myself for thinking about it. "And stupidly tempted."

He smirked lazily before pushing a shot glass my way.

For the next hour or so, I glanced at him too often. He caught me too often, too. Focusing on the conversation was nearly impossible. Instead, I found myself taking him in differently. He was another tatted-up bad boy, much like Madigan and Lincoln.

Funnily enough, I'd always found them safe. Being *attracted* to that type was safe. Because it was—in general—purely physical. Skin-deep, like their ink. A temporary thrill.

With my background, I had something wholesome and comfortable in mind for my future. Stability and normal hours, with a lot of focus on family. I needed to create a good home for my daughter so she wouldn't have to go through what I'd done. Not that I blamed my parents for my fuck-ups, but history was never innocent, and they'd played a part.

"What do you say, Casey?" Jameson's hand landed on my thigh under the table, causing me to jump slightly.

"What?" I replied dumbly.

Madigan chuckled. "We're talking about callin' it a night. You ready to go?"

Yes and no. It would probably be *wise* of me to hightail it out of here, except I had a problem. I was half hard in my jeans, and I wasn't thinking with the head on my shoulders.

Nevertheless, I nodded and emptied the third beer I'd had since I lost count.

The head rush hit me like a wrecking ball when I stood up. "Shit." I blinked and gripped the table, my free hand not-so-subtly adjusting my crotch. At least I made the guys laugh. "I need t-to take a leak." Even I heard the slurring in my voice. Jesus. "I'll be right back."

I stumbled out of the bathroom and dropped the paper towel on the way to the bar. I'd never understood unscented soap. Okay, fine, allergic people, but that place was sort of where you wanted a nice scent the most.

The bar was clearing out. I closed my tab and didn't even react to the amount of money I'd wasted on, well, getting wasted. Bleary-eyed and foggy-brained, I walked out and took a deep hit of the fresh sea air. It smelled like rain, and I wanted fries.

"Where's Madigan?" I joined Jameson on the boardwalk and looked around me. Only the lights from the row of restaurants and bar lit up my closest surroundings. The parking lot was...*that'a way*...and out of the dozen lamps on the pier, only one worked.

"I told him to beat it."

Ruh-roh.

The thrill was back, and it sent a jolt through my system. "Am I gonna regret something in the morning?"

He shook his head and slipped his hand into mine. "Come on. Just a short walk."

Yeah, toward hell.

Not that I was complaining. I let him take the lead and wasn't too surprised when we ended up on the pier. It wasn't windy tonight, which I wasn't sure was a good thing or bad. Washington weather otherwise had a knack for sobering one up.

I heard the ocean just fine, though I couldn't see it. Everything was pitch black except for the lone light that shone farther out on the pier. A shudder rolled through me in a heavy, sluggish way. The alcohol had a tight grip on me, effectively ramping up the lust and pushing down any rational thought.

"Madigan gave me a big-brother speech about not hurting you," Jameson mentioned.

"Sweet of him." I considered it and side-eyed him. "I'm not sure you could."

"Good." With that said, he guided me over to the railing and backed me up against it, his hands gripping the wooden bar to cage me in. My pulse kicked up as he leaned down a little, his hooded eyes intense and gauging my mood. "Goddamn." He cupped my jaw and searched my eyes. When I swallowed, his mouth quirked up in a sensual little smirk. "How the fuck haven't I noticed how gorgeous you are before?"

I exhaled a shaky laugh. "Booze will do that for you."

He shook his head and inched close enough to slide his nose along my jaw. "Tell you what, next time we see each other..." He pressed a soft, wet kiss at the corner of my mouth. "If I don't find you just as hot then, I'll run through the Valley naked."

I grinned. "Now I don't know what to hope for."

He chuckled huskily, and a beat later, his mouth covered mine.

6

"Oh God..." I moaned and clutched my stomach, strangely torn between nausea and desire. I could sense the sun shining through the window from behind closed eyelids. I was never drinking again. Fucking ever. Though, I might revisit Jameson if he was up for it. He was certainly *up* for it last night.

I rolled over and threw a pillow over my head, and of course, that slammed a screaming headache into place.

Perhaps I was one of those pain-sluts, 'cause my cock was still hard. Despite nausea. Despite headache. In the back of my mind, hazy memories of Jameson and me making out like teenagers kept the lust flowing through me in a steady current. We were at it quite a while, all hands and mouths, and it stayed there. We were good boys.

"Exactly what I needed tonight," he'd murmured in between two drugging kisses. "Fuck, you can kiss."

So could he.

The downside was the forceful reawakening of everything I yearned for. The pain rivaled my headache.

I touched my lips and sighed, having a feeling I wouldn't be able to sleep more. I needed to take a leak like whoa, and I itched to shower and brush my teeth.

With an unhappy grunt, I threw my legs over the edge of the bed and sat up as my feet hit the floor. Soft carpet. Not hardwood. What the...? I cracked one eye open, only to groan in sheer misery. I wasn't at Lincoln and Ade's, dammit! I'd completely forgotten just how wasted I was last night. After enjoying some kissing and groping with Jameson, I'd said fuck it and decided to crash on Lincoln's yacht. I had the keys, after all. And it'd been *so close*.

I scrubbed at my face, then surveyed the room. I suspected I'd landed in the bedroom in the stern of the boat. The area wasn't...pointy, like the bedroom in the bow. Light, soft carpet and matching walls and bed linen met the contrasts of the bed frame and cherry wood paneling. It was the design for pretty much everything on the yacht except the third bedroom that Lincoln had specially ordered to make two young girls happy. In there, a rainbow had taken a shit.

Scratching my arm absently, I hauled myself out of bed and stumbled into the bathroom. Time for a complete scrub-down. Then I was going to hunt down painkillers.

Half an hour later, I stepped out of the little bathroom along with a wall of steam. My nipples weren't too fond of the temperature drop, so I put on my tee from last night. Securing the towel around my waist, I exited the bedroom and walked down two steps to reach the middle area of the boat. There was a fully stocked kitchen, which struck me as a little odd, but most of all, there was a cupboard reserved for medicine and every lotion necessary for the guaranteed sunburns I got in the sun. Not that I had any plans to put myself through that torture.

Two painkillers in hand, I opened the fridge and shook my head at the waste. Every shelf was full, and it was gonna go bad before Lincoln and Ade came back home.

The yacht's soft bobbing on the water was taunting my nausea, so I poured a glass of OJ and downed the painkillers. Then I took a seat in the large booth that was the dining area. It would probably seat all of us, and I eyed the table with suspicion.

Knowing Lincoln, this spot was already tainted. He would've christened the yacht with Ade here.

I grimaced and leaned back, my hands landing in my lap. I had nothing planned today, so it was difficult to get my ass in gear. Instead, I stared out the window and waited for the headache to become a face on a milk carton.

It was a pretty day. The lower deck came fairly close to the water level, and the sun bounced off the dark blue surface. What were those islands, though? I leaned closer and squinted. It couldn't be the Chinook Islands—wait...why the fuck were these three islands so fucking *close*? You couldn't see the Chinooks—of which there were five, by the way—from the goddamn marina when a boat pointed toward them. It was completely the wrong angle.

I shot up from the table and rushed the fifteen or so feet to the other side, all but plastering my face to the window next to the kitchen area. No boats. Open water. Confusion gave way to the shock that shot through me. Had I drifted—no, that was ridiculous. A sixty-foot yacht didn't fucking drift out of the marina because it felt like it.

"What the fuck!" I gripped my hair, panicking. This was how it was going to end for me. Someone had kidnapped me—or stolen the yacht and they were going to kill me to get rid of me. Or it really was a kidnapping, and they were gonna demand a ransom for my freedom. Lincoln was loaded. Come on. Big-time producer and former guitarist in one of the biggest rock bands in the world.

I was being punished for my friendship with a famous person.

Fuck my life!

"What the *hell* are you doing here, Casey?"

I spun around at the sound of the angry voice coming from the stairs that led to freedom.

Ellis!

"*You* kidnapped me?" I yelled.

He did a double take and looked at me incredulously. "I did *what?* For God's sake, I'm borrowing the boat from Lincoln. You're not supposed to be here."

"I agree!" I glared, offended by the suspicion in his own glare. Did he think I'd snuck on to the boat to tag along? "So why don't you turn this raft around and take me home—*Now.*"

He gnashed his teeth together and pinched the bridge of his nose.

"What're you waiting for?" I threw out my arms.

"Lower your voice," he snapped. "Why are you shouting?"

"Because it makes me feel better!" I shouted.

Except, that kind of deflated me. I scratched my head and glanced around me, half expecting to see life as a little more colorful now that I wasn't going to sleep with the fishes. But everything was the same. The cream colors with the dark wood, the sun shining outside... No ransom for Casey's life.

"Why are *you* pissy?" I asked him. "I'm the one who's hungover and in serious need of a floor that doesn't move. It's not like I wanted to crash your party."

Ellis groaned under his breath and switched to rub his temples. "This was the last thing I needed, Casey. You can't even fathom it."

My brow furrowed. Worry trickled in and grasped on to the cobwebs of my hangover illness. "Did something happen?" I did remember him expressing he wanted to get away. Was this it? Was the yacht his white Bronco?

Ellis was going to dodge. I could tell. He sighed heavily, and I just knew he was seconds away from glossing over something that should be highlighted. So I put my foot down—figuratively.

"I'm not giving you an out here. Sit down," I told him. "Tell me what's going on."

That earned me a glare, though it was weaker than the previous one.

I took a seat at the Table of Defilement, and he followed, stiff as a stick and with his mouth pressed into a grim line.

Despite his rigidity, he looked more casual than ever, albeit weary. The suit was gone. Even his standard casual wear of slacks and pullovers was missing. His white tee looked brand-new. Had I ever seen his legs before? In a pair of cargo shorts with pockets on the sides, he was displaying a fine set of calves.

I had a thing for legs. Thighs, calves, the lines of muscle...

I shook my head and got my deprived ass back to the topic at hand.

"I can't stay at home anymore," he said tightly. "There isn't much to say. I need a break, so I called Lincoln and asked if I could borrow the boat for a couple of weeks. He said yes."

"Yeah, I, uh, I can do the math on that one. You don't strike me as one to steal a yacht."

"But I strike you as a kidnapper?"

"Exactly, so let's get back to the part where you can't stay at home." I wasn't gonna let him derail *nothin'*. "What's going on, Ellis?"

Landing his forearms on the table, he slumped his shoulders while he stewed. His jaw clenched, and he cracked his knuckles. I winced even though there was no sound. Nasty habit. Jesse often did that, too.

"Did you and your wife fight?" I prodded.

He shook his head minutely. "The opposite, I suppose. I told you about this—how easy it would be to go back." I remembered, and it made me sad. I didn't believe for one second he should stay in a lifeless marriage because it was easy. "It's so incredibly fake, Casey." He scrubbed at his face and blew out a breath. "I knew from the moment she suggested a nice dinner at home that it was going to be a disaster."

"Disasters aren't generally easy," I noted.

"No, and it wasn't." He shook his head, staring at the table. "I felt suffocated and had to close myself off in a way I've never done before. It was terrible." He paused. "I fled like a coward after dinner. Spent the night in my office, then called Lincoln and made arrangements to get away for a while."

I nodded slowly, figuring he'd picked up the other set of keys at Lincoln and Ade's house. It was a wonder we hadn't run into each other, and something made me curious.

"Did you sleep here last night?" I asked.

He lifted his brows a fraction. "I did. Whiskey knocked me out, but how you slept through several hours of traveling along the coast is a miracle."

"We're in Canada?" I sort of half shouted. Technically, this wasn't a big deal. We already lived closer to Vancouver than Seattle, but Christ, another country made it sound so far away from home and, and, and *drastic*.

In my defense, twenty minutes ago, I thought I was in the marina.

The look he gave me said it was possible he thought I had a flair for drama.

He wasn't necessarily wrong.

"I didn't say I was going north," he replied impatiently. "But, no. We left Port Angeles a while ago. I filled up on fuel there."

That meant... I squinted at nothing, visualizing a map. He'd gone a little south, and now we were on the way alongside the Olympic Peninsula toward the open sea. This was bad. We were nowhere near the comfort of Camassia and our calm waters. I *liked* that part of living in an inlet with more islands than I could count. Land was never too far away.

"All right..." I wrung my hands and looked out the window. We weren't moving at the moment. If we had been, I would've feared he had an accomplice on board. "So, uh—" I cleared my throat. "How are we on the matter of taking me home? Once I know, I can calm my tits and be a better listener."

It was his turn to clear his throat, and he shifted in his seat. "Problem is, if I see any more of Camassia today, I'm not sure what I'll do. I have a friend outside of Port Renfrew who's letting me spend the night in—"

"That's in Canada," I interrupted.

"Gold star for you. It's on Vancouver Island, yes—"

"But it's *Canada*," I repeated. "*Whole* other maple leaf. What's wrong with staying in America?"

He frowned. "Do you hate Canada or something?"

"No..." What of cell service, though? "Can I check in with Haley there?"

His mouth twisted, and something in his eyes grew gentler. "It's Canada, Casey, not outer space. This shouldn't be news for you. You travel quite a bit with Lincoln and Ade."

I lifted a shoulder. "I have Haley with me then, and I use the hotel Wi-Fi for blogging."

"Fair enough, but yes, you'll be able to call Haley. It's only for one night. I need to clear my head. Then I can take you home tomorrow morning. Okay?"

Well, what choice did I have? I didn't want to be a dick. He clearly needed the space. Besides, I wanted to know what *would* have happened if he returned to Camassia today. Would he panic? Get anxious? In which case, I'd honestly like to know why. This was serious shit.

What plans did I have, anyway? None whatsoever.

"Okay." I nodded once. I wasn't going to freak out and admit I wasn't born with sea legs. It was all good. Twenty-four hours on a yacht in waters so deep that a dozen Loch Ness monsters could have an orgy underneath us and we wouldn't know.

Cool.

As it turned out, I'd slept 'til noon earlier, so we'd been on our merry way for a long time. We still had hours to go before we got to Port Renfrew, and I did my best to sleep through it. Failing horribly. I kept lifting my head off the pillow to look outside and see if I could spot land.

I couldn't.

Ellis was obviously driving, and he'd made it pretty clear he wanted this time to be alone, so I couldn't bother him with my nervous chitchat.

If I ever wanted to get away, I'd stay on land.

After tossing and turning a couple hours, I gave up and left the bed. My options on clothes were limited, and I ended up going commando in my jeans from yesterday. My T-shirt smelled all right. Then I went upstairs to the upper deck...and froze.

Much like in a car, there was a driver's seat and a passenger's seat. Ellis used neither, opting to drive while standing. He gave me a cursory nod and slid his Ray-Bans down from the top of his head, but that wasn't what made me all but drop my jaw.

Holy mother of... There was land. I'd stupidly been looking out the window of the wrong side of the boat. Land was everywhere. I'd never been so happy to see Canada. Shit, it was stunning. Mountains and valleys covered in thick forest—not unlike back home—and steep cliffsides, waterfalls... *Land.*

I needed to see more. This part of the upper deck had an indoor feel with a large sunroof and tinted windows on the sides. I passed the driver's section and lounge area to sit down on the edge of the massive sunbed. Foamy. I tested the bounce a second.

There was none.

Then I was back to staring at the mountains and valleys to my right. It was different seeing land from the ocean. More immense.

I breathed in the salty air, ignoring the slight chill—and the wind in my hair. Fuck, it was gorgeous. Not a cloud in sight, either.

We'd slowed down significantly.

My nausea and headache were gone, and I leaned back, my elbows hitting the soft padding, with the first sigh of contentment for today. Maybe being out here wasn't too awful. Maybe it would even do me some good.

The sun on my skin felt nice.

Movement from Ellis caught my eye, and I frowned when I spotted him leaving the console. With a map in hand, he shifted over to the lounge where he sat down on the large L-shaped sofa and fanned out the map across the table.

I gaped at him.

"What the fuck're you doing?" I sat up straight.

Ellis glanced at me, confused. "Pardon?"

"We're—" I waved a hand at the wheel, panic rising. "We're *going!*"

Looking over at the two empty seats by the wheel, he furrowed his brow before facing me once more. "It's on autopilot. I'm going to set the course so I can make us some lunch. I assume you haven't eaten."

"Auto—" I squawked. Very cool of me. "Motherfucker. Autopilots on *boats?*"

Ellis became impatient. "For chrissakes, Casey, you've been on boats before."

"I don't think cruise ships count," I shot back. Or parties on sailboats that didn't leave the marina.

If the boat was out on the water, someone was driving it. It was kind of like a rule.

Ellis broke that rule and told me, while failing to hide his aggravation, that he'd give me the ins and outs later. He promised we were safe and that everything was fine. He said if I was overly worried, I could sit by the wheel and make sure we didn't leave our course while he fixed us something to eat.

I didn't want to be a bother, so I didn't mention that we were out on the sea. There weren't any roads or signs to let me know the *fucking* course. I decided to wing it. It was too late to save my dignity, but dammit, I could keep us alive by making sure we didn't come too close to land. Funny how that worked. Land was my favorite thing in the world. Now I was going to veer away from it.

I didn't touch the wheel even once. Ellis knew exactly what the "road" looked like, and he'd picked a moment where he was confident enough to step away altogether. The autopilot did the work, and I sat there like a schmuck.

"Can I help?" I called down the stairs.

"No, that's okay," he replied. "It's better you make sure we don't crash and die a fiery death."

"I realize you're mocking me, but—"

"Then let's leave it at that, Casey."

I snapped my mouth shut and ran a hand through my hair, figuring it was best not to push it. He was funny when he was testy, and I had a knack for poking the sleeping bear. Instead, I sat back and twiddled my thumbs, eyes searching for my next distraction.

The yacht's manual would work.

I flipped through the pages and snorted at some of the terms. God forbid we call it bedroom or kitchen. It was VIP Aft Cabin and galley. The lounge area behind me was evidently a saloon, as was the dining area next to the kitchen—'scuse me, galley.

Reading about the hydraulics entertained me. I found such things fascinating, same with the freshwater system. Tapping my cheek absently, I thought of the park I was going to design in Camas, the neighborhood south of Downtown. I'd be on a tight budget, but there was such a thing as saving money by spending a little extra of it. Rainwater harvesting came to mind. The park should be *useful*. With a filtration and purification system, it would be free drinking water. Or it could generate electricity for what the solar panels wouldn't cover. A green park, in every way imaginable. I liked this idea. Much to ponder.

The smell of herbs and something fried was followed by Ellis resurfacing from the galley.

"Goodness." I stared at the two plates he carried. I spotted two minor mountains of fries and what looked like strips of fried fish. Lettuce, cucumber, cherry tomatoes, dressing, and ketchup. Yeah, I followed him to the lounge, because hey, the autopilot could drive us. "You make the best kidnapper, Ellis."

He smirked briefly.

I liked him better without shades. Now I could read him easier.

The sofa was huge and the table was low, so I got comfortable and held my plate close instead. Spillage happened to adults, too. I didn't think Ade would appreciate ketchup on the cream-colored couch. Which was a stupid color for furniture, by the way.

"You can cook." I smiled, adding it to his list. "What else can you do?"

"I can tie a cherry stem with my tongue." He was messin', but I thought that was an impressive skill. A *sexy* one.

Shit.

A memory from last night came back to me. Did I admit to being infatuated with Ellis?

I winced internally and threw a couple fries into my mouth.

Wrong man to get attached to that way.

It was what it was, though. It would fade.

"Where does one pick up a skill like that?" I asked. "College?"

He nodded, stabbing a piece of fish with his fork. "I was a fun guy once upon a time." He took on a pensive expression. "Perhaps a bit too fun."

"How so?"

He chewed what was in his mouth and reached to grab a remote off the table. My eyebrows shot up as he pressed a button that made the top of the table slide to the side, revealing the inside of the...well, box. It was a giant-ass cooler. "You know of my parents?" He grabbed a bottle of orange juice for himself and a can of Pepsi for me. He knew I liked Pepsi.

I nodded slowly, still stuck on the futuristic fridge. "I've heard stories. Thank you." I accepted the Pepsi.

"I managed to get a full ride through college," he said. "A scholarship was the only way I knew I could escape my folks."

Made sense. His father—Lincoln's dad's brother—was a seemingly normal guy up until he met Ellis's mother. She was... I couldn't even say religious because there was nothing wrong with that. Being part of a cult, however, was. The stories I'd heard bordered on abuse. Like not letting Ellis have supper until he recited a prayer correctly.

There was an uncomfortable tug in my chest at the thought. I'd known about this for years, yet now, when I was getting know Ellis better, it put things in a new perspective. How the fuck did he stay sane in a home like that? I was glad he'd escaped.

"College must've been liberating." I tipped my head, studying him.

"Indeed. To the point where I almost forgot the part where I was supposed to study." He let out a chuckle and dragged a fry through the pool of dressing. "I partied quite a bit my freshman year."

Understandable. Who wouldn't? He was finally free. Then he'd gotten his act together, presumably. Otherwise, he wouldn't be sitting here with a couple degrees now.

"Any regrets?" I asked. Because that was really all that mattered, wasn't it?

"I wouldn't say regrets." He chose his words carefully. "It's... complicated. I'm not sure how to explain it."

It's complicated.

I grimaced at that. I couldn't exactly fault him for using the term; I did it plenty myself. Excuse me for not enjoying when *others* did it.

I ate in silence for a while, unsure of what was okay and not. Respecting his wishes came first, so if he wasn't in the mood to talk, there was little I could do on the front of learning more and eventually be of help.

"Can I ask you something?" he asked.

"Anything." There was that weird jolt of excitement again. Whenever he initiated conversation, I had half a mind to fist-pump the air.

"What would you say you crave the most in your life?" Jeebus. When he asked, he asked big. I opened my mouth to respond, and he held up a hand. "Not a wisecrack, Casey."

Aw, man. I *did* crave more of this garlicky dressing, though. That was no wisecrack.

I set down my plate next to me, drawing patterns in the ketchup with a forked piece of cucumber. Flicking my gaze to his plate, I noticed he didn't have any ketchup. Was that another thing he'd done for me because he knew I liked it?

It was slightly disconcerting to know so little about him and, at the same time, have no clue how much he knew about me.

I slumped my shoulders in defeat. In the end, I wasn't going to lie. I was an honest man, even when it made me feel ridiculously exposed.

"I crave death to stereotypes," I muttered.

"That was..."

"Not what you expected to hear?" I smiled wryly.

He smiled back and shook his head. "No, not really. Care to elaborate?"

I didn't mind too much; I just wanted him to open up, as well. "If you go first, Elusive Ellis. What do you crave most of all right now?"

That required some thinking, but he didn't reject it. Opening his OJ, he took a big swallow from it and then fidgeted with the cap. "In short, connection. Connection and affection."

Ouch.

He peered out the window, a crease forming between his brows. "I remember I used to love simple touches. I think it's from where I derive energy." No wonder he often looked so tired. He was deprived. Something I could relate to. "There was a time Marilyn and I couldn't keep our hands off one another. It wasn't even always about sex. Just—that level of closeness.

Although..." He furrowed his brow in thought. "I think it was more my thing than hers, to be honest."

I swallowed and nodded with a dip of my chin. I wasn't hungry anymore, the food—as delicious as it was—sitting like a rock in my stomach.

He kind of nailed it with those words. Connection and affection. It was from others I got energy, too. When I spent too much time alone, I grew frustrated, restless, and moody. Like something was missing.

"Sounds familiar." I cleared my throat and moved the plate to the table. I was done eating.

"About those stereotypes," he hedged carefully.

"Yeah, fuck them." I forced a smile and set down my pop, too. Needing some distance, I scooted back to the corner of the sofa and stretched out my legs. "I never fit into any premade molds, and there's nothing like *seeing* the moment your date realizes you're not their type."

Shouldn't that shit stop hurting by now?

This was what I'd planned on blogging about the other day before I'd chickened out. I guess it was one of those subjects that crossed the line for me. Honesty was a must. Complete vulnerability was harder.

"What premade molds do people tend to have you in?" he asked curiously.

"Depends what they know of me beforehand and if it's a man or a woman," I replied. "Most of the time, though, it's that I'm not manly enough." Bitterness crept in.

Ellis seemed confused. "You're joking, right?"

"Nope." This applied to both men and women. Actually, when I dated men, I was either-or. Not masculine enough or not feminine enough. After three years of constant dating, it was sort of crushing to never be enough. "People can't place me."

With my criminal history, I was expected to be this badass motherfucker.

I had learned several useful lessons in prison, and none of them involved being able to hold my own. My one strength was that I was fast. I loved running. Going up against someone else in a fistfight, however? No, I'd had Lincoln to protect me. I didn't fight. I fucking *hated* violence.

Lincoln was released one year before I was, and I spent the following months in and out of hysteria. I turned to self-harm so I could medicate myself halfway into a daze. I closed myself off whenever I could so I wouldn't fall apart. I wasn't strong in that sense.

Explaining this shit to Ellis put me on edge, but as always, it was best to get it off my chest. If he found me ridiculous or too weak, he could move on. No time wasted.

"I'm not one of those flamboyant types, either," I went on, tracing an invisible pattern on the sofa. "I like sports, beer, and being in charge." Well...half the time, at least. "Then, I also like a good bargain, Beyoncé, and pleasing the people I love." My brows knitted together, and I trailed off a bit.

Was it that I didn't take myself seriously? A handful of people I'd dated in the past found it embarrassing when I goofed off in public. For Halloween, one better believe I was in a costume, too. It made the girls smile like loons. I had no issues shaking my ass, being the life of the party, or having fun at my own expense.

When your daughter was your world, it was difficult to care about what happened on the outside. Yet, others seemed to care so fucking much about image and what strangers thought.

Enough, already. Lighten the mood.

I blew out a breath, then mustered a smirk. "It's not easy being someone who burps the alphabet one second then giggles like a schoolgirl the next."

Ellis didn't buy it. Resting his forearms on his knees, he studied me with an open expression.

I tried again. With a grin that probably came off more self-deprecating than cocky. "I'm complicated."

He shook his head slowly and brushed a hand over his mouth. "You seem perfectly fluid to me."

Yeah...and who the fuck wanted fluid.

7

The sun was setting by the time we reached the inlet that led to Port Renfrew. Ellis slowed down, leisurely navigating his way between sailboats and other yachts. A few were even as extravagant as this one.

Boat people had a thing for waving and saying hi. Unfortunately, I wasn't feeling social at the moment. Ellis hid out in the driver's seat, and I lay down on the sunbed. These waters were calm, as was the wind, so I removed my T-shirt and threw it over my head.

Saying hi was one thing, but seriously. When you had to shout at the top of your lungs for a nearby boat to even hear you, what was the point?

The only one I cared to say hi to was Haley. The connection was spotty, so I had to resort to texting Adeline, who responded with a "The girls are having a blast. Love you!"

I managed to let her know I'd have shitty cell service 'til tomorrow before I lost the connection again.

I inhaled deeply, willing myself to relax. Willing the concerns to shush. The foamy sunbed was perfect and didn't stick to my skin. Memory foam—that was it. I'd splurged on a pillow like this at home, and here I had a whole fucking sunbed in that material. I sank down comfortably on it, and if I didn't have qualms about sleeping on the open sea—under the stars—I would've ditched my bed.

I did have qualms, though. And mosquitoes found me delicious.

"Have you managed to clear your head any today?" I asked, hoping he heard me. It wasn't too noisy anymore.

"Perhaps a little." There was a comfortable stretch of silence before he spoke again. "I really only had one thing planned for today."

"What's that?" I lifted the T-shirt a little to see how low the sun was getting.

"Throw a couple burgers on the grill, open a too-expensive bottle of Scotch, and watch the sunset."

I smiled sleepily to myself.

Sounded like a nice evening, and he certainly deserved it.

With the soft fabric of my tee over my head, I soaked up some sun and dozed on and off for a while, the gentle movements of the yacht oddly lulling for a guy who wasn't a big fan of the water.

At some point, it became completely silent, and it was a low, mechanical whirr that roused me. *"Lights out!"* I sat up straight, disoriented. The sound—fuck—it reminded me of the lock systems in prison.

"What's that sound?" I asked, clearing my throat.

"Just lowering the anchor."

Oh. I scrubbed at my face, shaking the memory, then peered around me. "Shouldn't—" *there be a marina?* Ellis had mentioned a friend... We were in the middle of a small cove now, though. Surrounded by forest and cliffs on all sides.

I twisted my body and looked behind us. A river, I guessed. How long had we been traveling upriver for?

"Missed the sunset," I heard Ellis mention.

Yeah, it'd recently disappeared behind the tree line. The remaining light danced across the sky and would fade soon enough. And then what? *Blair Witch* meets *Jaws*? A forest wasn't enough; we had to be dumped in a huge puddle of water, too.

"Are we *staying* here?" I asked.

Ellis nodded and stretched his arms above his head. "A friend has a vacation house here. You can see his dock over there." He pointed. "No need for an extra permit, no rent to stay at the port."

I followed the direction and saw a red house nestled among the trees on a hillside across the cove. Okay, so we'd be in the Canadian Amityville instead. Fuckin' A. We were going to die one horrific way or another.

Oh God. The forest was alive. I heard it. Rustling trees and cooing owls. Or whatever it was.

"Do you have no sense of self-preservation?" I stared at Ellis.

His eyes flashed with mirth. "I take it you're not tagging along for a midnight swim later?"

"You're out of your fucking mind," I replied flatly.

He chuckled and headed downstairs.

Well, shit. Fuck if I was staying here alone. Scooting off the sunbed, I was quick to follow him below deck. At least down here, I could pretend I was in a house. On land.

Ellis disappeared into the bedroom at the front, only to return with two hoodies. "It gets chilly, and I presume you don't have extra clothes on board."

No, nothing other than the pullover I wore last night. And my tee that I not-so-conveniently forgot on the sunbed. I wasn't going up there to get it, that was for damn sure.

"I didn't plan to be kidnapped, so, no." I accepted the hoodie with a nod of thanks and pulled it on. *Jeeesus*, the man smelled good. I didn't expect a full-body shudder. "I, uh... Actually, I wasn't planning on crashing on the yacht last night, either."

"You mentioned a hangover." He inclined his head and opened the fridge. "Hot date at the marina?"

I snorted and half sat on the dining room table. "I did have a date, but I blew it. Couldn't bother to give many fucks last night for some reason. Then I met up with Madigan and—you've heard of Jameson, right?"

He nodded, getting busy with burger fixings.

"We got wasted, and then Jameson and I exchanged some saliva before I thought, hey, that boat is really close. I'll just sleep there."

Ellis spared me a brief frown. "Lovely description."

"Fine. We held hands and made kissy faces. Better?"

He sighed and gathered all the food on a tray. He was evidently dead set on his Amityville barbecue.

It made me nervous, which seriously sucked. I didn't want to be a scaredy-cat.

Running a hand through my hair, I eyed the stairs, knowing I was acting like a goddamn head case for being even slightly anxious. Would I need Ellis to check if there were monsters under my bed, too?

Also, when I was nervous, I lost whatever little filter I had in the first place.

I rambled. "Basically, we were three single guys who complained about dating while getting hammered in the wrong way and talking about some men we find really hot. Your name might've come up once or twice."

Ellis did a double take, the shock evident. "My name, what? I mean, who would—"

"I did." I stood up straight. Now the words were out there, and it temporarily settled the nerves. It gave me something new to focus on, and right now, that was to own what I'd said. No big deal. I hoped he found it flattering. "It can't come as a surprise that you're attractive as all fuck."

His lips parted. Then he swallowed and promptly closed his mouth before he looked away. Oh, holy shit, I'd managed to embarrass him. In a highly adorable way. His ears tinted red, and he cleared his throat.

"We should get dinner started."

I watched him stalk out and upstairs, my mouth twisting up. *Don't poke the bear.* If only that wasn't so *fun.* Lord, what would happen if I flirted with him? Would he keel over?

If I was going to brave the Canadian night in the middle of nowhere, I was going to need entertainment.

Ellis handled the grill. It was a portable one that he set up down on the bathing platform—at fucking sea level. I stayed up on the deck, in the lounge area where I made sure the sunroof and all windows were closed, and maybe I located a few blankets, too.

I'd enjoyed several sleepovers with Haley and Lyn in a blanket fort. Fuck anyone who said they were only for kids.

It got dark quickly once the sun set, and only a reddish glow was left where the sun had disappeared. The night sky was taking over, black inch by black inch, star by star. Not even sexy black inches.

I stole Ellis's previous spot on the sofa too, because there wasn't a chance in hell I was going to turn my back on the darkness. Only a mosquito net separated us from the rabid wilderness.

I couldn't see Ellis, which bothered me, but I saw the thin pillar of smoke from the grill, smelled the delicious burgers, and heard the sizzle and pop of the fire. My T-shirt was still on the sunbed, on the other side of the net. Beyond saving.

Was I a loser or what?

This morning, I remembered holding my stomach and vowing never to drink again. Empty words, of course. I was chugging beer already.

When Ellis trailed up the steps along the side of the boat, I was ready for my second beer. He unzipped the mosquito screen and appeared with a plate of burgers. The tray on the low table was full of condiments and vegetables, and my stomach rumbled. I'd have to repay him somehow for the awesome meals. Maybe I could make my famous pancake breakfast tomorrow.

"Is it that cold?" Ellis sat down next to me and eyed the blanket covering my legs.

"Don't be silly. This is my armor." I leaned forward and plated a burger, ignoring his amused expression. Then he did something stupid. He reached for the magic remote, and instead of turning the table into a cooler, he dimmed the lights a *lot*. "What're you doing?"

"You do know the light attracts the insects, yes?"

We had the net...

Then again, a million moths smashed up against the netted screen didn't sound appealing.

"Okay, I'll allow it," I muttered.

Why were people so fucking fascinated with the outdoors? I enjoyed a good hike here and there, and the trails above Ponderosa and Westslope up to Coho Pass were spectacular for a long run. Then when darkness loomed ahead, you went *home*. Fuck tents. And rock-star yachts.

"What plans am I ruining tomorrow when you take me back to Camassia?" I wondered.

"That's the thing about vacations. I haven't made many plans." There was visible discomfort at the notion of going home tomorrow, yet he spoke with ease and even managed a somewhat casual shrug. "I get back to work on September fourth. Until then, I'm going to take it easy. Do some fishing, hiking, reading...thinking." Sucking some mayo off the side of his thumb, he used his free hand to retrieve a folded-up brochure from one of his many pockets. "After dropping you off, I'm going here."

I took a bite of my burger and leaned in to see better in the shitty light. "Oh, wow. That's beautiful." The pictures showed thick forest, a suspension bridge across a narrow canyon, and an impressive waterfall. "Where's this?"

Ellis gestured toward the river that brought us to this cove. "There's a smaller river a couple miles north. I thought I'd take the tender and get there in half the time it would take if I hiked."

"Tender—I know that word. It's a small boat." If you lived in a coastal town, you picked up on these things. For a Detroit kid, it was something.

"Very good," he chuckled. "Yes, there's a tender in the storage under that sunbed." He nodded at the home of my discarded T-shirt. "Hopefully, I'll bring back dinner at the end of the day."

I nodded. So he was going fishing in a tiny motorboat. Upriver. Mountains and forest everywhere, and little springs with waterfalls for swimming. Why the hell was I feeling jealous? Because it sounded *fun*. It would be during the day.

"You'll have fun." I smiled.

The smile faltered as it dawned on me how much I felt like staying. Fuck the yacht and the water and the hiking; I wanted Ellis's company. I liked being around him. There was a warmth to him that I wanted to soak up. At the same time, I wanted to ease his aches. There were constant traces of sadness and weariness in his eyes. I hated that part.

Ellis shifted a little on the couch. "I don't suppose I can convince you to stay an extra day?" At that, my heart rate picked up. "Problem is, I wouldn't be able to get you back in time for work on Monday—"

"That's fine," I said quickly. 'Cause, fuck yes, this was happening. "I can call in sick. I'm pretty tight with the boss." This meant another night on a boat, and I didn't even care. "Does that mean we can do the waterfall swimming tomorrow?"

"Sure." For one moment, the sadness was gone from his eyes. It flooded me with contentment and stupid longing.

"I thought you wanted to be alone," I said, side-eyeing him.

"So did I."

The next morning, I faced a big dilemma about what to wear—until Ellis introduced me to the Starboard Crew Cabin. It was a small extra space designed to be whatever you needed. There was a bed you could flip down from the wall, a utility closet, and even a damn washing machine. I could wash my Friday night clothes.

"I packed to stay away for a month, so there's my closet, too," he said.

I ended up borrowing a pair of black trunks and a long-sleeved army-green tee.

When I reemerged from my bedroom after changing clothes, he was waiting in the kitchen.

"How did you sleep last night?" he asked.

"Let's not talk about it, okay?" I tightened the drawstrings of the trunks. Ellis was a size or two larger than me. Maybe three. "By the way, I'm making breakfast."

"Have at it." He stepped aside with a faint smirk playing on his lips. "You weren't attacked by any sea monsters?"

Oh, you.

It was quite possible I'd slept like a freaking baby, but he didn't need to know that. I focused on breakfast instead. "Don't you have something to do?" I pulled a carton of eggs and some other shit from the fridge. "Maybe get the little raft out of the big one?"

"We're going to Port Renfrew first," he replied. "One of the battery chargers is acting up."

I chewed on the inside of my cheek as I measured what I needed for the pancakes. "Every cabin has a charger." One of the few things I'd noticed. It'd be a travesty if my phone died.

"Ah, for the boat—not a phone charger."

Right. Duh.

"So we'll be parked there for the day while we're out?" I questioned. "Or, um, docked. Whatever."

His mouth twitched, and he nodded once.

All right, then.

"But I guess I can start driving if you're making breakfast." He pushed off the wall he'd been leaning against. "Let me know if you need any help."

Hell no. He'd done too much for me already. Besides, a breakfast tasted better if it was a surprise, and he hadn't tried my main act.

We were only an hour or so outside of Port Renfrew, and in that time, I prepared everything for a quick breakfast as well as food to bring on our outing today. A couple rolls were getting stale on the counter, so I sliced them thin and threw them in a pan with butter and cheddar.

I added some extra salt to the pancake batter after taste-testing the first one.

Orange wedges, water, pops, a couple apples, and a handful of candy bars went into a cooler. I'd been around boat people enough to know that the cooler would just be lowered into the water when we stopped for a break. The cheesy bread followed once I'd gotten rid of excessive grease and bagged them. There were also some leftovers from lunch yesterday that we could finish off.

While I waited for the pancakes to cool off, I prepared four sandwich wraps we could eat before we took off.

Then, magic. My famous pancakes and the toppings.

Watching Ellis secure the yacht in the Port Renfrew tourist marina was going to become spank-bank material. He radiated masculinity and concentration. Ray-Bans on, another pair of cargo shorts, and a tee that stretched across his chest, the white fabric a contrast to his subtle tan. Goddamn those Hayes men. They didn't turn lobster red in the sun.

"Can you open the tender garage, Casey?" He climbed up on the dock with a thick rope. "We should be out of here in ten."

"Okay." I rose from the sofa and trailed down to the bathing platform. As I opened the storage, my eyebrows shot up at the sight of what was inside. Yacht architects needed more recognition. What they did to utilize every nook and cranny was nothing short of amazing.

The tender looked like one of those inflatable rescue boats. Of course, since this belonged to a man who pissed liquid gold, it had to be fancy. Leather seats for two near the back, and an open surface at the front for two people to stretch out and have a merry time. More than that, there was a fucking jet-ski behind the tender.

Well, the garage was open. I didn't wanna make a wrong move, so I returned to the lower deck to grab the cooler. Better safe than sorry, I opened the fridge to grab another couple of pops. I could inhale those suckers.

I closed the fridge, then frowned when I spotted two receipts stuck under a magnet.

"Un-fucking-real," I blurted out. Fuel receipts. In the span of twenty-four hours, Ellis had spent nearly a grand on diesel. I couldn't believe it. Yachts were a *menace*. And he was going to make a ridiculous detour to take me all the way back and spend that amount again? Guilt slammed into me with enough force to knock the air out of my lungs.

How would I pay him back? I did all right these days. I could even set some money aside every month, but vacations that were literally a thousand dollars a night were way out of my price range.

I was going to blame Lincoln for this. Fucking rock stars.

I left the lower deck, feeling glum, and reached the bottom platform just as Ellis came back. Someone was going to look at the battery charger, he told me.

"I wish you'd told me how pricey this water castle was in fuel consumption," I muttered. At his look of confusion, I added, "I saw the receipts on the fridge."

That didn't make him any less confused. "What about them?"

"Oh, boy. Never mind." I blew out a breath, understanding now he was one of *those* people. The saying went, "*If you have to ask how much it is, you can't afford it,*" and he was one of those who didn't ask. "Just...let me know if there's anything I can do to pay back—" *Shit.* My eyes widened. "I didn't mean for that to sound sexual. *Although*...it's certainly not off the table."

He coughed and glared for a second, though he couldn't hold it. Not when I blasted him with my megawatt, lopsided grin.

That's when he sighed. "You're something else, Casey Teague."

Yup. I was complicated, right?

The tender boat was featherlight in comparison to what I

expected, and between Ellis's strength and direction skills and my...being here, we got the little boat in the water in a jiffy.

It looked like I was gonna poke him with some flirting, after all, because when he had one foot in the tender and the other on the yacht, I couldn't resist. "Has anyone ever told you how delicious you look with your legs spread?"

He grabbed the cooler from me. "No, you'd be the first. Thank you for being gentle."

Sad day for me; he'd figured out my game and didn't let it ruffle his feathers this time. On the other hand, now I could add witty to the list. I *loved* witty comebacks.

"In fact..." He pointed at a duffel on the platform, which I handed over. "I barely felt anything."

"What the—" I stared at him, incredulous. Did he really go there? Oh, he did. That sly, sexy son of a bitch. "You actually... *Wow.*"

He laughed, and the rich, heartfelt sound was fucking gorgeous. He needed to laugh more often.

"Just get in the damn boat, Casey."

Yes, sir.

Ellis liked to go *fast*.

Fuck it, so did I. If this little boat capsized, I wouldn't worry about getting a Titanic over me. I'd just swim to the closest shore, which in this case was a minute or two away on either side. The seats were comfortable, the excitement in my stomach was constant, and the sun was shining. It was the beginning of an awesome day.

I'd finished eating, so I offered to take over. He'd only had a couple bites of his wrap.

"Are you sure?" he asked over the wind. "I'd like to get there sometime today."

"Oh, you're real funny." I scowled as he grinned.

It was a beautiful grin. Someone's spirits were getting higher.

He did eventually concede, and it was time for me to reclaim some of my coolness. I could go fast as hell, dammit. When he rose from his seat, I slid into the one he left, and he pulled the cooler closer to get his food.

To be a dick, I reached over and stole his shades. If I'd known I was going to get kidnapped, I would've brought my own.

"You don't ask first?" He raised a brow.

"You didn't ask before you kidnapped me," I pointed out.

The rumbling of the motor cut him off before he could argue, and then I stepped on it. I absolutely loved to drive, and this almost topped being in a car. Flying over the bumpy water turned it into a ride that belonged in an amusement park.

"I didn't think you had it in you," he said with a smirk.

I flashed him a lazy smile and a wink, then slid on his shades.

8

I hissed at the cold, gently rubbing the sunscreen across my neck. Clutching the bottle, I stepped over to the front of the boat and sat down on the floor. Here, I could stretch out my legs and, most of all, *not* have the sun grilling my neck.

"How are you feeling?" Ellis returned to the driver's seat and eyed me in concern.

"Crispy." I blamed the fast driving. Slicing through the air at high speed meant I didn't feel the onslaught of the sun. Then when we took a break and I twisted my body to unpack our lunch—holy fuck. I sure felt it now. "Sometimes, I think I was made to be a pasty gamer who lives permanently in a basement."

Ellis's mouth twisted up. "There's still time."

"I don't like gaming." So I was shit out of luck.

He winced. "Lost cause, then."

I liked this new development. We were touching on bantering territory. My favorite.

Removing my shirt, I hung it around my neck to give it a shadowed break—a well-deserved one. "When will we be at the waterfall, you think?" I asked, pouring more lotion into my hand. No need for the rest of me to get burned, so I began applying the sunscreen on my chest, abs, and arms. They were pretty abs. I'd worked hard for them.

Ellis cleared his throat and stared into the forest. "Shouldn't be long. According to the map, it was a couple miles past the suspension bridge."

We just drove under that. I would've missed it if Ellis hadn't pointed it out. It was high up.

He told me if we had time, we should hike up there and cross the bridge. I laughed at the sexy lunatic. If I didn't like deep waters, I sure as fuck didn't like dangling above air on a bridge made of rope and rickety boards. Crazy talk.

Done with the lotion, I sighed contentedly and leaned back against the edge of the tender. "You can drive. I think I've found my sweet spot."

He let out a chuckle. "I thought the point of this break was lunch."

"Oh, right." I sat up straight again and reached for the cooler. "Are you ready to taste my magic, Skipper?"

I realized how dirty that sounded.

So did he, and he snorted and shook his head. "I know how this works. I say yes, you drop a pun filled with innuendo. I say no, I don't get lunch."

"Win-win for me," I laughed. I dug around the cooler and found the box I was looking for. "Okay, so these are my awesome pancake sandwiches. We've got cream cheese, sundried tomatoes, and bacon as crispy as I am. And we've got sausage, eggs, and mushrooms in the other. Which one do you want to start with?"

"Good lord in heaven," he muttered. "Am I having a side of diabetes with that?"

"Possibly two."

"Bacon, please."

"Can't go wrong with bacon." I tossed him a wrapped sandwich and told him there were enough to get some clogged arteries, too.

He unwrapped it carefully and gave it a sniff before he tried it.

Then everything shot straight to hell. He closed his eyes and let out a low, gruff groan, and I zoned out for a while. That *sound*... I shuddered violently and swallowed dryly. I'd need to hear that sound again.

"Fuck, Casey."

I gusted out a long breath and adjusted my trunks.

I did get to hear that sound again. Ellis devoured two-and-a-half pancake sandwiches and didn't hold back any sounds of pleasure, so by the time we arrived at the waterfall, I was strung tight and in serious need of a cold shower. I had no funny comeback to anything. Whenever I as much as glanced at him, my only thought was to pounce.

Damn them straight men.

Once Ellis steered us to the rocks, I was out of the boat, and I helped him secure it before I looked up at the waterfall. It offered a break from my other musings. The fall was beautiful—smaller than I expected. I estimated it was about thirty feet high, and with the river so narrow and forest so close, the area looked like a well-hidden secret.

Leaving the boat behind, we climbed up the ten or so feet of rocks and boulders to get to the waterfall's pool. A smile played on my lips, because despite my thoughts on overnight adventures in the wilderness with beasts and otherworldly savages, I absolutely loved nature. It was my biggest inspiration at work. I always wanted gardens and backyards to be functioning, much like nature. We lived on a planet full of natural resources. Everything had a purpose and a job. Perfect harmony.

I landed on a large, flat boulder, and the only thing out of place was a candy wrapper left by a stupid person. "Idiots." I picked it up and opened the cooler to grab one of the empty bags from lunch. We could throw the trash in there now, I reckoned. "What?" I noticed Ellis was watching me, all observant-like.

He shook his head, a ghost of a smile appearing. "Nothing."

Guess who wasn't a *talker*.

Whatever, I needed a cooldown—stat. The water was almost clear, revealing the blurry, rocky bottom of the pool. As I retightened the drawstrings of my trunks, I spotted a log here and there, too. Pebbles and sand filled the cracks.

Ellis got his shades back.

Lastly, I removed the shirt around my neck and took a deep breath. This was going to be cold as *fuck*. Stepping closer, I said, "If I scream like a girl, don't hold it against me."

He laughed quietly and sat down on the boulder. "It shouldn't be that cold."

I smirked to myself. For once, I knew what I was talking about. When I was close enough, I toed the water surface and shivered. Yup, definitely cold. "You see the patterns in the rock up there?" I pointed to the mountainside from where the water rushed out. The swirling, pitter-pattering, gushing sounds were naturally mouthwatering. It was the sound of a life source.

"Yes?" Ellis's forehead was creased when I glanced at him over my shoulder. "You mean with the cracks?"

I nodded. Layers upon layers of flattened rock. "Right. Exposed bedrock—and the water comes directly from the mountain. So unless there's a reservoir at the top of the mountain, or a heat source nearby, water from any aquifer is gonna freeze your nuts off." *Here go my nuts.* I sucked in a breath and then dove in before I could chicken out. Oh my fucking—God. I stiffened, my body screaming. Then the rush reached my head, and it was rejuvenating and goddamn perfect. The cold soothed my neck and woke me up, and I resurfaced with a hissed curse and a grin.

Tasty water, too.

I pushed back my hair and squinted at a smiling Ellis.

"I want to hear more about your job," he said as I told him, "You should get in."

We grinned.

There was a silent agreement of sorts. He stood up to get ready to join me, and I prattled on about the waterfall. The slightly milky blue hue of the water was probably due to dissolving limestone, which was common in the several hot springs on the island. As he removed his tee, I did my best not to gawk at his perfectly sculpted chest by sharing a story from school. A group of us went up to Tofino to study the tidal pools for a project, and...yeah, that was cool. Fucking hell, he looked good.

He looked at me quizzically. "What was the purpose of studying them? I can't see the connection, I suppose." Between that and landscape engineering.

"Geology and hydrogeology—big part of what I do." I swam backward a little, my mouth right at the surface, as he stepped closer to the edge. "The more I know about nature, the more I can utilize it."

"That makes sense." Hands on his hips, he eyed the water with a level of reluctance. He didn't stall either, though. He released a breath, then dove in gracefully.

I smiled and tasted the water, only to cough a chuckle when he emerged with a vicious, "*Motherfucker.*"

I tsk'd him and told him he had such a potty mouth. Not that he cared. Not that *I* cared. Because only a wet Ellis was hotter than a dry Ellis, and all I could do was stare. *Jesus.* Water sluiced down his broad shoulders, his already dark hair turned black and glistening, and the lines of his muscles looked more pronounced.

I was pretty sure I silenced the shrinkage alert. My cock certainly worked in cold water.

Down, boy.

Dunking my head underwater seemed like the best option. Then, distance.

An hour of chilling in the water, catching some sun, and talking to Ellis was all I needed to realize I had a problem on my hands. We didn't touch on any particularly important topics, keeping it at music, film, and a bit about our jobs, but it was enough for my brain to start making notes. *We have that, that, that, and that in common.* I was hopeless. This happened every damn time I carried a torch for someone.

It was nothing new, and to be honest, I didn't mind it too much. Outlandish scenarios were amusing. In my head, I'd been married at least a dozen times, lived in several countries, and ended up with more children than I could count. A new *possible* life paved its own road every time I met someone I clicked well with. Then...none of those had been married, nor had they been straight—if they were men. Lastly, I'd called none of them family.

Ellis ticked all those boxes.

Getting out of the water, I dug around his duffel bag for two towels and kept one for myself. I fanned it out across half a boulder and sat my ass down with a bottle of sunscreen and my shirt. The sun was brutal today, and I definitely complained about it to Ellis.

He chuckled, swimming lazily in the water. Closer and closer to the waterfall.

"If it makes you feel any better, it's going to rain tomorrow," he replied.

It did make me feel better.

I bet spending a day on the boat watching movies while the rain pattered down would be cozy.

Hmm. But I was going home tomorrow. Ellis was going to spend a ridiculous amount of money on fuel to get me back to Camassia. Then he'd return to his vacationing in this area, exploring hidden gems like waterfalls, good spots for fishing, maybe sit back and read a book before watching the sunset...

Great. I'd officially turned into a willing captive.

I was a kidnapping slut.

Once I'd dumped another generous amount of sunscreen on my body, I draped my shirt over my shoulders and lay back to absorb some of the heat I'd lost in the water. Fuck, it felt nice. Goose bumps rose on my skin, the sun's warmth blanketing me until I felt snug as a bug in a rug.

I missed Haley. The thought of her horrified squeals at the cold water here put a smile on my face, and I hoped I could show her this place someday.

"I could get used to this." I closed my eyes and yawned, crossing my ankles and folding an arm under my head. "I think I need my own minion factory so I can take vacations more often."

Ellis's quiet laugh sounded closer than I expected. He must've left the waterfall.

"Is that a thing? Minion factories, I mean."

"Well, you have one," I said drowsily. "Hundreds of employees these days..."

"A bit of an exaggeration, drama queen." He was coming out of the water, judging by the sound of it. "I expanded a couple years ago. I wanted more than advertising."

I knew he'd moved; that was about it. "How did you expand—*goddammit!*" My eyes shot open as icy droplets of water pricked my skin like fucking needles. "You asshole!" I reached out and smacked his leg out of instinct, and he laughed.

"I couldn't resist." He smirked down at me, then took a step back to arrange his towel next to mine.

"I'm extremely disgruntled," I decided. "Were you a bully as a kid?"

He snorted and sat down. "Are you telling me you wouldn't have jumped at the opportunity to do the same to me?"

I waved a hand. "We're not talking about me now, princess."

"How convenient for you." He pulled the cooler closer and rummaged through it for drinks and snacks, and it took long enough for me to drop the banter. I was still curious about this expansion at his work. Hell, I was curious about everything where he was concerned.

"Before you shook your head over me like a *dog*...you were talking about expanding your business," I told him.

"Mm." He inclined his head and opened a bottle of water. "We went from advertising to include PR and production. I didn't have space for a photography studio at my old office."

And now they did. I'd have to pay a visit sometime to razz him. Maybe bring lunch. "Does that mean you get sexy models parading all over the place?"

"Yes, Casey. I turned the building into a catwalk. You nailed it."

I grinned. He had the hottest fucking drawl when he went into deadpan mode.

Goddamn, I really didn't wanna go home tomorrow.

We left the waterfall sometime later to be able to get back to Renfrew before it got dark.

"We never did any fishing," I mentioned. "Did you even bring the poles?"

Heh...poles.

"Plenty of food in the fridge." He slowed down and steered us toward the yacht, the area outside of the marina packed with sailboats and people enjoying the late-afternoon sun. "Worst-case scenario, I'll add some spices and butter on you." He eyed me over the rims of his shades. "You look about cooked and done."

"You can eat me *any* time." I palmed my forehead and winced. If I didn't know better, I'd think I was running a fever. "How red am I?"

His mouth twitched. "I'm sure there are those who are drawn to skinny tomatoes."

Oh, fucking wonderful.

I wasn't skinny, though. Maybe in comparison to a tomato, but that was *it*. Building up my company had also built up my body a bit. I wouldn't have nobody knockin' that shit down.

As we reached the yacht, Ellis sidled up along the bathing platform and killed the engine. Then he was out of the tender, and he extended a hand to me.

I grabbed the duffel and the cooler, then his hand. "I'm gonna go call Haley before we're out of cell service again."

"Good idea." He nodded. "I'll get everything ready here—wait." The second I had both feet on the yacht, he gently clasped my shoulder, his expression blending into one of concern. "Kidding aside, you're not very red, but you did burn yourself today." He placed his other hand on my forehead.

The close proximity made it harder for me to suck air into my lungs. My eyes searched his face, greedy and taking advantage of the opportunity to get a better look. The rough stubble was glinting in lighter shades in some places, bleached by the sun. Same with his hair; a few streaks of a lighter brown were appearing. He was all warmth and kindness. From the silver and the crow's feet to the rich brown and the soulful eyes.

"You should put on some after-sun lotion," he murmured, lowering his gaze to look me in the eye. *Hi.* He'd just noticed how close he was. He swallowed and furrowed his brow slightly, then removed his hand, cleared his throat, and looked away. There was a silent *whoosh* of tension going with him as our contact broke, and I managed to draw a breath.

I was screwed, wasn't I?

"I'll, uh..." I gestured vaguely toward the dock. "I'll go call Haley."

He nodded and stepped back.

I found a bench outside a tourist info center slash ice cream shop and spent a good twenty minutes listening to Haley telling me about all the cool rides and pretty princesses. I wore a stupid smile and got misty-eyed, and *fuck*, I missed her like crazy.

She was my hugger. When I felt particularly lonely, a Haley hug made all the difference. It lessened the pressure in my chest.

"But, Daddy? Uncle Lincoln won't wear his crown anymore." There was a pout in her voice. "Just that one time."

I chuckled and rubbed at my eyes. "Will you bring home a crown for me? I'll wear mine, I promise."

She giggled. "Yes! Auntie Ade picked a blue for you. Mine is blue also."

"Perfect. Then we'll wear matching crowns," I told her. "What're you guys doing today?"

"I dunno..." She got quiet when someone spoke to her in the

background. "Oh, um...we're going to, um, Paris?" It was Adeline who confirmed it, and Haley added, "Yeah, Paris. What's Paris?"

"It's a beautiful city." I smiled, absently pressing a hand on my neck to check the sunburn. "I'm sure you'll have tons of fun. Will you take pictures for Daddy so I can see when you get home?"

"I'll take lots!" she promised. "We gotta go, Daddy. I love you!"

"I love you too, baby. So much. Give Lyn a hug from me, will you?"

"I will!"

The call disconnected, and I rubbed at my chest, in desperate need of one of her hugs right now. Blowing out a breath, I leaned back for a second and glanced over at the yacht. Ellis was on the upper deck with the mechanic who'd brought the new battery or charger or whatever it was.

I needed to shake the melancholy before I faced Ellis again, so I did what any self-respecting person did in this situation. I went meme hunting. Finding a handful that were sufficiently funny, I added them all in a blog post and told my readers I'd be back soon.

Then it was time to be the funny guy again.

9

I offered to cook dinner when we got back to the little cove, and it worked well enough to distract me and stow away the last of the *blah* feelings. It also helped that I could sample the bourbon I used to make the sauce with.

"That's the—"

"Jesus!" I jumped and spun around to see Ellis in the doorway to his bedroom. Or cabin—whatever.

"—third shot. That I've seen you take." His mouth twisted up.

My racing heart twisted, too. He looked delicious coming out from his shower. "They're baby sips, not shots. I'm sampling." And he needed to go get dressed. Wearing only a towel could get someone killed, and not him.

"If you say so, you lush." He chuckled and walked over to open the fridge. "What's for dinner?"

You?

"Cajun chicken, bourbon sauce, and rice—and the salad you're going to make while I shower." I turned my back on him before I'd be forced to watch him chug water, too.

"That sounds delicious." He came up behind me and carefully felt my neck. The light sensation gave me tremors, and I stiffened. "No more sun for you. Does it hurt?"

I couldn't speak all of a sudden, so my "only a little" became a head shake.

Stupid fucking side-effect of my crushes. I turned into an awkward spaz sometimes.

Luckily for me, I got my shit together as quickly as I lost it. "If you wanna be my cooling pad, you're hired." 'Cause it felt amazing.

He laughed under his breath and turned his hand over. Fuck yeah.

"So good," I mumbled, struggling to keep my eyes open. The chicken wouldn't fry itself though, so I forced myself to function. When the oil started sizzling in the pan, I dropped a dozen chicken bits in there, then checked the rice.

"Do you enjoy cooking?" Ellis removed his hand—a fucking travesty—and leaned back against the counter next to me.

"Depends. If I'm cooking *for* someone, yeah—a lot." I poked at the chicken, keeping my eyes on it. Otherwise, I'd burn it too damn easily. A lesson I'd learned several times. "I guess I'm like that with most things." I frowned, thinking about it. Was I a typical *couple person*? Was everything more fun if I did it with someone?

I wasn't sure that was a good thing. People should enjoy their own company too, right?

Fuck if I knew.

"You thrive in a relationship," Ellis murmured.

I hesitated, and I didn't know why I was reluctant to answer. "Maybe." Perhaps I was reluctant because it became even more glaringly obvious how much I hated being alone.

I didn't worry about being one of those who jumped into relationships for the sake of it. I wasn't *that* desperate, and I didn't drag it out if the person I dated wasn't right for me.

Despite the difficulties I had finding someone who wanted me for me, I did succeed on occasion, and I wasn't a stranger to calling things off. But, yeah...with the right person, I loved to become a unit that nurtured what they created.

"Might be a theory that has too little practice." I added another teaspoon of honey to the sauce to take away a bit of the sting from the bourbon. "My success rate with relationships isn't the best."

The longest one so far lasted approximately a year.

Go me.

Pleasure surged in my gut when Ellis devoured dinner. I was such a fucking pleaser. Sitting on the sofa in the upper deck lounge with my plate in my lap, I stared at him—discreetly, I hoped—long enough to almost forget to eat my own food.

"What does Three Dots stand for in your company?" There. Good distraction. I'd borrowed a pair of sweats from Ellis after my shower, and it said "The Three Dots Agency" along the gray pant leg. He wore the same sweats, only in black.

Ellis leaned forward over his plate, chewing on a piece of chicken while he glanced at the print on my leg.

Had I stumbled upon a secret? He looked like he didn't want to answer. Of course, that made me want to know the truth even more.

"You couldn't have asked another question?" He offered a small, rueful smile. "Like what's my favorite color?"

"I won't be derailed that easily, but I guess I can let it slide for now." I forked up some rice and salad drenched in hot and sweet bourbon sauce. "I don't think you have a favorite color."

He cocked his head, curious. "What makes you think that?"

I chewed and swallowed, then reached for my Pepsi. "You're

way too practical to get hung up on personal preference." Additionally, he was a man in marketing. It was little about what he wanted and a whole lot about what others wanted. "If I were to guess, I'd say you think every color is great for the right purpose. Or something like that."

His brows lifted a fraction before he took a swig of his beer and returned to his food. Which was frustrating. He was being elusive again, dammit. Had I nailed it or not? I couldn't say I'd given it a lot of thought. It was just at the top of my head. He was practical. And I couldn't remember him favoring a particular color in shirts, ties, his car...or anything. He was *great* at matching, when I thought back on it. He knew aesthetics. He put thought into that.

"For as long as I've known my wife, she's thought my favorite color was blue." He wiped his mouth on a napkin, done with his dinner. "Apparently, I wore a blue shirt on our first date." Leaning back against the cushions, he let out a sigh and peered up at the tinted sunroof. "It never occurred to me that I was supposed to have a favorite color. It was one of those silly little things."

It was a silly thing. Something I asked my girlfriend in junior high about. If you knew someone's color, you were *in*. You knew that person then.

There wasn't an ounce of truth to that. No one knew me better than Adeline and Lincoln, but I doubted they gave a flying fuck about freaking colors. The notion was ridiculous. Yet...after eleven years as someone's wife? Seemed like Ellis's wife should know. Maybe. Again, it was relationship territory where I was a novice.

Lincoln undoubtedly knew Adeline's preferences, though. It happened when you paid attention to the details.

"Have you told her it isn't blue?" I asked, because communication was a thing.

"No."

My forehead creased.

Ellis lolled his head along the back of the sofa and faced me with a grim, sober look in his eyes. "I haven't cared enough."

Depressing. They seriously needed to divorce—or fix things in a way that made them happy about their relationship.

Ouch.

I averted my eyes and frowned, that last option suddenly appearing with a spike of jealousy. No good. It tightened my gut uncomfortably, and the next breath felt heavier in my chest.

As soon as I got back home, I'd have to do some damage control on this infatuation of mine.

"Come on, we're going outside." Ellis rose from the sofa and dimmed the lights.

"Uh, no?" I wasn't stupid. The bugs that found me delicious were on the other side of that screen. And nighttime away from any civilization took darkness to a whole other level. "Why would we—"

"I want to show you something." The lunatic grabbed my plate from me and set it on the table. "Let your eyes adjust."

With that said, he dimmed the light further until it died out completely.

"Adjust to what? *Death?*" I stiffened, seeing absolutely nothing. Well, when I turned my head toward the stairs that led to safety, there was a sliver of light under the door. There were also a few glow-in-the-dark stickers by the console, as if someone would be stupid enough to drive the boat in the middle of the night with no lights on.

The unzipping of the screen had me whipping my head in the other direction, and I cursed. He was going to invite those bloodsuckers to feast on me. I was only wearing a T-shirt with my sweats. At least he was in a hoodie.

"Have you lost your goddamn mind?" I demanded.

Ellis let out a carefree laugh that happened to be traveling closer. Then he was right there, unless it was a monster's hand that grasped my shoulder, a thought that gave me shudders.

"Don't make me carry you, Casey."

There's an idea.

Irritated and jumpy, I stood up to get this over with quickly. Afterward, I was going below to hide out in my cabin.

"Fine," I replied curtly. "I'd say show the way, but that's—" He grabbed my hand, warm fingers slipping between mine. I went blank for a moment. "I, uh, sh-yeah. Okay, that works."

I swallowed my nerves, and Ellis guided me out of the enclosed lounge and into the wilderness. His eyes must've adjusted quickly. He had no problems finding the sunbed. He patted the mattress and told me to get comfortable.

"You wanted to show me something," I pointed out.

I sure as shit didn't need to have a fucking seat.

"I do." The patient bastard yanked me closer, and with a gentle nudge, he made me sit down on the edge. "Lean back."

My mouth ran dry, the annoyance on a temporary hiatus, as he followed and got settled right next to me. Shoulder to shoulder. What the hell was going on? His hotness was confusing things. He let go of my hand, and my eyes had gotten used to the darkness enough that I could see him pointing skyward.

"Look up, Casey."

I threw a disinterested glance toward the sky, only to do a double take and stare. *Holy fuck.* I'd never seen the Milky Way that clearly before. Millions of stars shone brightly along the streak our planet called home. The dust clouds gave a yellowish, purplish glow, and the sky shifted in colors of the darkest black to silvery beige.

"Shit," I whispered.

It was breathtaking.

As my eyes adjusted further, it became nearly overwhelming. Starry nights weren't unheard of, but clouds were definitely more common. Sunny days were a nice break from the regular overcast. We'd gotten lucky with a hot summer like this one, and now, evidently, even luckier with nights so clear we could see the Milky Way.

A calm washed over me, making me acutely aware of the dead silence around me, all while being comforted by it. It was another break. A break from society and all its demands. No clocks, no artificial light, no buzzing, no nothing. The wind rustled through the trees here and there, that was it.

The motions of the yacht being on the water were barely noticeable. Whatever little there were only lulled me deeper into a state of relaxation.

I released a long breath, my gaze traveling across the sky.

"I named my company after the ellipsis." Ellis's quiet voice broke the silence. "Three periods—or dots—meaning continuation. When I get stuck or feel defeated, it's my reminder that some things will go on as long as I make them. A story isn't finished until it ends with a period."

I let his words sink in. Gaining more understanding of the man next to me was becoming increasingly important to me. It probably wasn't good for me when push came to shove, though there was nothing I could do to stop it. I'd soak it all up.

Now I could add sentimental to his list. I liked it.

Three dots... Like his closing symbol whenever he commented on my blog posts.

"Life is full of choices," he murmured. "After getting away from my parents, it would've been easy to give up." And he'd chosen to go on. To continue.

I turned my head his way, able to make out only contrasts and shadows. "Is that something you struggle with? I mean, since you didn't want to talk about it earlier."

"No." He took a deep breath and let it out slowly. "I suppose

I'm just terrified of my next choice in life." To divorce or not, I guessed. "I can't ignore it anymore."

Made sense.

I looked up at the stars again, slightly unsettled. The faintest chance that he was going to stay with Marilyn bothered me, and it was disturbing how hopeful I became at the "I can't ignore it any longer," as I assumed it probably meant he was going with divorce.

I shook my head and did my best to get rid of the thoughts. I had no business worrying over that.

If there was anything I should worry about, it was the fact that I was returning to Camassia tomorrow.

"What're you thinking about?" Ellis wondered.

Honesty was the only option, and I hoped for the best. "That I don't want to go home tomorrow."

He turned on his side and pushed himself up a bit, supporting his weight on his elbow. "So don't."

I chewed the inside of my cheek. I could see the glint of a reflection the starry sky gave his eyes, the sharp features of his gorgeous face, but his expression was impossible to read.

"You can take a few days off, can't you?"

I could...

I shouldn't, though. Something was off with me. Missing Haley, feeling too fucking lonely, and this newfound attraction to Ellis would result in a major pity party soon. I could feel it.

On the other hand, I had the self-restraint of a heroin addict, and if he was okay with me being here, I wouldn't be able to refuse.

"Are you sure?" Because I wasn't.

He nodded slowly and lifted his hand. The physical contact was brief; he brushed away some hair from my fore-head, yet it was *too goddamn much*. It wasn't okay, it wasn't normal. Tension flooded me—frustration, longing. Then his hand was back, this time lingering in a ghosting touch along my neck.

He asked how it was, if I was in pain from the sun. I merely stared at his lips moving. Was he shifting closer? It sure felt like it. Holy shit, no, this wasn't happening.

Except, it was. Ellis leaned down, and I managed to suck in a breath right before he carefully pressed his mouth against mine. I sort of checked out; nothing made sense, and I went with it. I mirrored his cautious testing of the waters, keeping the kiss slow and light.

I shivered as he cupped my jaw. His long fingers caressed my skin with such care that I could fucking weep. This was *Ellis*. It was beginning to sink in. Ellis goddamn Hayes, married and allegedly straight, was kissing me. One unhurried kiss ended, only for him to wet his lips and start another. More pressure was applied.

I let out a quiet groan that seemed to set him off. He deepened the kiss further, and when my fingers found the hair at the back of his neck, he was the one who made that sound.

"Did you hit your head?" I mumbled into the kiss. "You know I'm not a woman, right?"

"Very aware." That was all he said before he went all in. As I hauled in a quick breath, he took advantage and stroked the tip of my tongue with his, and then we were making out.

It was the single most drugging yet comfortable experience in my life. My body roared to life, demanding to be heard and sated, and even then, the moment was languid and swimming in safety. *He* was safe. Or I was just thoroughly screwed in the head.

"Ellis..." Fuck, he tasted amazing.

He stroked my shoulder, slowly shifting down to my chest, and grazed his teeth along my bottom lip. "Yes?"

I shuddered. "No, I just wanted to say your name."

He smiled. He *smiled.* He was smiling into a fucking perfect kiss that he shared with me, another man. I moaned under my breath and pushed my tongue into his mouth, to which he whispered a ragged curse and moved closer. Closer and closer, until he was lying half on top of me. I mumbled my approval and slipped a hand down to his thigh so I could hike it over me.

"Shit." I blinked, seduced beyond words. Sparks of excitement shot through me as he left my mouth to nip at my jaw and neck. Heated, sensual kisses followed, and he got more handsy. "Fuck." Needing to feel more of him too, I snuck my fingers under the hem of his hoodie, encountering warm skin. Judging by his shiver, he didn't mind.

I traced his ribcage and the trail of hair under his belly button.

"Christ, Casey." He swallowed and trembled, then kissed me harder and gripped my hip. "I want to feel you."

I nodded and went for more of that kiss. If he asked me now, I'd probably give him my kidney. Whatever he wanted to *feel*, he could have.

What he did want turned out to be skin on skin. In between kisses and increasingly needy caresses, we got rid of our shirts, and he rolled on top of me, gathering my hands above my head.

"Holy—*Jesus.*" I inhaled sharply and rolled my hips at the feel of his cock. The cotton of our sweats did fuck-all to hide that he was hard as a rock. So was I, but I wasn't pretending to be straight. "Seriously... You're gonna give me a complex." I eye-fucked his chest before I got one of my hands free to stroke his sternum, his defined pecs, and feel his sparse chest hair. I was damn quick to get my mouth on there, too. "You're stunning, Ellis."

He groaned quietly, lips lingering at my temple. "So are you."

Really?

I kissed his neck, an openmouthed one to get a taste, then peered up at him. "Do you think so?"

He nodded and lowered his face to mine, and I was gone again. Lost in the passionate movements of his mouth, the taste of his tongue, and feel of his hands. I moaned and tipped back my head when he brushed his thumb over my left nipple. *Shit, that works.* He was insanely affectionate and seemed to be studying me for reactions. More than that, he appeared to be as starved for physical touch as I was.

Yet, it wasn't enough. The pressure was building up, and my breaths were getting too choppy. I acted on instinct, both hands free now, and slipped them underneath his sweats. I palmed his sexy ass and pushed him down on me, earning myself a low growl of pleasure from him. He responded further with a slow, firm thrust, and then the chase was on.

"Look at me, Casey," he whispered huskily.

I opened my eyes, unaware I'd closed them to begin with.

I thought getting trapped in a gaze was a myth, but fuck me if he didn't accomplish it. A million things went unsaid in a silence that stretched between us. He searched my eyes; I searched his. I saw the hint of vulnerability, I saw the exhaustion, I saw the deep hunger. He had a shit-ton to say but couldn't. It was okay. I kissed him, hoping it told him it was okay. *It's okay, it's okay, it's okay.* Right now, I just wanted to give him whatever he needed.

A shudder ripped through him before he started moving again. To get more friction, I snaked my calves around his and met every push. It became a mission of mine, to give him as much pleasure as I could.

Having no clue about his experience with men, or how far he was willing to go at the moment, I stuck with what I did know. I poured everything into each kiss, and I touched every inch of his body that I could reach. The affection—I craved it for myself as much as I craved to give it.

"Oh, fuck." I stifled a gasp, taken aback by the sensations from the soft cotton brushing against my balls. It was a contrast to his hard cock pressing against my own. The rasp of his stubble on my cheek or jaw or wherever he kissed me only fueled the need to get off. *Now*. Little spurts of precome created a wet spot in my pants, and it didn't take long before the smell of sex invaded my senses.

"I need to come." He spoke into a messy kiss, his voice strained and breath ragged. "Ah hell, Casey..."

I cursed again, the shivers setting off one after another. Our hoarse groans mingled in the chilly air, and I flushed as the ball of lust dropped lower and lower. When desperation came into play, every touch was rougher and laced with urgency. Screw the goddamn rhythm—I lost all patience. Devouring Ellis in another kiss, I ignored my protesting muscles and ground my pelvis against him.

He hissed, grabbed my jaw, and pushed forward harshly. It sent fire through me; I was fucking gone. My orgasm slammed into me, the force eliciting a choked gasp. I went rigid and clenched, and a fleeting thought of having his impressive cock pushing in and out of my ass rendered me completely useless. Several ropes of come soaked my sweats in what had to be the most satisfying release I'd had in ages.

Watching Ellis get off was almost as satisfying. He shuddered and rocked into me, face awash with tension, jaw clenched...before he let out a gritty moan and all that tension left his body.

"Oh God..." My voice shook from the ecstasy.

I blinked and looked up at the Milky Way.

Ellis's labored breaths hit my neck in the silence that followed, a silence that went from blissful to heavy in a matter of minutes. Clarity, you bitch. We did all kinds of things in the heat of the moment, and I didn't know what I'd do if his eyes flashed with regret once he lifted his head. I wanted this to be a memory to hold on to forever.

I sighed, grasping at the lingering contentment. I didn't want to worry before I had reason to. I didn't want my past to seal the fate of the future. Being jaded sucked. Being *afraid* sucked even worse.

A kiss to my neck settled the immediate fears, and I relaxed. *Thank fuck.* No one with regrets dove for post-sex kissing.

Tilting my head, I was there when he captured my mouth in another long, unhurried kiss. Goddamn, he was a master in the art of kissing. He had me hypnotized with a few lazy strokes of his tongue, and he evoked the most visceral reactions from me. It was as if he pulled all the strings and knew exactly which one caused whatever he wanted to reveal.

"Will you spend the night with me?" he whispered, ghosting his hand over my hip.

I shivered and nodded, meeting his gaze. Yeah, he could definitely have my kidney, too.

10

I slept like a baby that night too, despite the fact that I woke up several times. Twice to seek out Ellis's warmth, once when he sought out mine, once to do some thinking—though I just ended up staring at our discarded clothes on the floor—and once to brush my teeth.

After washing up last night, I'd borrowed a pair of white boxer briefs from Ellis. He wore the same kind, and he wore them ten times better. I stared at his ass and muscular thighs, then yawned and went under again.

Sometime later, I woke up wrapped around him. My forehead was perfectly nestled between his shoulder blades, and he was deliciously warm. The sound of heavy rain gave me an internal smile. I fucking *hoped* it would be one of those days. Sheets twisting, rain coming down, all the cuddles we could take, pillow talk, breakfast and lunch and dinner in bed...

I'd read about those days. They were on my bucket list.

Unless Ellis had a habit of kissing fingertips in his sleep, I deduced he was awake when he kissed mine. One brush of his lips for each finger before he returned my hand to his chest.

The man knew how to pull at heartstrings.

Elusive Ellis had been promoted to Puppet Master.

"Morning." I cleared my throat to get rid of the sleep from my voice.

"Good morning."

I pressed my lips to his back. "What're you thinking about?"

He hummed tiredly. "That it's lovely to be the little spoon, too."

I grinned then laughed under my breath. "I'm happy to take turns."

"*Good*," he murmured and rolled over, gathering me close. Lifting my chin, he planted a firm, sleep-laden kiss on my mouth. "Don't go anywhere. I'm gonna get us some breakfast and coffee."

I'd won the lottery. So far, so good. If I had my way, I'd cross something off my bucket list today. And the fact that it was with him—and how that mattered even more—was only slightly troubling. I could feel I'd hit the risk zone of developing deeper feelings for Ellis.

He untangled himself from the sheet we shared and left the bed.

"At the risk of sounding horribly cliché..." I lifted my brows and placed a hand under my head. "I hate to see you leave, but I love to watch you go." Because goddamn, his ass, his broad shoulders, his...his all of him.

He rumbled a morning laugh and shook his head.

Once he was out of the cabin, I got up, too. I needed to take a leak and freshen up, and I brought my phone with me. I had cell service here and there and saw a message had come in at some point last night.

Wish you were here, Casey!

It was a text from Adeline with a photo of Lincoln and the girls. Bent over slightly, he was at their level, and he was pointing at something on the river that put big smiles on Haley and Lyn's faces.

I grinned, zooming in on Haley's beautiful face. Even with the tug at my chest, I was happy we were where we were. She was having a blast with her aunt and uncle, and I...I was with Ellis.

After flushing the toilet, I washed my hands and started brushing my teeth. I grabbed the phone again and took a selfie where I winked and fired off a pistol shot at the mirror.

I wish you were here, too. In the bathroom, specifically. Because sharing is caring.

"Dammit." No service. I'd have to send it later instead.

I was back in bed a minute or two later, and it was possible I buried my head in Ellis's pillow to see if it smelled like him. And it did. It was a scent I could bottle and sell for a shitload—to myself.

A voice at the back of my mind was getting increasingly louder about the uncertainties of where all this with Ellis was leading, and a giant ball gag couldn't silence the warning. Maybe, if I tried really hard, I could get *one* day before I went there.

Things were bound to get complicated. Gut feeling.

When I heard Ellis returning, I dragged myself up and leaned back against the headboard. I scratched my bicep, scanning the room. It looked much like the one I used on the other side of the yacht, only this one was a bit bigger and looked more lived-in.

The smell of coffee hit me as the door opened, and my stomach growled. I wasn't sure what I wanted the most—the food served on him as a plate, or me being the plate. I wasn't choosy.

He set a tray with two plates of heated leftovers and two cups of coffee on his nightstand, though what made me cock an eyebrow was something already on the little dresser. How the hell had I missed that? A bottle of baby oil was hidden poorly behind a box of tissues.

I didn't mention it.

Ellis got comfortable next to me before handing over a plate and a mug.

"Thank you." I blew off some steam, then took a careful sip of the coffee. Ahh, sweet nectar.

He cleared his throat, picking at a piece of bacon with his fork. "I realize you have questions."

I stifled my smirk and took another sip. "Only a few hundred."

He nodded with a dip of his chin and sighed quietly. "I'm not sure I have answers for any of them."

Side-eyeing him as I began eating, I thought of questions I knew he'd be able to answer. Answers I probably wouldn't be afraid of, because there were several of the crappy kind. The "What happens now?" hung heavy in the air—or maybe only I felt it—but that was an answer I wasn't ready for.

"Is it only a need for comfort?" I avoided the word he'd used. Affection. It was what he craved, affection and connection.

"No." He shook his head and wouldn't look me in the eye. "I'm having issues keeping my hands off you even now. I'm very much attracted to you."

Well, hey. I smiled around a mouthful of bacon and chicken smothered in bourbon sauce from last night. Except, the bacon was new. "I'm very much attracted to you, too."

He huffed, most likely finding me insufferable. "I get formal when I'm uncomfortable, all right?"

"You get cute as fuck, too," I pointed out.

In response, he sighed and sent a skyward look to—I assumed—ask God for help. Because I wasn't easy.

I could be a good boy, though. I quit the teasing and inhaled my food so I could sit back and savor my coffee. Coffee was the most important meal of the day, anyway.

"Have you been with men before?" I wondered.

Another headshake. "I've... It's complicated. I've been attracted to men before, but nothing like..." At last, he faced me, and he narrowed his eyes. "It wasn't until *you*. Seeing you more often, getting to know you better—God." He released a breath and drank from his coffee mug. "I cannot for the life of me get you out of my head."

I beamed at him, half self-conscious, half falling for him.

I couldn't just sit here after hearing that, nor was I eloquent enough to say anything, so that left one thing. I grabbed our plates and set them on the nightstand; our coffee followed, and then I hitched a leg over his so I could straddle him.

"I like being in your head." I lifted his chin and kissed him briefly. "It means we're square."

He was good at shaking his head this morning. "You don't understand." His hands did the talking by sliding up my thighs while he thought of what to say. "I think I've reached the point where I could wax poetic about your goddamn eyes."

"My goddamn eyes..." I locked my fingers behind his neck and nuzzled his jaw. This moment—this one right here—was the best part of any relationship I'd been in. Before they left, before they realized I didn't fit their mold. "What about my eyes?"

He closed his, and he rested his forehead against mine. "They're fucking beautiful. It usually takes hours in editing to get that intense blue." More than half self-conscious now. Jesus. He opened his eyes again and searched my face, a faint smile tugging at his mouth. "At the risk of inflating your ego, you could be a model. Those eyes, the fair skin, and with the jet-black hair? But it's more than that." He continued before I could splutter something about my features. Was he losing his mind?

"You wear your life like an outfit, in a way. There's an edge about you—"

"I'm definitely not edgy." I had to interrupt, and I was honestly wondering if we were still talking about me. No one had ever called me edgy.

"You are, though." He ghosted his knuckles along my jaw. "Don't you think people see it? You check your surroundings more than others do. You're alert." Except, I missed the baby oil on the nightstand. "You're easily triggered by sounds. You tense up and scan the area if anything's out of place."

I sat back and frowned. The little things he mentioned... They were second nature and nothing I thought of. It wasn't how I would describe myself at all.

Getting to know myself through the eyes of another was strange.

For the record, I *didn't* think people saw any of that.

So why did Ellis?

"You've been through numerous experiences that've made you more guarded." He gathered my hands in his, palms up, so he could brush his fingers up the insides of my arms. My scars had faded and were barely visible. "Your childhood wasn't easy, either. Then prison, learning about Haley, Kendra leaving..."

Maybe I didn't like this anymore. I withdrew my hands and thought of lighter topics—

"And you hide," he said.

My gaze flashed to his.

The bastard was smirking. "You're doing it right now. You may be a refreshingly honest man, Casey, but you have fears that you stash behind your humor."

"Are you psychoanalyzing me?"

He smiled. "I've only paid attention."

"You make me sound like a boring textbook case."

"You're anything but boring," he corrected mildly. "Being a

textbook case is also one of the broadest definitions known to man. I'm sure we're all textbook cases. Cause and effect, coping mechanisms—we're textbook human."

I swallowed and looked down between us.

I put myself out there all the goddamn time; I was honest, I spoke of what I wanted, what my goals were, I wasn't afraid to take initiative, and I didn't let fear of rejection hold me back. But motherfucker...what was it gonna take? Should I shout to the entire goddamn world that I was lonely as fuck and despising it? Was I supposed to believe good things about people when I knew they'd eventually take off?

Actually, I did believe there was good in people. Otherwise, I wouldn't be drawn to them. It was just extremely hard to stay positive at times. In a world where everyone seemed to be looking for their idea of perfection, I wanted someone who didn't mind a few flaws.

I remembered an ex-boyfriend of mine. He was the first man I dated after coming out as bisexual, and he eventually dumped my sorry ass over a stupid argument we'd had. He'd spoken up about self-harm and how those who did it only wanted attention, which... Christ, we didn't talk for three days afterward, and then I got a text about us not working out.

I thought he was genuinely wrong, but we were different people. We had different backgrounds. There were certainly things I was ignorant about, and it often took personal experience before we got it. His ignorance on one matter was a flaw I would have been happy to overlook if it meant we could meet in the middle once the moment wasn't so infected. I couldn't see his perspective; he couldn't see mine. Then he'd ended things before we could even try work it out.

I wondered idly what the last drop would be for Ellis.

"Casey?"

Okay, time to pull my shit together. "Yup." I lifted my gaze and smiled stiffly.

"I hide things, too. I hope you didn't take that as a personal attack."

It was what it was. "I don't think concealing some things makes me any less honest."

"I agree with you." He smirked softly. "In my case, however, it does. I haven't been honest with myself in so long that I've forgotten who I am." Once again, he grasped my hands and pried them open, the insides of my arms facing up. "Since that night at the restaurant, when you came over to my table, I've been trying to do better, starting with acknowledging what I want—to myself. And much of it is thanks to you."

I chewed on the inside of my cheek as he traced a finger over a crisscross scar on my wrist. "What *do* you want?"

"Right now? You."

I suppressed a shiver and took a slow breath. It was fucking vital I didn't get ahead of myself. He said right now. There were no promises of tomorrow.

"I want to be completely open with you." He inched closer and pressed his lips to my collarbone. "I get the feeling you'd take a stream of consciousness with immediate acceptance. You're safe."

I'd thought the same about him last night. At the same time, I felt ridiculously exposed.

Something told me he had the power to tear me down pretty good.

"You can tell me anything." It wasn't my place to judge, and I knew how much that shit could hurt, not to mention ostracize. "I have no expectations—as long as you keep doing *that*." Because his mouth on me was fucking wonderful.

His lips stretched into a smile, and he nipped at my shoulder before trailing kisses up my neck. "In the spirit of transparency, then... It's amazing to touch you." His hands roamed my back, making it too easy to be seduced. "I could watch you for hours. Read your expressions, learn your reactions."

I grinned a little and kissed the side of his head. "Because I wear my life on my sleeve, right?"

He hummed. "You do. You cut me off earlier, so maybe I should continue."

"Oh yeah, let's see what you've got. I still don't think I have an edge."

He chuckled quietly, and then he captured my mouth in one of his unhurried kisses. "Let's see..." Before he could go on, I stole a deeper kiss where I could taste him properly. *One for the road.* "Mm—fuck. You wear your fatherhood with pride, often in the shape of nail polish and macaroni jewelry. It says a lot about you."

I laughed breathily. Was it so wise to discuss this while I was getting a serious hard-on?

"You struggle with anxiety sometimes, too," he whispered. "That's when you wear a ratty old beanie."

That one was a gut punch. My grandmother made me that the year before she died. While I was in prison, I rarely took it off. Until Lincoln was getting out; I gave it to him, though he gave it back to me when I was released on parole.

"How do you notice these things?" It wasn't something I advertised.

"Hmm, well, to be fair, I've always paid extra attention to you," he murmured into another kiss. "I've admired your openness since day one. It's quite ironic, actually."

"How so?" Wanting to feel more of him, I scooted off of him so we could lie down instead. It was about damn time I got reacquainted with his ass.

Side by side, I could kiss him some more all while slipping a hand underneath his boxer briefs. He groaned under his breath as I gave his ass a firm squeeze and pulled him closer to me.

"For saying you're complicated," he replied, out of breath, "you never complicate communication. Simple truths are simple truths for you."

"And it's not for you?" I explored his scruff with my lips and made sure he felt my cock against his thigh.

"Christ—no. I hide too, remember? Behind expectations and the norm."

The *norm* could fuck off harder than fears.

Fuck conversation, too. For now.

Sensing his willingness to follow rather than lead at the moment, I took charge and told him to turn around. I wanted to get up close and personal with his back and thighs. And ass. Definitely ass. Mostly his ass.

His legs and thighs could wait 'til later, even.

He hesitated, then rolled over to be the little spoon again. "Should I worry for my virtue?"

I chuckled and stroked my knuckles over his shoulder blade. I fucking loved the definition of his muscles. Down, down, circling a birthmark...down, past his perfect back dimples, until my fingers played with the waistline of his underwear.

"Are you okay with exploring a bit? Just fingers."

"God, yes."

I flushed with heat. "Then, no, nothing to worry about." Impossible to keep the sex out of my voice now. I helped him get rid of his underwear, and my own followed. "It's like I was just given the key to the candy store."

He tossed a smirk over his shoulder, and I leaned over and kissed him before he could say something cute.

"I wanna make you come," I mumbled into the kiss. "Get me the oil over there."

That ended the amusement, and his eyes grew darker.

With the bottle of baby oil in my hand, I instructed him to lift his leg while I got him slick. He was about the discover how much I loved the feeling of bodies slipping and sliding together. I poured a generous amount into my palm, ready to tease the wit out of him.

At the first contact, Ellis sucked in a breath.

I stared hungrily, my hand sneaking between his thighs. My cock throbbed as I rubbed oil in sensual strokes along his most sensitive areas. Under his tight balls, between the cheeks of his ass. I teased his sac with brushes of my fingers, and when I flicked a glance at his cock, I saw it was getting harder and harder.

"Goddamn." Ellis turned his head and moaned into the pillow.

Scooting farther down, I kissed his shoulder blade and reached between his legs to slick up his erection, too. This was probably as much for me as it was for him. Getting my hands on his cock for the first time was making my mouth water.

He hissed and thrust into my fist. "You're dragging it out."

"Damn right, I am." I swiped my thumb over the glistening head and gave the next upstroke a slow twist. Then down again, I applied pressure along the thick vein on the underside of his cock. He liked that one. Noted for the future. "I think your cock was made to be sucked and choked on."

"Jesus," he panted.

It was enough. It wasn't, but it had to be—for now. I shifted higher again and spent some time rubbing the spot between his cock and ass. I cupped his balls, rolling them in my hand, not releasing him until every inch was coated in oil and he was groaning.

In a selfish moment, I grabbed my cock and pushed it between those delectable cheeks. *Fuck.* I swallowed dryly as a heavy fog of desire weighed down on me.

"I could come like this." I fucked the tight, slick gap slowly, and every time the head of my cock brushed against his opening, he let out sounds of pleasure. If nothing else, he was curious about taking more in his ass. He would in a minute.

"*Casey...*" He growled.

I chuckled huskily and dropped an openmouthed kiss on his shoulder. "Patience."

Sex shouldn't be rushed. Ever. Unless I was the bottom. I needed things when I needed them then.

For the purpose of prolonging the moment, I did have to give him a break before I lost my composure. I gave my cock a few firm strokes and then reached for the oil again. We were going to have to change the sheets after this. Fingers dripping with oil, I found my focus—on his pleasure. I slid a hand along his ass, my index finger slipping between to tease his hole. Ellis grunted and pushed back, and to keep him on his toes, I didn't wait. I forced my middle finger deep inside him.

"Fuck," he exhaled sharply. He stiffened for a beat, only to relax when I went back to slower movements.

I wasn't even part of the equation anymore; it was only about him, and I felt like I could do this forever. Fucking him gently, watching the excitement take over, hearing his reactions, seeing the muscles in his body strain... It went to my head. I wanted him more than ever, and the physical bit was just a portion of that.

He took a second finger with a hiss and a groan, and then he was carefully meeting every thrust. I pushed in; he rolled his hips. Tilting his head back to me, he wordlessly conveyed what he wanted, and I lowered my face to kiss him.

"Sexy as all fuck." I nibbled at his bottom lip before swiping the tip of my tongue into his mouth. "Let me know when—"

His gasp cut me off, and that kind of answered the question. I brushed my middle finger over the rough surface inside him, caressing it in slow, persistent circles. Every time my fingers entered him, I made sure I rubbed him there.

"Fist your cock," I told him. He did, and the sight made me jealous of a goddamn hand. "Stroke yourself and match my pace."

Applying more oil, I began fucking him with three fingers, and that was the magic number, it seemed. For the first time, as far as I knew, Ellis cursed as much as his cousin, and he pushed back quicker. It spurred me on, and I fingered him faster, harder, deeper. Our kisses turned bruising, and the smell of sex was back.

"Fuck, I love this," he whispered. "Oh, hell." He shuddered and screwed his eyes closed. "It's—fuck, more. Too intense."

Did that mean it was too much or he wanted more?

There was no time to dwell on it, because he tensed up, his jaw set and abs more pronounced. A second later, he let out a gritty groan and started coming. Burst after burst shot out of his cock, landing on the mattress and his chest.

I was pretty sure I forgot to breathe. I definitely forgot I was still massaging his prostate, and it was his breathy growl that snapped me back to what I was doing. Carefully easing out my digits, I excused myself and hoped he'd let me indulge in taking care of him. It'd been over a year since I last got to do any boyfriend stuff, and though I was far from his partner, fucking sue me. I was gonna draw us a bath, so help me God, and we were gonna cuddle in the hot water.

11

"What're you doing? No, no, no, let me." I took the camera from Ellis and checked the settings myself.

"I'm perfectly capable of operating a camera, Casey."

Clearly, he wasn't. "We're hopefully photographing whales, not stars," I argued. There was no need for the ISO to be that high. "Lord. At least you're pretty." I left him behind the wheel and shuffled over to the sunbed while I readjusted the ISO on his camera.

After being holed up in bed for two days, we needed this. We went hiking this morning before saying goodbye to the Port Renfrew area, and now we were heading down the coast to do some touristy whale watching. I'd hit up Google to find out the town of Sooke was a perfect location for that. We wouldn't be there until tomorrow, but there was no harm in checking out the waters along the way.

"I'm around cameras all day at work," he pointed out.

I furrowed my brow at him. "I drive to work every morning. That doesn't make me a mechanic."

He sighed and set the boat on autopilot, then walked over

and sat down next to me. "How does a landscape architect get into photography, anyway?"

"He's on a budget and creates his own portfolio." There. I peered through the camera, satisfied with the light. Now we just had to wait for whales to appear. "I think I deserve a kiss."

He snorted. "For being a jackass?" Such language. Nevertheless, he grabbed my jaw and planted a kiss on me. "I'll go get our lunch."

I nodded and did my part by getting the sunbed cozy for us. The camera was ready, there was a cooler of pop and beer, and soon enough, a few blankets and pillows, too. We'd been up at the ass-crack of dawn for our hike, so I was hoping we could nap later. The weather was nice, meaning we could nap outside.

Ellis brought up our sandwiches and mentioned we'd need to go to a store tomorrow. We were running low on food.

I'd already thought of finding a store, 'cause I was hoping the lone condom in my wallet would need a box of friends at some point. Ellis was getting bolder by the hour, it seemed, and I was only waiting for the green light. Slow and sweet was making my soul happy; however, sometimes a guy needed to get railed.

I fucking itched to get my mouth on his cock, too.

"How would you define gender fluidity?"

I coughed around a mouthful of my food and gave Ellis a frustrated look. This wasn't the first time he'd broken a comfortable silence with heavy topics, and it always threw me. I could rarely figure out where his thoughts were, and then he'd blurt out something that took me by surprise.

"In general, or...?" I cleared my throat into my fist and reached for a Sprite. We were out of my precious Pepsi.

"No, on a personal level. You're fluid."

I felt for him. He had a *lot* going on—a lot changing—so whenever he came off as a bit more tense or uncomfortable, I ignored it and paid attention to his questions instead.

"Not about my gender," I replied. "I'm just a guy, but I guess I'm fluid when it comes to stereotypes." I was learning that he struggled with society's expectations the most, so I went there first. "I don't give a rat's ass about what's considered feminine and masculine. If I enjoy it, I enjoy it. I don't put labels on stuff —unless it's Haley's clothes. I admit, we go nuts with our label maker."

He shook his head in amusement.

After the label-making comment had settled, he ate in silence, lost in thought.

"Do you think they'll ram the boat?" I whispered.

Ellis laughed under his breath and gave my hand a squeeze. "I highly doubt it."

We were the worst whale watchers on this planet. We'd killed the engine and Ellis had lowered the anchor outside of a tiny inlet, and now we were lying on the sunbed even though we could *hear* we had company.

I was too content to move.

He'd tilted his head back earlier to confirm it was a pod of orcas.

"Where's the camera?" I murmured drowsily.

Ellis grunted and felt around blindly, and then the strap of the camera landed on my chest. Cracking one eye open, I saw he was holding it, so I took it and flipped off the lens cap.

The Lifetime Achievement Award for Laziness went to me. I held up the camera and took photo after photo in the direction of...you know, the water. Who knew, maybe I caught something on film.

Ellis rolled onto his side and grinned into the kiss he pressed to my shoulder. "We're terribly spoiled, aren't we? People pay a lot of money to see orcas."

I was too busy taking a selfie to reply.

"What're you doing?" he chuckled.

"I'm making love to the camera. Care to join me?" I angled the camera a bit and flashed a lazy smirk.

"In lovemaking? Sure." Funny guy. Sexy guy. He raised himself up and decided to steal the blanket from me. Then he began leaving a trail of kisses along my chest and stomach. "I was thinking about what you said earlier...about gender identity. And whether you identify as male or not, my attraction for you is definitely stronger because you're a man."

"Oh, yeah?" I bit my lip, watching as he played with fire. Or, the drawstrings of my sweats. With his mouth. Fuck, he was dangerous. A tremor ran down my spine when he left an open-mouthed kiss at the bottom of my happy trail. The sight turned me on, and I instinctively lowered the camera to eternalize the next kiss.

Oh God.

As he gave my sweats a tug, I lifted my hips so he could push them down.

Thank fuck I was going commando.

Ellis wet his bottom lip and wrapped his fingers around my cock, and that was all it took for me to stop thinking with the head on my shoulders. The camera landed somewhere behind me, and I wove my fingers into his hair.

This was his show. While he was opening up more and more, he was an introspective man. He did a lot of his thinking and reasoning in the privacy of his head, and it wasn't until he'd made up his mind that he included others. And now—

"*Jesus.*" My eyes nearly rolled back as he took me in his mouth. And now...he was evidently ready for oral. Good fuck-ing...*hell.* I shuddered, feeling his tongue swirling around the head. Funny how I went from semi to rock-hard in seconds around him.

Everything he did was always so damn sensual. He didn't rush or half-ass anything. When he was in, he was all in. *There's a thought.* I needed him inside me the minute he was ready for it. For now, I resigned myself to suffer his teasing. He hummed, taking me a little deeper, and used his tongue a *lot.*

"Shit," I breathed out, tensing up. One second, I was lifting my head because I couldn't *not* see this. The next, my head hit the pillow because the pleasure built quickly and stole my self-control. I groaned and accidentally swiveled my hips, effectively burying myself deeper. "Sorry."

He shook his head, eyes closed, and tightened his lips around me. He was fucking *into* it, a realization that made me relax and enjoy it more. A breath gusted out of me, and he stroked his way up my thigh until he had my balls in his cupped hand. Rolling them firmly, tugging gently, he drew ridiculous whimpers from me. Motherfucker, he was gonna make me beg, intentionally or not.

"Ellis," I moaned. "Fuck—I need to get off." I rubbed his neck, my pleading wordless at first. *More, please.* I encouraged him closer, to take me faster, and the bastard managed a smirk around me. "Don't be mean," I complained as I lost my breath. The pressure grew and grew, and it pooled lower. "Please make me come."

He made another deliciously husky humming sound, and thank fuck, he complied. He sped up and moved his hand to grip the base of me tightly. That sent me right to the edge, and my thighs and abs clenched. Sucking in a breath, I screwed my eyes closed and shook his shoulder in warning. He had to get his mouth away from me.

"Close," I hissed.

He didn't move an inch, and the wet sounds pushed me

over. My orgasm cracked down forcefully. Bursts of my release filled his mouth, and I felt his tongue shifting back as he swallowed. The fact that he didn't hurry to end the moment drew another shiver and more come from me. I was goddamn spent. Mush, liquid, *fluid*—a groaned giggle escaped me. If he asked me about fluidity now, I'd take it in a literal sense. I couldn't move a muscle.

"*That*...sound." He breathed heavily, his forehead landing on my thigh. "Casey, that was fucking adorable."

"Shut up." I planted a hand over my heart and felt it race. "Oh God." I swallowed dryly. "I was unintentionally punny in my head, okay? Happy accident. Fuck—I think you sucked the brains out of me."

I was making no sense.

Ellis chuckled and kissed his way up my body. His *cock*... Oh boy. Just like that, my desire woke up again. It was finally my turn. His cock pressed against my leg, and there was no need to tell me he wanted to get off.

First things first, though. I squinted up at his handsome face. "You swallowed."

He lifted his brows a fraction. "Is that a bad thing?"

"No, it's just... I don't do that, so you don't have to. I mean, if you want to—fucking A—but don't feel like you—"

He kissed me.

I sighed contentedly.

"I loved tasting you," he whispered. "I only do what I'm comfortable with, or what I want to explore."

"Okay." I kissed him back, though I kept it chaste. "I hope you don't mind that I spit. I never liked the texture."

"This is a bizarre conversation." He dropped lower to kiss my neck, seemingly unruffled. "Why would I mind?"

He'd be surprised, and I told him as much. Then, because I was me, I rambled on. An ex once told me he felt like I didn't want him enough if I didn't swallow. I ended our relationship and ordered a T-shirt that plainly said: "I spit." And another guy I fucked around with casually a while back stated my deep-throating skills—because I was a goddamn champion at that—were wasted because I didn't go all the way. Go all the way? Fucking hell. Idiots. But, nevertheless, it'd made me somewhat resigned to admit that I didn't like swallowing—

"You can be quiet now." Ellis's murmur cut me off, and he planted a firm kiss on my lips. "Firstly, I think I remember that T-shirt." He smirked faintly. "Secondly, you lost me at deep-throating. Who the hell cares about the rest?"

"A lot of people—"

"It was a rhetorical question."

I narrowed my eyes. "You interrupt a lot."

He smiled. "Sorry, still thinking about the deep-throating."

Oh. Well. I could do something about that. "I've been freaking dying to get my mouth on you, so I'll be happy to demonstrate. Stand up."

Ellis shuffled off the sunbed, his forehead creased. "When someone gags, it's usually a sign that says I've gone too far."

I grunted as I yanked on my sweats again. "No problem." I sat up and scooted toward the edge of the bed so my feet touched the floor. "I don't think I have a gag reflex, to be honest." I scratched my nose, thinking back on how thoroughly my theory had been tested. For science, of course. "Anyway. The rougher you get, the hornier I become. I'm a bit of a cock-sucking whore, so don't go easy on me."

His lips parted, and his eyes darkened. It abruptly ended another, uh, *interesting* conversation.

He stepped between my legs, then grasped my chin and dipped down to kiss me on the forehead. "At the risk of sounding like a crass, inconsiderate bastard..." Then he brushed a soft kiss to my cheek. "Be careful what you wish for, my beautiful Casey." Those words made me shudder, and he pressed the next kiss to my other cheek. "I like the idea of you being a whore for my cock."

"Holy shit," I mouthed to myself. My mental state took a nose dive to be a perfect bottom boy for him, especially if he showed more of this aggressive side. "Please be as crass as you want—whenever the fuck," I told him. "God, Ellis."

"Noted." He straightened and tapped my jaw. "Open wide."

I licked my lips and parted them as he pushed down his shorts and wrapped his fingers around his cock. He was hard and ready to go, yet he stroked himself as if he were in no hurry whatsoever. The patience this man had...

"Don't suck on it yet." He teased me, sliding his cock along my tongue. My mouth watered, and it was fucking difficult not to wrap my lips around him. He was larger than average, so it was impossible to avoid him completely, and every time his warm skin brushed past my lips, that spot tingled. "Look at me."

I flashed my gaze upward and struggled not to grin. He didn't hold anything back; he smiled and stroked my upper lip as he pushed his cock deeper.

If he kept his up, I was gonna drool.

He told me how sexy I was, and the thing was, he didn't have to tell me. It was indescribable to be able to *see* how much he desired me. It was written all over his expression. Then when he told me I could suck him as hard as I could, I nearly choked on both eagerness and saliva. Wasting no time, I closed my eyes, took him down my throat, and swallowed hard.

"*Fuck.*" He tensed up and moved his hands into my hair, gripping it firmly. He took a minute or two to test the waters, and again, I was the one who suffered. Ellis was turning me into an addict, though at the same time, I loved how he called the shots his way. He wasn't going to let me take control here.

I breathed deeply through my nose and let my hands make

him feel even better where they could. As I swallowed around him repeatedly and traced him with my tongue, I squeezed his ass and massaged his sac. He shuddered when I scratched his thighs, so I made sure to do that again.

"Hell, you're tight." He exhaled and slid one hand to my throat. That made me moan, knowing he was feeling the ridge of his cock pushing that deep. By now, he knew I was loving it, and he withdrew slowly, only to shove his cock inside again, this time faster and harder.

After that, he relaxed and fucked my throat the way I wanted him to. Lust flared, my skin flushed, and I had to give my junk a squeeze to relieve some pressure.

It only got worse when he lost the last shred of composure. The moment it became all about his pleasure, I was rock hard once more. He groaned, cursed, and hissed, one hand fisting my hair, the other stroking my throat. He became rougher and rougher, and my eyes welled up because I fucking *wanted*. I wanted more, all of it, everything. He had my body buzzing with excitement.

"Casey...you really are a little slut for cock, aren't you?" He'd noticed I was hard in my sweats. "I can't get over how— mother*fucker*," he groaned. "How...goddamn exquisite you are— even more with my cock buried in your throat like this. Shit."

I couldn't take it. He continued to abuse my throat perfectly, and I stuck a hand down my pants and jacked my cock. The urgency changed into sheer desperation, and by the time his thrusts grew shallower and irregular, I was ready to come.

His warning came out in a low growl that set me off. He pulled out a couple inches, no more than I would let him, and then my release tore through me, coating my hand and the inside of my sweats. My groan must've sent enough vibrations up his cock to push him over the edge, too. Hot come flooded my mouth, for once disturbingly arousing. Not a chance in hell I was gonna swallow, but damn, it was intoxicating to take him.

Ellis staggered back until he hit the couch, and he managed to tuck himself back into his pants before he landed flat on his back. He threw an arm over his face and panted.

I killed my smirk and went over to the railing, then spat into the ocean. It was my contribution to keep the water salty.

"Are you okay?" I asked, pausing where he was. Mouthwash and a clean pair of pants were next on my list.

"Give me a minute, please."

I grinned, close to ecstatic, and headed below.

12

It probably wasn't wise to call what I shared with Ellis a relationship, but whatever it was shifted that day on the boat. He grew more comfortable and assertive, not to mention bolder—and not just in the bedroom. He became more personal, even. He didn't ask me questions to figure out things for himself as much; he asked to learn about me.

My heart took a minor hit when he asked me to dinner the following day.

Don't fall for the married man.

Divorce wasn't the end to complications. It was the start of several new ones. I knew even if he did end up getting divorced, there was no sunset to run off into on the horizon. Not yet, anyway.

We docked in Sooke early that afternoon, and I excused myself to check in with some work shit and to call Haley. In the meantime, Ellis spent way too much on fuel again.

Not for the first time I'd touched land in the past week, I was hit by my vertigo the moment I left the yacht. Fucking crazy that I'd be more used to being on the water.

Work was easily dealt with. Haley, not so much. It was too

late in Europe, and she was already asleep, so I ended up talking to Adeline.

"She misses you. They've both been fussy today."

"No lie, I'm glad to hear it." I rubbed the back of my neck and took a deep breath. A group of tourists passed me, following whom I assumed was a guide of some sort. It was a stunning harbor—massive and surrounded by hilltops and forest—so I could see the appeal to explore the area. "I'm kidnapping them as soon as you get home."

I wanted to build a blanket fort and get a pedicure. Lyn was a pro at the latter—minimal scarring from the nail filing. There would be cookies and milk, too.

Adeline laughed softly. "Won't you have a house to get ready?"

I waved a hand. "Not much to do." I'd been smart and hired a painter the minute I'd been handed the keys. The old floors had recently been prettied up, the kitchen and bathrooms were new, and the little backyard was mine to play with. Moving in the furniture was all that remained. "Haley's requested a pink room with white polka dots. I'd fuck that up on the first dot."

She laughed again. "Fair enough. No polka dots for you?"

"Funny." I grinned. I wasn't picky and had randomly chosen a gray color. The living room and the guest room would be left white for now. "So you've done Disney, you've done Paris—what's next?"

"Lincoln wants a couple days on a beach, so I think that's the plan," she answered. "The others are going home tomorrow, too. Adrian's got school coming up." True. The new semester would start in a few weeks, and he was one of those high school teachers who loved his job. He'd spend an eternity getting everything ready. "Okay, so back to the girls staying with you..." There was a noise in the background, papers rustling. "Lincoln has a big project and will stay in Seattle for a bit, and you know how cranky he gets if I'm not with him." Even truer. "If we stay at the condo... Let's see, we get home on a Tuesday... So, 'til that weekend?"

I nodded. "Sounds good. I can pick the girls up in Seattle. No reason for you to drive up here just to drop them off."

The familiar excitement of being with Haley—and Lyn—built up rapidly inside me. However, one thing was new. When I thought of shit we could do, my mind strayed to Ellis. What did he think of kids? Other than what was required for the uncle role he played for both of them. Thinking back on birthday parties and dinners, I knew he certainly didn't *dislike* children. He put thought and effort into gifts and had accepted the invitation to a tea party once or twice, but beyond that? No clue. He wasn't the type of uncle who spent time with them unless we were there.

After finalizing my plans with Adeline, I was ready to get off the phone and get back to Ellis. I had a few more days of keeping my head firmly stuck in the sand; I was going to worry about later...well, later.

Ade had another agenda. "So how's work?"

Who cared? It was fine. I answered on autopilot as I watched Ellis leave without me. He couldn't very well stay by the fuel dock.

"Interesting," Adeline noted. "Why are you lying to me?"

I frowned. "What?"

"I got your message the other day. Your pretty bathroom selfie?"

Oh. Yeah. I smirked. I'd sent it as soon as I'd had cell service. It was too good to keep to myself. Although, this didn't make me a liar. "You're welcome."

She made a noise. "Casey. I recognize the bathroom. Are you on the yacht with Ellis?"

Well, fuck. I ran a hand through my hair, unsure of what to

say. The situation suddenly got sticky. I didn't know what Ellis was comfortable divulging, and though the cat was out of the bag in terms of where I was, there was most likely a correct angle to play this.

It hadn't been my intention to be vague or untruthful; it'd come naturally to not mention it. Which on its own was slightly disturbing. I didn't do lies. Once upon a time, I ended up in prison for being a shitty criminal. Was I turning into a serial killer? They had to start somewhere. Sometimes all it took was one lie.

"To be fair, he kidnapped me," I stated. "I got drunk—as I do —and I spent the night on the boat because it'd been closer than your house. The next day, I woke up in the middle of the ocean. What's a guy to do?"

Apparently, that was too much for her to process.

―――――――

Once Ellis had been directed to a spot for visitors, he left the boat to join me on the dock. He'd put on nicer clothes, slacks and a button-down, and I was in sweats and a T-shirt. If he thought we were going to dinner like this, he was batshit crazy.

"I'm not a fashionista, but I do have some sense of decorum," I told him. "Either I change on the yacht, or I drag you out shopping."

He slid on his shades and tossed me something. I caught it— my wallet. So we were going shopping.

"I want you in something nice for our date." His mouth twisted into a careful smile, confirming that our dinner was, in fact, a date. He was getting more dangerous by the minute. "I may have a fantasy."

Let's talk about that.

"What kind of fantasy?"

"It's not entirely sexual, you animal." He chuckled quietly and gestured toward the parking lot farther away. "But the thought of seeing your ass in a pair of nice dress pants might've sparked something."

I could do dressy for him. "Ellis Hayes likes my ass. This is going in my diary."

He laughed.

"I also made reservations for dinner," he added conversationally. "Our car's over there."

He'd been busy while I was on the phone. I learned he'd ordered transportation to take us to a shopping center, after which we were returning to the harbor for six o'clock reservations at a hotel slash restaurant frequently used as a wedding destination.

I threw a glance over my shoulder, looking back at the dock. Was this safe? Ellis was clearly on a mission to explore something he didn't have in his marriage, something his wife was exploring elsewhere, too. But what the fuck would happen with the poor schmucks they explored with? Namely, me.

If I were bitter, maybe I would feel used. Being with him now, though, that was impossible. I needed this too much to resist. I'd live out the delusion until it came crashing down around me.

"You might have some shit to explain to Ade later," I said, ridding the worries in my mind. "She knew I was with you, so I told her you kidnapped me."

He chuckled, so I hoped that meant he wasn't concerned about people knowing we were on the yacht together. "You and your kidnappings."

I wouldn't be a kidnapping slut if I didn't mention them often, now, would I?

A couple hours later, I crammed myself into a stall in the men's room to change clothes. I didn't enjoy fashion much, but that didn't mean I didn't know it. I'd walked straight into a store and found a pair of charcoal slacks that made my ass look fuckable to straight men, and then Ellis and I had stopped at a coffee shop for a light snack. During which I'd suffered his testy grumpiness because I hadn't showed him the damn pants. Lastly, I'd found another store where I bought a blue shirt. Or "midnight marine," as the saleslady had called it. Was there even a lunchtime marine?

I wasn't buying new shoes for just one date, so I'd warned Ellis he'd have to settle for my black Chucks.

"They're very you. I wouldn't want anything else," was his answer.

Don't fall for the married man.

Pushing up the sleeves of my shirt, I checked my arms to make sure the scars weren't too visible. Despite that they'd faded to the point where some people didn't even know of them, I was self-conscious about it. More so in the summer when my skin got...*maybe* three-quarters of a shade darker, and my scars stayed the same color.

The final touch was the free sample of a cologne I'd snatched up, because fuck, I loved free samples. I was one of the reasons that marketing strategy worked so well. When crap was free, I entered a store with my wallet open.

I ran a hand through my hair and then stashed my old clothes in a bag before exiting the men's room.

Ellis's reaction made the shopping worth it. He pushed away from the wall and cursed under his breath, his gaze growing predatory and heated.

That reminded me: "We gotta buy rubbers," I blurted out. His eyebrows shot up, and I cleared my throat. "Don't look so surprised. You have to realize I'm putting out tonight."

"Oh, I do?" He gathered his wits and stepped close enough to press a kiss to my jaw. "I guess we have one more stop before dinner, then."

Yeah. To buy a wholesale box of condoms.

"Evening. Reservations for two under Hayes."

While Ellis spoke to the hostess, I peered around us to take in what I could only describe as one of the most romantic locations I'd ever been to. It was a resort for couples, no doubt. The Victorian estate sat on a hillside that faced the harbor, and the large terrace was full of tables, candles, white roses, and a ceiling covered in ivy. This, all of this, combined with the setting sun was looking more and more like the recipe for a future heartbreak.

I had half a mind to jokingly scold Ellis and tell him you didn't take casual lovers to places like this one.

"This way, please." The hostess smiled and guided the way to a table near the edge of the terrace. Down the grassy hill, a path lined with tiki torches led to the water.

We were left alone with two menus after ordering drinks.

Ellis opened his menu. "You once told me first dates are awful."

I quirked a brow.

He offered a small smirk, keeping his gaze on the chef's recommendations. "What if I wanted to change your opinion?"

Well, I—huh. So, he was a man with a plan. "Pretty sure you're exempt to that rule, Ellis. We already know each other."

"Sure," he replied slowly, pensive. "As family. We've never dated."

No, I would think I'd remember if we had. "True, but you

won't freak out or judge me if my prison time comes up. You know I have a daughter, and you—"

"Yes, I know all that." He smiled and closed the menu. "That doesn't mean we can't talk about it—as two men on a date. What, you don't think I have questions? Merely knowing you've spent time in prison isn't enough for me."

What did he mean by that? Ellis had a way of keeping me relaxed, so I couldn't say this was putting me on edge. There was a big, fat spell of uncertainty now, however. We'd hit a new level of exploring, one I wasn't sure I could recover from as easily.

I took this crap seriously. The bastard was going to make me fall in love with him.

"You can ask me anything." I made sure to keep my expression composed, and then I scanned my menu absently. "That means I can ask you anything, too."

"Of course."

Of course.

It felt like stepping onto a minefield. Maybe he did believe I could ask anything, though that meant shit-all if I still wasn't ready for the answers. Or rather, I was less ready than before. And that spoke volumes; I'd gone too far as it was when the answers mattered that much.

Not that any of this was going to stop me from diving in headfirst.

When a waiter appeared with our drinks, we ordered the rack of lamb with Hasselback potatoes and Cabernet sauce. According to the chef, it was *c'est magnifique*, and who was I to argue with someone who knew French?

Then we were alone again, and I figured I might as well get us started right away. "What more about my time in prison is there to know?" Because to be honest, he knew more than just how long I'd been there. He knew I'd succumbed to peer pressure as a kid. Anything to get friends who accepted me. Instead, they'd seen an income. Three of us had gotten involved in stealing and breaking in, and being the inexperienced one, I was the fastest to get caught. I'd learned since then that my "friends" were regulars in jail and prison.

"What drove you to self-harm?" he wondered.

For fuck's sake, he could never start slow, could he? Like, how was the food there? Did we wear stripey uniforms? No, he went straight for the crap I didn't like to talk about.

I cleared my throat, forced to think back on those years. Unlike Lincoln, who'd spent ten years behind bars and still sometimes woke up expecting to go through our regular routine, I was only in prison for three, and I'd shaken most of the triggers. My brain had reprogrammed itself within a year, and now, only certain sounds and smells earned me brief flashbacks.

"I guess...in comparison, the first two years were easy because I was with Lincoln. It wasn't until after that..." I shifted in my seat, uncomfortable.

"So he was your first cellmate?"

I nodded. "I was terrified of him at first. I mean, he comes off as pretty menacing if you don't know him, but I had a nervous breakdown my first night, and he helped me."

Lincoln hadn't been nice about it, although given the stories about inmates I'd heard beforehand—while I was waiting for my sentence—he was a saint.

I remembered being shown to my new cell on the second floor. I'd been told it was a reasonably quiet block with very few problems, which meant absolutely nothing to a sheltered dork from a wealthy family.

"It wasn't like in the movies," I said and wrung my hands in my lap. "Like when you hear the powerful echoes of barred doors shutting? It was none of that. It was quiet, and nobody gave a shit." In a way, that was worse. The cell door didn't close until it was bedtime, and when it did, it was with a mechanical hum and the soft *clank* of the lock being secured. "It was like being forgotten by everyone and everything." Even *sound* had forgotten me. I barely heard a noise. I recalled Lincoln's unimpressed once-over before he ignored me. *Nobody cared.* With the memory of my parents' disappointed looks, and worse, how they avoided facing me the last day of the trial, I felt completely fucking useless, unlovable, and invisible.

I stumbled through an explanation to Ellis on how I'd felt the walls closing in on me. Then how Lincoln had jumped down from his bunk to snap at me. *"What the fuck're you doing? Shut up, or I'll do it for you."* I hadn't even realized I'd been crying. The hyperventilating came next, and I'd been rocking back and forth and clawing at my skin when Lincoln decided to help me instead.

I'd clung to him after that. I'd told him I'd do anything if he kept me safe. *Anything.*

He'd accepted.

Ellis averted his gaze for a quick moment, his jaw ticking with tension. When he looked me in the eye again, his resentment was evident.

I halted him before he could express his distaste. "He did nothing wrong." I was firm on that one. "He took what I offered 'cause we change in a place like that." I'd only given Lincoln head, but even if it'd been more than that, I would've held my stance. Hell, because of him, distant suspicions of my possibly being bi became a lot more than a theory.

Nevertheless, prison dehumanized a person. Lincoln was closed off for many years; it was a coping mechanism to survive. We were objects on an assembly line, shuffled from station to station until the day was over. Morning showers, breakfast, work, lunch, yard time, dinner, bedtime. Lincoln had called us cattle and sheep. He wasn't wrong.

"He didn't make me feel like I was obligated." I ran a hand over my head to adjust my beanie, only to remember I wasn't wearing one. Right this second, I wouldn't mind it. "If anything, he treated me the way I needed to be treated. Sure, he protected me, but he also prepared me. He was a goddamn drill sergeant. The only thing he forced me to do was way too many push-ups."

Ellis's mouth twitched, though I could tell he wasn't entirely convinced. At the same time, I knew *he* knew that his cousin was a good man. Which left only a thing or two to be worried about... Me?

"I don't like the idea of you getting hurt, that's all." He confirmed my thought—possibly my wish, too—and took a sip of his wine.

"I hurt myself more than he ever could've done." I supposed that put me right back on track. I sighed quietly and followed Ellis's lead and took a swig from my wine. "Thanks to him, the two years we shared a cell were relatively easy. I took minor smacks from others, and he took care of the rest." So, most of my rude awakening didn't hit me until the day Lincoln was paroled. When he left, he took away the only sense of security I had. More than that, despite his promises to be there for me—and to be honest, I'd only half believed him—I lost my only friend. "Then he was gone." I mustered a small, empty smile. "The anxiety was back. I might as well have been new again."

Ellis didn't reply. He covered my hand on the table with his and just listened.

Goddamn him. Goddamn *me*. I should've gone with an abridged version. But goddamn him for making the words tumble out.

"There isn't much more to say about my last year." Because most of it was a blur. I was in and out of panic. One nervous breakdown after another, until I noticed the prison doc gave me meds every time I was brought in. They didn't increase my visits with the counselor. Just more medication. Antidepressants, sleeping pills, anxiety meds... "I took the easy way out and hurt myself so I would get sedated."

At times, it was methodical and planned to the last detail. Other times, I harmed myself during my panic attacks and was less aware of the severity of the damage. And that was how I ended up at the hospital and was labeled suicidal. At that point, Lincoln was granted special clearance to visit me, even though it was generally not allowed for parolees to visit inmates.

"Lincoln told you about the move then, didn't he?" Ellis asked. "I think I remember him saying something about that. He really didn't like Michigan much."

I nodded. Lincoln hadn't been out more than a few months when I learned he had everything planned out and that I was coming with him to Washington when I was paroled. He'd grown up in Camassia before he headed to LA and became famous.

It got a little easier in prison once I realized Lincoln hadn't been full of shit and empty promises. He was going to keep his word and make me a part of his family. By then, it'd expanded to include a pregnant Adeline, Jesse, Abel, and Madigan. The band of misfits was born.

Shortly after we arrived in Camassia, Ellis joined our family.

He looked lost in thought, though there was a faint smile playing on his lips. "You and Lincoln wouldn't cross a street until the light turned green when I met you."

I grinned. True enough. Parole kind of kicked your ass. There were rules and restrictions coming out of the woodwork, and we didn't wanna risk anything and get sent back to prison.

Our conversation, thankfully lighter now, took a quick break as our food arrived. I was grateful the heavy topic was over, making it a hell of a lot easier to enjoy my meal. The chef had been right, too. It was magnificent.

"You were super quiet back then," I recalled.

He inclined his head. "Since Lincoln and I were never close before, it took me a while to find my place in our family."

That made sense. I remembered Lincoln telling me about it. Other than being ten years Ellis's senior, Lincoln hadn't been close to Ellis because their fathers had that huge falling out when Ellis's dad decided to become a cult nut. It wasn't until years later, while Lincoln was in prison, that his dad—Keith—and Ellis started talking.

"Then you took a chill pill," I concluded.

He laughed quietly. "It helped that Lincoln called me Uncle Ellis when Lyn was born."

Shit, that was a crazy day. I'd never been around babies before. Hell, neither had Lincoln. He'd been a mess. It was before he was through his parole too, so he was bitchy as fuck about not being able to calm his nerves with a couple shots of whiskey.

Ellis shook his head fondly, stuck in a memory, no doubt. "Little Miss Nova-Lyn."

I smiled, and God, I missed that cheeky monkey, too.

"Were you there when he and Adeline fought about the names?" I asked.

"I caught the tail end of it when I arrived at the hospital," he chuckled. "Lincoln was yelling, 'But I bought a whole fucking book with baby names, and now we're not gonna use any of them?' right as Adeline screamed for an epidural."

I could laugh about it now. Back then, not so much. My nerves had been shot by the entire baby business. Adeline had been in so much pain, and Lincoln had tried to postpone their argument. She'd insisted they'd settle it before Lyn was born.

Lyn had been Lincoln's first suggestion—after Janis Joplin,

which carried some sentiment between him and Adeline—and she'd loved it. Then he'd bought that book...and he'd added Nova to the list.

Being as headstrong and stubborn as they were, *everyone* was thankful for Madigan's idea that they'd use both names.

Naming Haley had been a lot easier. It was just me.

My grandmother's maiden name had been Hale, so I'd changed it up a bit. It'd taken me two beers to decide.

"You were the next to become a father." Ellis's wistful expression made my next question obvious.

"Do you want kids?" I wondered.

He stared at his meal, considering his reply carefully. "For a long time, yes, I very much wanted to be a father. But it's a matter of chemistry for me, and I can't imagine raising a family with Marilyn. It wasn't for us." He pushed some food around his plate. "If I were married to someone with whom I had a more nurturing relationship, it's possible I would've wanted a child more than I do today."

The answer was so *him*. It was his favorite color all over again. He liked blue when it fit the moment. He liked children when it fit the relationship.

It made me think. He'd said there was a time he wanted kids, so maybe that was for himself—if he wanted them in general. Then, meeting Marilyn, it changed because of the nature of their marriage.

"You're the type of man to start a family with."

My head snapped up. Holy smokes, that was blunt—even by my standards. "You think so?"

He dipped his chin and slid together his knife and fork on his plate, finished with his meal. "I'm—I'm going to be honest with you, Casey." Something was making him uncomfortable. "The past several years, I've lived a bleak existence—at least in comparison. Then I look at you and the life you live with Haley

—same with Lincoln and Adeline—and it's full of color and warmth."

I didn't know what to say, other than warmth and color were exactly the description I'd use for the time I'd spent with him recently. The passion was there, like a current.

"It's what you've brought to my life on this trip," he finished quietly.

I smirked and felt my cheeks get warmer. "I was thinking the same."

As ready as I was to jump into bed with Ellis by the end of the evening, I suggested we walk back to the yacht. The sun had set, but the marina didn't look any less beautiful. I estimated it would be about half an hour to reach the other side where the boat was, and we weren't alone. Every now and then, we'd pass a sailboat where laughter among friends and the clinking of glasses rang out.

Growing up near Lake Michigan, I wasn't unaccustomed to dinner parties on fancy water castles. Only then, it'd been suffocating and tedious. It'd been me and my Game Boy and stuffy old rich folk who exhibited their wealth with caviar and art.

In my parents' circle, a boat never left the marina. That wasn't what a sailboat or yacht was for. It was merely a half-a-million dollar, portable party venue. Camassia Cove and this entire area—big difference. You couldn't live in Washington, outside of Seattle, if you weren't outdoorsy.

"You sailed as a kid, right?" I tilted my head in Ellis's direction.

"Hmm? Yes. Every Saturday."

I snorted softly. "Was everything running on a schedule?"

"Mmhmm." He nodded slowly and slipped his hand into

mine. I threaded our fingers together, side-eyeing him. He appeared content as fuck, which was always nice, but I had questions about his childhood. Thankfully, he didn't seem too reluctant to offer up the deets. "We didn't eat seafood; it was considered dirty, but my mother—how do I put this," he muttered, the question rhetorical. "She looked down on other communities, so when her own religious leader spoke of the importance of giving to the poor, which essentially included anyone who wasn't a Disciple of Abraham, she donated whatever catch my father and I brought home on Saturdays."

"Good lord, the cult had a name?"

He chuckled under his breath. "I assume most do. We were originally called The *Divine* Disciples of Abraham, but someone pointed out that it might contradict our humble lifestyle."

"No kidding." This was making my head spin. I'd watched enough documentaries to know children escaping cultism were often traumatized in one way or another. "How did that life not mess you up? Sorry if that sounds ignorant."

"No, it's okay. In short, it was public school." He gave my hand a squeeze. "You know how my parents met, yes?"

Sort of. I nodded, recalling the gist of it all. His dad had moved south and did his residency in a hospital in Flagstaff. Ellis's mom was from that area and had volunteered at the hospital.

"Right," he continued, "so my mother was the granddaughter of the founder, and at least a dozen people in his inner circle—that I know of—left Arizona to start branches elsewhere. To recruit and expand. For whatever reason, she managed to recruit my father, supposedly a man of science, but that was the extent of it. When they moved up here, there was no community to fall back on, and it posed a dilemma when I was old enough to start school. Either she homeschooled me according to her faith, or she let me go to public school—with normal children—so she could focus more on being the village idiot with her propaganda."

He was trying to make light of the situation. I couldn't muster any humor to pick up on it; instead, I lifted our hands and kissed our linked fingers.

"I knew from an early age that she and my father were the different ones, and once I figured that out, all I had to do was persevere."

"I can't imagine." I shook my head, picturing a young Ellis. Childhood wasn't supposed to be about hoping to get out in one piece. "Christ, college must've been *insane*." We'd talked about this before, and now, knowing more of how it started—yeah, definitely couldn't imagine. "I wonder if that's what an Amish Rumspringa's like."

Ellis looked at me incredulously, his mouth pressed together as if he were suppressing his amusement. It was futile. The mirth showed in his eyes plenty. "I'll go out on a limb and say that's offensive to the Amish. As far as I know, their religion isn't abusive, and it's a choice—"

"You nitpicky bastard," I laughed. "I meant how college must've opened up a whole new world for you."

"Oh."

I snickered and bit his shoulder, 'cause I felt like it.

We walked in silence for a few minutes, the dinner settling, the contentment solidifying. I wouldn't wanna be anywhere else right now. It was a good feeling. I didn't even begrudge anyone their happiness as we passed more people having various dinner parties on their boats, and that was personal growth. Or me being happy, too.

"There's one thing linked to my childhood that's come to my attention lately. Or at least I believe it's linked to that somehow." It was rare for Ellis to think out loud, so I kept my mouth shut. "Everything has always been better than the alternative—the alternative being how I grew up. My freshman year in college, for instance. I was constantly amazed by the fact that I didn't have a curfew. I could eat whenever I was hungry, anyone who didn't tell me what to do was a friend, and Sundays were the most relaxing days. No amount of studies before an exam could top the stress of having to pretend I worshiped the way my parents did."

Fuck, it hurt to listen to this. *I could eat whenever I was hungry.* Because before, he hadn't been able to do that.

"Makes sense." I hugged his arm. "You couldn't take much for granted before."

"Exactly, so what if I want more now? I used to find happiness in the littlest things, and now it feels like settling. What I've had for the past eleven years isn't enough anymore. I want... something else."

We reached the dock where the yacht was, and I could only say what I'd been saying for a while. "Whatever you do, don't wake up one day with regrets." Then I thought of what he'd said about his agency. Three Dots. An ellipsis for a continuation—to represent choices and the option to go on. "You have to choose, Ellis. For yourself."

He sighed quietly and slowed down until we stopped between two streetlamps, one of them broken. "What if I've already chosen?"

"Have you?" I faced him.

That earned me a narrow-eyed look and a smile. "When I mentioned wanting something else, you completely missed your cue to ask me *what* I want."

Was he fucking kidding me? "You have no clue how hard it is to stay objective here, princess. Goddamn, there's a shitload I wanna say and ask, and I might slip at times, but I won't push you in any direction you don't want to go, and that means I'll—*umph.*"

He felt the need to cut me off with a kiss. "There. Quiet. *Princess.* After spending this time with you, how the hell can I not choose this?"

This, being...?

He gave me another kiss, gentler this time, lingering. "I won't assume, and I have a lot to deal with when I get home," he murmured, "but if I were to call you and ask you to dinner again, would you agree?"

This, being *me.*

I swallowed nervously, my stomach tightening. "You have to elaborate on that."

Thankfully, he got it—and hopefully why. He could be asking for more exploring, he could be asking for me specifically, and I needed to know.

"I want more with you, Casey. Do I stand a chance...despite everything?"

I didn't know what the *despite* entailed, and screw it, he could have all the chances he wanted. Holy fuck, this was surreal. It was suddenly more than okay to hope, 'cause it looked like I had a shot with Ellis Hayes.

"Of course," I said, all cool and shit. Then the face-splitting grin kind of ruined it for me.

He smiled and kissed me firmly, and the notion of butterflies was disturbingly real. My gut flipped as if I was stuck in a permanent somersault, and though joy surged forward unlike anything else, it was scary, too. People often changed their minds when shit got real. People often *left* when shit got real.

My track record was stacked against me.

"It's slightly nerve-racking, isn't it?" He cupped my jaw and deepened the kiss, causing my head to spin. "Exhilarating."

"Terrifying," I muttered, out of breath, and I swept my

tongue into his mouth. His kisses made me understand the hot-for-someone saying, because he literally made me run hotter. "Thing is, I already like you a crapload, so if you could minimize the damage if you change your mind, that'd be great."

Ellis eased out of the kiss with a few chaste ones, his brow furrowing. "You have doubts."

"Shit happens," was all I could say.

"Hm. Then it doesn't matter what I say. I'll show you instead." He took my mouth once more, then nudged me toward the boat. "For what it's worth, what I feel about you isn't fleeting. I know the difference between—never mind, it's not fleeting."

Feelings changed all the time, and that was my bitter past speaking. *That* guy needed to shut the fuck up. I was never going to be able to predict the future. What I could do was to enjoy the present and fight for an awesome tomorrow.

That's what I chose.

13

"**I** need you again..."

We kept saying that to each other all night. This one was him. I woke up from a light sleep to his soft kisses on my shoulder and his heavy, hard cock pressing against my ass.

I groaned, yawned, and stretched, pushing my ass up to meet him. It was all the invitation he needed, and he quickly rolled on another condom and slicked me up with lube. His *fingers* were...a fucking godsend. Burying my face in the pillow, I hissed as he fingered me in that sensual, maddening pace of his. It needed its own goddamn trademark.

"I can't get over how amazing you feel." He pushed inside me with a deep moan.

We worked up a sweat every time, neither of us satisfied until we'd found that perfect slip and slide of our bodies. He stayed close, his chest to my back, and withdrew his cock just to shove it right back in and make me cry out through gritted teeth.

Ellis was solely responsible for turning me into someone who was loud in bed. It was new to me—and fucking mind-blowing. The pleasure was sharp and darted from one erogenous zone to another, never failing to pass through my crotch.

And I tensed up more for each thrust in order to intensify the bolts further. Shit, it was sex on a new level, and he was there. In my head, around me, inside me.

"Harder," I growled.

I hissed as he grabbed a fistful of my hair and exposed my neck. I got on all fours and grabbed the headboard with one hand, and then I looked over my shoulder while he gripped my hips and positioned himself. He drove deep, and I pushed back. The sharp bolts were back, an equal amount of pain and pleasure.

The sounds and the intoxicating scent of us filled the air. At one point, the slapping of skin matched my heart rate. It pulled me under in some sort of drug haze.

"Jesus, Casey." Ellis panted and yanked me back to his chest once more. My eyes rolled, and he swiveled his hips to get deeper while his hand found its way to my throat. "So beautiful. Sexy, mouthwatering." He curled his fingers around my throat loosely, cursing when he felt my Adam's apple move with a swallow. "Perfect little ass."

I kinda blacked out after that. My body was out of control and my mind even more so. I followed the ecstasy like an addict and didn't know I was close until he stroked me a few times and set me off.

I didn't remember collapsing.

Dreams were packed with foggy images of us having sex—or maybe they were memories? Either way, they woke me up sometime later, and I blinked blearily. *Ouch.* I winced. Every muscle in me protested, and my ass was so sore it wouldn't surprise me if he was still buried in me. Alas, he was snoring lightly next to me.

"Oh Christ." My head hit the pillow after checking the time, and I noticed how hoarse I was. Only, instead of having been to a rock festival, I'd had a whole night of insane fucking. Hours and hours of panting and wheezing had effectively stolen most of my voice. "Ellis," I croaked. "Wake up."

He made a noncommittal sound in his sleep, so I struggled through the aches and stole his sheet. His ass was fine as hell this morning... My mouth went dry at the sight of it. One day, it was gonna be my cock that took him, but for now, I was still in bottom mode. I couldn't fucking believe it—or how it was even possible—but I wanted him again right now.

I was such a whore.

"*Ellis*," I groaned and pressed my semi against the mattress. "I need you again."

Not here, though. The second the thought hit me, I wrinkled my nose and squinted around us. The cabin was a war zone. The sheets were an uncomfortable mess, there were clothes everywhere, the air was bordering on stifling, and we were a tad too sticky.

"Mmm, five minutes, baby..." he grumbled. "I think you drained me."

Well, hey. That was new. *Baby.* "It'll take us about five minutes to fill a cooler with sugary pop and go outside." Fresh, crisp air, a sunbed waiting for us, and the sky catching on fire. Seemed like a perfect way to welcome the morning.

I managed to get Ellis to agree, and then we were moving like zombies to get out of the sex sauna.

We didn't even put on underwear.

"You know what would be perfect now?" He rubbed the sleep out of his eyes.

"Yeah. More sex." I snagged three condoms and the lube, then opened the door to head upstairs.

He followed me with a few soft drinks. "That too, but I was thinking we should go for a swim."

He was funny.

Everything in the color white on the upper deck shone in

orange, reflecting the new day starting, though it would be another twenty minutes or so before we caught the first glimpse of the sun. The best part was the fresh air.

The forest was almost completely silent.

"I'm serious, Casey." Ellis came up behind me and stroked my chest, his hands colder after holding the pops. He nipped at my neck. "Join me, please?"

I frowned at him, finding him fucking crazy, then watched as he took the steps down to the bathing platform along the side of the boat.

"We should have you committed!" I hollered, and I instantly recoiled at the echo of my voice. Hoarse or not, it carried. I half expected to see a flock of birds lifting from the trees.

Ellis laughed warmly, sounding like he'd been to a festival, too.

It didn't take a genius to figure out I hesitated a whole lot, but eventually, I trailed after him. I reached the platform in time to see him dive in, and I instinctively cupped my junk and shuddered.

He's naked and soaked in there.

I chewed on the inside of my cheek, picturing him.

Unlike the time we went swimming at the waterfall, he didn't surface with a feral hiss because it was so cold. No, if anything, he looked relieved.

"You have to get in. It's nice," he told me. "Think of how sexy it would be to feel each other up in the water."

"That's the only reason I'm even considering this." I stepped closer to the edge and peered into the water. The pitch-black water. "Goddamn you, Ellis Hayes." I rubbed the back of my neck, nervousness settling like a rock inside me. "Okay, fine." Releasing a heavy breath, I dove in and already regretted it. *Cunt, fuck, douchenozzle!* After sleep, *everything* was cold. Suddenly, the waterfall swim seemed like a hot spring. "Fuck this," I coughed, already on my way back to the ladder.

"Oh no, you don't." Ellis swam after me and grabbed my foot.

I was hauled backward and let out a highly manly yelp before I went under.

When I reached the surface again, I was locked in Ellis's arms, and he covered my mouth with his just as I was about to curse him out.

"*Umph*—you—fuck." I panted, surrendering. I was a defeated popsicle. Or cocksicle, whichever. "You...cretin! Shit." My hands had found his solid chest. I did love his chest.

"Now I can do what I didn't have the courage to do at the waterfall." He gave me a wet kiss. "Kiss you all I want, touch you everywhere." He proved his point by gliding a hand along my ass cheeks, two fingers slipping between and brushing over the sensitive skin.

He knew how to change my mind about getting out of the water.

"Keep going." My ass clenched, and I grasped his shoulder. Shit, around him, I was one needy puppy. Insatiable, as well.

"Or..." He smiled and brushed his nose to mine. "We could enjoy our swim before I maul you again."

There was nothing wrong with mauling. One couldn't really have too much of it. So why the fuck was he swimming away from me? That was goddamn criminal.

"Lie back and appreciate the moment, Casey." So that's what he was doing. Most of his magnificent body was submerged, with his gaze and part of his chest facing the sky. *He* was the one I wanted to appreciate.

I looked up, though. "Yes, Dad." Last time I followed his direction, I'd seen the Milky Way and then...then I got him. I wasn't disappointed this time, either. It was a peaceful war between east and west. Midnight black and stars on one side, fire and pale blue on the other.

I sighed contentedly. The man had been right. This was kind of wonderful.

"Do you ever miss your parents?" he wondered.

"Way to ruin the moment," I huffed. "No, can't say I do. They hurt me pretty fucking bad." At times, I wondered what hurt me most, being in prison or being disowned by my parents *because* I was in prison. "These days, I'm even relieved. I wouldn't want them around Haley." The thought of their uppity, narrow-minded bullshit made me shudder. "I hope you don't miss your folks."

Ellis's mother and father were part of the very rare breed that my pacifist ass would get homicidal with.

"Goodness, no." He snorted quietly. "I can relate to the relief, particularly when speaking of my mother. I ordered pizza when I heard she passed away."

No one could blame him for that. I would've probably ordered cake, too.

Ellis's dad had died of a fatal heart attack the year after I left Michigan. According to Lincoln and Keith, Ellis had been quiet a day or two, then moved on with his life. Keith had mourned the brother he'd grown up with, not the orthodox nut job he'd died as.

"Did you always want to work in landscaping?" Ellis asked next.

"If we're quizzing each other, isn't it my turn?"

"Let me think... No."

I grinned, angling myself to float closer to him. "Since you made such a valid point... No, not at all." Once upon a time, I thought I was going to be a software engineer. "I guess there's been an engineer in me since I was a kid, but... The landscaping part was because I was in prison. Not being able to go outside whenever I wanted...? And the monotonous lifestyle. Every day was the same."

When the day came and Lincoln told me to get my ass to the nearest college, I didn't have a fucking clue what to go with. Adeline sat down with me, having gone through something similar where she didn't know what she wanted to do with her life, and she helped me narrow it down. From my time in prison, I knew I wanted to use my hands as much as my brain. I needed variety in my work atmosphere as well as my schedule.

She'd gotten us into the field of landscaping, and after some research, I found the profession *landscape architecture.*

"It just clicked for me, I guess," I finished. "What about you? How did you get into marketing?"

It was a big leap from Trapped by Cult to CEO of a big agency he'd started himself.

"My freshman year in college, I took as many classes as possible that were related to human behavior." What he said sparked a memory. He'd once mentioned being driven by understanding people. Presumably to make sense of why some shitheads acted the way his parents had. "I didn't have any interest in working in psychology," he went on, "but I saw how readily it was used in sales and marketing. The art of manipulation."

I tilted my head in his direction.

"It can get utterly nasty and dishonest in marketing." He paused. "To sell a cure, we often have to make up a disease first, and in my naïve days as a student, I wanted to change that."

"Did you?"

"Not even close," he chuckled softly. "I do have fairly high standards. I'm in a position where I can afford to choose what client and product to represent, but at the end of the day, the honest truth is too boring to market. It has to be explosive somehow."

I wasn't too surprised to hear that. In general, we became bored very easily today. We were spoiled.

We'd forgotten there was a difference between wants and needs, and unless someone told us we needed something, the chances of us buying it weren't as good.

"Can I visit you at work sometime?" I asked. "I'm trying to picture you as a boss."

He let out a laugh. "Having problems envisioning it?"

"Yeah... You're too nice."

"Hmm. I'm not going to demonstrate that side of me, but you're more than welcome to stop by the office." He swam closer to me, and soon, I felt his fingers gripping my wrist. "Have I told you how much I enjoy getting to know you better?"

"Every complicated quirk of me?" Back in a vertical position, I treaded water and circled him until I was behind him.

"You're not complicated." Goose bumps rose across his back as I kissed the spot between his shoulder blades.

"So you keep saying," I murmured. "In all seriousness, though...it's strangely fulfilling to get to know myself through your eyes. I like the way you see me."

"Same here." He turned around and pulled me close, encouraging me to wrap my legs around him. "I've learned a lot about myself by talking to you."

"For the better?"

"Always." He rested his forehead to mine. "Enlightenment is never bad."

Maybe.

I searched his steely eyes, having run out of words, and pushed back some hair from his forehead. Then I covered his mouth with mine because I needed again. *Needed, needed, needed.* Why did it feel that way? Superlatives were generally used to highlight and emphasize; they weren't supposed to be so fucking accurate. I'd told partners I found them irresistible before, but that didn't mean I literally couldn't resist them physically. With Ellis, though, all bets were off.

I didn't know he was moving us back to the boat until my leg hit the immersed ladder behind me. He pushed the tip of his tongue into my mouth and reached for the handrail to the ladder, then deepened the kiss further. My weight was fully supported, meaning I could let my hands wander.

"Shit." I sucked in a breath as he rubbed the head of his cock between my ass cheeks. "I wish we could fuck here."

"One day." It sounded ominously like a promise. Promises were dangerous, so I kissed him before he could say something else.

Holy fuck, he felt good. The cold water eased the soreness, whereas his cock heated me up and made me crave more. Namely, that big cock shoved up inside me. Since I couldn't have that, I settled for his teasing.

Sliding my hands up his biceps, I felt his muscles flexing underneath his flesh. One of his hands had disappeared between us, but I couldn't see clearly. For one, the water and my cock obscured the view. For two, his hungry kisses kept stealing my attention.

"Are you stroking yourself?" I muttered, out of breath.

He nodded, breathing just as heavily. "I want to come—right here." He pressed against my hole, and for the goddamn life of me, I couldn't kill the whimper before it slipped out of me. If my desperation wasn't clear earlier, it was now. "And when I do..." He grazed his teeth along my bottom lip. "I'll think of the day I get to fuck my come deep inside your perfect ass and watch it drip."

"I..." I had nothing. My mind went blank. Until the images he'd just pushed into my skull were everywhere. It was all I could see and think of. "*Fuck*, Ellis. I want it. I wanna feel it." Because I knew I would. I'd feel the heat pulsating across my skin, and the thought made my mouth water. *Think of what could follow.* "For the love of—only you would make me wanna do that to you and then use my tongue to clean you up."

Ellis groaned and screwed his eyes shut, the idea evidently not unwelcome. One day, maybe—fuck, I could beg for that to happen. As the pressure grew yet not nearly enough, I wrapped my fingers around my cock and jerked myself to my own fantasy. How would he react to my tongue-fucking him? I'd tease him for all the teasing he'd given me. I'd go gently and softly until he fucking begged.

"I'm close," he breathed out through clenched teeth. "Ah, Casey—fuck..."

My undoing was when he started coming and I felt the first pulse of his release ghosting across my opening. I clenched, *hard*, my entire being wanting him to just slam in and fill me up. My orgasm rocked me unsteady, and everything was a reaction to his actions. One moment, his cock slid slowly between my cheeks, drawing a heavy shudder from me. The next, he jerked forward and almost entered me, and the spike of pleasure hit me sharply.

The second my climax subsided, I knew it was the last one I could handle for a while. I fucking *hurt*. How many times had we gotten off last night? I must've come four or five times at least. My skin was crazy sensitive, too.

"You're g'na have to...carry me." I could barely speak, for chrissakes. My brain felt like it'd been dipped in cement.

"Are you okay?" Ellis swallowed, his voice strained and breathy, and I managed one nod before my forehead hit his shoulder. "Did I wear you out?" Smug bastard.

He totally had, though.

"I'm only glad I...I didn't make a just-the-tip joke. 'Cause I was getting ready to beg when you came."

He chuckled through a tired groan and hugged me to him.

"I'm glad you didn't. I would've caved. Christ—I need to sleep for a week to recover."

Sounded about right.

"Let me draw us a bath. I can give you a massage if you want?" He palmed my jaw and made me face him. I blinked sleepily. "Adorable."

"Yes on the massage. No on the bath—because I'm not sure how to get there."

He thought that was funny. "I've got you." He kissed me briefly. "I promise."

Oh no, I couldn't allow him to promise me things.

14

If no promises were made, they couldn't be broken. On our slow, yet too-fucking-fast, journey back to Camassia, I interrupted Ellis every time he tried to make promises. I didn't even want him to reassure me of anything. My hopes were already way up there, and I told him the truth. In the event that something happened, one promise fewer could at least diminish the risk of any resentment. Ellis was the last man I wanted to resent.

"Well, aren't you a ray of sunshine, you stubborn man." He nipped at my jaw, hands on my hips.

"That's us, Princess and the Ray of Sunshine." I batted away his hand as it dipped too low. He had to get back to driving the water raft, and I was gonna fix us some lunch.

He shook his head, amused, and returned to the wheel. "I told you once you hide other things. Remember?"

"My cock needs to stay hidden at the moment. Fucking like bunnies causes chafing."

"Jesus," he muttered and slid on his shades. "Definitely not what I was referring to."

Yeah, I know.

We'd already established I hid some fears behind humor, however reluctant I was to admit it. Sue me.

Fucking like bunnies was what we'd done our last few days on the yacht. Tonight, we were scheduled to be home again, and I could feel myself retreating. Mentally, anyway. I couldn't bear to retreat physically, nor did he deserve any skittish behavior from me.

Heading below deck, I dug out the ingredients to improvise a pasta dish. You couldn't really go wrong with pesto, mozzarella, and tomatoes.

Docking in the marina at home put a rock the size of Mount Rainier in my gut. Whatever little I'd brought with me and bought along the way was packed in the bag from the store where I got my Date Pants, and I was back in the clothes I'd worn the night I got kidnapped. Anxiety about work was creeping in, as well. I'd played hooky way too fucking long and had a lot of catching up to do.

The low rumble of the engine was exchanged with dead silence, and Ellis grew quieter as he secured the boat. He'd told me he planned on sleeping on the yacht for a while, though he was returning to work shortly and hoped to talk to his wife tomorrow or the day after.

Back to normal, we go.

Ellis approached and took a seat next to me on the sofa. He gave my leg a gentle squeeze. "Ready to face reality?"

I scowled at him. What was he *thinking*? "It doesn't help when you put it that way, jackass. It implies the trip was a fairy tale and now everything's ending."

"You truly are a drama queen." He gathered my hands and

kissed them. "Allow me to rephrase so it'll suit Your Highness. Are you ready to face the more grim facets of our reality?"

My mouth twitched. I fucking loved the way we bantered.

I was going to miss it.

"You have my new address," I told him quietly. This reality he mentioned was sinking in. Vacation was over. "I have thirty-six hours to get the house ready before I pick up Haley and Lyn in Seattle. If I'm not at home, I'm at work."

I'd sent a text to Madigan and a few friends who were able to help out on such short notice, so putting all the furniture where it was supposed to be wouldn't take more than a few hours.

Ellis nodded with a dip of his chin. "Give me a week—two at the most. I'd like to have the conversation with Marilyn out of the way, and I need to look for my own place." Before, he'd mentioned he needed to process, too. That was the scariest part.

"Take all the time you need," I replied. "I can be awesome at waiting. More awesome than Sherlock fans waiting for the next season."

"I...don't know what that means."

I waved a hand. "It's a brilliant TV show. I'll school you in Netflixing one day."

He smiled then grasped my chin and tilted my face for a kiss. "I look forward to it."

Right. Me, too. For now, though, this was it.

I woke up the next morning anxious about...everything in my life, really, and I got ready on autopilot. Shower, brush my teeth, jeans, my gray "I spit" tee... I hesitated in front of the boxes in the hallway, then grabbed my beanie, too.

After stacking the boxes of clothes in the bed of the truck, I left Lincoln and Ade's house and drove down the hillside. The guys were coming over in ten minutes, which meant I was running late. I'd promised to bring breakfast, something I'd hoped to have done once I'd picked up the rest of my shit from work.

As I drove onto the quiet little street five minutes away from the marina, I spotted Madigan's car outside my new house. He and Jameson stepped out when I parked behind them.

"Morning." Madigan took a sip of his coffee. "We're ready to build muscle."

I mustered a grin and dug out my keys. "I guess you guys can warm up with the boxes in the back. It's all clothes." I liked that I was the owner of a house with a picturesque picket fence, although it needed a coat of paint. As I bent down to scrape some rust off the handle, Jameson sidled up next to me. "Hey. Thank you for coming."

He smirked and leaned close to speak in my ear. "I had to prove a point, and...yeah." He nuzzled my jaw and skimmed a hand over my ass. "Still gorgeous."

I spluttered a chuckle and straightened. "Hands off the merchandise, you flirt."

He winked, then headed over to assist Madigan.

I shook my head, amused, and opened the gate. Even with the rising anxiety because of my stupid—not unfounded, but sometimes irrational—fears, a sense of pride swelled in my chest as I looked up at my new house. Two stories of all *mine*.

The old brick offered a vintage feel to it, but it'd been painted not too long ago, and the pristine white made me happy. It went fucking perfectly with the ivy that slithered up the little porch, not to mention the plants and flowers I had planned for the flower beds. I was saving those for next spring, though.

After unlocking the door, I returned to the street, only to veer right to my driveway. "There're some boxes in the garage, too. They're all labeled." It was mostly going up in the attic. "If you bring this in, I can go get the rest of the stuff from work, and I'll be back with breakfast. That okay?"

Madigan nodded, heading inside with two boxes in his arms. "You know what I like."

Before I left, another two buddies showed up, too. I made quick introductions before I took breakfast orders from everyone and then took off. I wanted to hurry so they didn't get stuck with the most tedious work.

I worked up a sweat getting all the furniture onto my truck. Feeling bad for having left my employees alone for nearly two weeks while I was with Ellis, I told Beth to order pizza for lunch for the three of them. It'd been a good month, so I'd add a bonus to their paychecks, too. I didn't take vacation days very often; I'd needed to get away more than I'd initially thought, but it hadn't been fair to leave without notice. Even if they handled everything great on their own.

All in all, I was gone an hour and a half, and the guys were hungry when I got back to the house.

I unpacked the food, filling the kitchen island with coffees, teas, muffins, bagels, and whatever else they'd ordered. "Your misspelled names are on the beverages, guys. Dig in."

Jameson lifted his latte. "'James On.' Seriously?"

I pressed my lips together to stifle my laugh, though Madigan's cup always did it for me.

It just said Bob. He'd long ago given up on baristas getting his name right, so he used Bob.

Other than the occasional KC, they tended to know how to spell my name.

"Have you talked to Jesse lately?" Madigan asked me.

"Maybe a few weeks ago. Why?" I tucked into an egg sandwich in between sips of my coffee.

"Lincoln's worried about him."

I furrowed my brow. "Is something wrong?"

Jesse was...an interesting character. I loved the guy, but he frustrated the crap out of me, too. He struggled a lot with the concept of family; he went looking for it in the wrong place. His biological dad was dead, and his mom abandoned him when he was around ten or eleven. Ade and Lincoln would do everything for him, and the thing was, Jesse *needed* them, yet something kept him from accepting it. As far as I knew, it'd been like that since Lincoln got out of prison.

Jesse didn't belong in LA, something I'd told him many times. Much like me, he thrived when he was around family.

"We don't know yet," Madigan replied. "He's partying a lot, though. Drinking heavily."

Aw, man. We had to do something if it was getting out of control.

"So next time he's home to visit, we don't let him leave." I liked my suggestion.

So did Madigan. "That's what I told Lincoln. Jesse doesn't stand a chance."

That was reassuring. We could be a force to be reckoned with.

When everyone left around three, I continued almost frenetically. No one was around to distract me, meaning every thought was occupied by Ellis if I rested more than a minute. The couch was pushed into the living room, a new rug and coffee table were put into place, and the entertainment center was reassembled before I ordered Chinese for dinner. And I could eat at the same time as I sorted through all the DVDs and picture frames.

I focused less on Ellis's feelings and decisions and more on my own. It'd been an intense few weeks—not only the time we spent on the yacht—but the days leading up to it. The physical aspect was a nonissue; my attraction for him had probably always been there in a removed, distant sort of way. The rest, though? Fuck me, it was messing with my head.

We'd known each other for six years now, and every goddamn story, every anecdote, was changing. Everything I knew, my brain was trying to reexamine, and I didn't even know why. Because my feelings toward him had changed? Maybe.

I sighed and wiped sweat off my neck, noticing I'd stopped what I was doing. Damn that man for getting under my skin.

On the other hand, I wanted more. There was something intoxicating about having your heart in someone else's hands. Perhaps he didn't have a full grasp on all of it yet, but it was no doubt heading in that direction.

Get back to work, you sappy fool.

Grabbing a bottle of water from the otherwise pathetically empty fridge, I surveyed the kitchen, then the living room, and deemed the downstairs almost ready. A final touch of some knickknacks and setting up the surround sound system could be dealt with tomorrow.

Then I continued upstairs.

Haley was a priority, so I got cracking in her room. The polka-dotted walls were perfect, pastel pink and white, and the bed looked comfy under a canopy of multicolored drapes and string lights. Next were her clothes and toys, though she was old enough to organize some of her stuff the way she wanted it. I put together the shelving system and emptied the moving boxes in the nicer plastic ones that went on the shelves, and we could do the rest together.

I spent much of the next day in the fast lane of domesticity, too. I finished with the house, went grocery shopping, did some paperwork, *didn't* think about Ellis more than a few hundred times, and then prepared dinner. I had a feeling the girls were gonna be as exhausted as they'd be starving, so I wanted everything ready when we got back.

After that, there wasn't much to do, yet I had to keep moving. Otherwise, it would be too easy to have a seat in the kitchen and stare at my phone.

He's not gonna call anytime soon.

"Quit fucking obsessing." I smacked the wall in my shower, accidentally getting suds in my eye. "Serves you right, you neurotic asshole."

I stepped under the spray and washed off. Then autopilot took over while I shaved and got dressed, and I reasoned with myself for once. Ellis was a good man. He would never intentionally hurt me, so I had to stop believing the worst. Lastly, he wasn't gonna pay for what'd happened in my previous relationships.

There. I could be rational.

Then I was on my way to Seattle with a piece of cardboard that said "Can I have my daughter back now?"

As soon as I spotted Haley, my eyes smarted and I held up the sign. Lincoln was carrying her, and it was obvious she was looking for me in the sea of arrivals. Adeline walked hand in hand with Lyn and grinned tiredly when seeing my board. She leaned closer to Lincoln and Haley, pointing them in my direction, and then my girl wanted down. Fast. Her eyes widened, and this huge smile took over that I matched.

"Daddy!"

I picked up the pace as my heart did the same, not stopping until I was a few feet away from her. That was when I dipped down and grabbed her in my arms. I had no clue where the sign landed. It didn't fucking matter. Haley was finally home again, and it felt too damn good. My throat closed up and words eluded me.

Being a parent meant I was indestructible and a sitting duck all at once. Never had I felt this strong yet vulnerable at the same time. Ten feet tall, yet on my knees. I all but crushed her in my hug and peppered her face with kisses, and she giggled breathlessly.

Eventually, I had to ease up on the hold, and then we were just kind of staring at each other with big grins.

"I missed you." I swallowed hard and tucked a piece of hair behind her ear.

"I missed you, too!" A yawn cut her excitement short, and I chuckled at her as she rubbed her eyes with her fists. "Can we go home now? I'm hungry." She tugged at my beanie.

"Hell yeah, we can go home. Spaghetti and meatballs are waiting for us. And way too much ketchup."

"Yes!" She fist-pumped the air.

I spared Adeline and Lincoln quick hugs before I got down on one knee in front of Lyn. She got a better hug, and we exchanged an Eskimo kiss. She was thrilled about our plans for the week, which included fort-building, cookie-making, and Netflix-bingeing.

"I feel dismissed," Lincoln said.

Adeline laughed. "I think we're officially in the chopped liver category."

"You're not wrong," I told her and stood up. "Where's the luggage?" 'Cause I was ready to hit the road.

"Should be here soon." Lincoln glanced over his shoulder. Go figure, he couldn't be bothered to handle his own luggage. "Anyway." He faced me again. "Ade said you haven't called the sitter."

I shook my head. "I won't need her." A woman Adeline used to work with had recommended her daughter to watch the girls when our schedules clashed, but I wasn't meeting with any clients this week. "I'll be in the warehouse setting up the new office. Haley and Lyn can tag along." There was a couch and a laptop with movies waiting to be watched. Possibly more than a little ice cream, too.

Ade smiled and slipped her hand into Lincoln's. "Casey's gonna overdose on the princesses."

Fingers crossed.

Starting with spaghetti and meatballs while catching up.

Haley was so overwhelmed by her new room that once she was done squealing behind her hands, it got to be too much and she started crying. Flying halfway across the world probably hadn't helped.

"Do you like it?" I sat down on her bed in the corner, and she nodded and ran over to me. "What do you think, Lyn?"

While Haley climbed up on my lap and tried to hide her face in my armpit—which, frankly, I wouldn't recommend—Lyn was inspecting every surface more critically. Pausing in front of the window, she looked out over our little backyard.

Then she turned to me with a big smile. "This is so pretty, Uncle Casey."

Phew. It passed inspection.

Haley calmed down after a couple minutes, so I left them alone to explore while I heated up dinner. It was a good time to start a load of laundry too, 'cause Haley left with one piece of luggage and came home with two.

With the food in the oven—with a shit-ton of cheese dumped on top—I took the girls' suitcases to the laundry room and sorted out all the clothes. I smiled, hearing them stomping around upstairs.

Fuck, it felt good having Haley home again.

We didn't get much done the first three days. Haley and Lyn went from cranky to hyper while they readjusted to our time zone. Getting them to sleep on time was fucking impossible, but at least I got plenty of cuddles.

The weather today was...*okay*, so I decided to put the girls to use. It was never too early to learn how to pick weeds, and they could do that while I gave the picket fence a fresh coat of white paint.

Keith stopped by to catch up and have coffee, too.

Everything was fine on the surface. Being around the girls and talking to Keith was always nice, yet I couldn't shake the deep-rooted yearning Ellis had reawakened in me. I missed him.

Standing up, I used my arm to wipe sweat off my forehead, and I looked at the sky. With a bit of luck, the paint would tack up before it started raining.

A sleek black sedan drove onto the quiet street, and fuck me if I didn't recognize it. My first thought went straight to Ellis, and just as quickly, I dismissed it. It was his goddamn wife. Marilyn came to family dinners only on holidays, and if she arrived from work, that was the car she drove.

"This can't be good," I muttered under my breath. Thankfully, I could be quick on my feet sometimes, and I addressed Haley and Lyn. "Girls, why don't you show Pop-Pop Haley's new room? I bet he'll love the glow-in-the-dark stars you bought at Disney."

I hadn't loved attaching them to the ceiling, but that was another story.

"You gotta see them!" Lyn exclaimed, immediately grabbing Keith's hand.

"All right, all right." He grunted through a chuckle and rose from the lawn chair.

Haley darted up the small porch and ripped the door open.

Privacy: accomplished.

Marilyn parked in front of my house, grabbed her purse, and stepped out. How much did she know? Given the circumstances, it wasn't a matter of if she knew. I must've been the topic of at least one conversation for her to even know my new address. Which posed another question. Was Ellis aware of her being here?

She looked like the bearer of shitty news. Considering she worked in her family-owned funeral home, I supposed it was fitting. She wore a lot of black, and her hair and makeup were always impeccable. She was attractive—I couldn't deny that— though the frigidness to her made me instinctively want to take a step back.

"Casey." There was no warmth to her voice, either.

"Hey, Marilyn." I adjusted my beanie.

"Can we talk?" she asked curtly.

"Well, I..." *Fuck.* "I can't think of any reason why we can't." And that sucked. "What's up?"

She rested her purse at the top of the fence, and I pressed my lips together. Telling her it was newly painted wouldn't earn me any favors.

"I saw Keith and the children heading in, so I won't ask to be invited." How nice of her. "I, uh, I had an interesting conversation with my husband yesterday."

Fuck you.

Shit. Maybe I had some resentment toward her building up inside me. Probably a lot of jealousy, too. So fuck her. Fuck her forever and a day for the fortune of being able to call Ellis her husband.

He's divorcing her. Calm your tits.

I folded my arms over my chest, waiting. I wasn't gonna ask.

She cleared her throat. "Perhaps it's best I show you." Opening her bag, she dug out a—oh, fuck. A camera. "I found this in his bag when he stopped by to do laundry. I was only going to check the battery when the last taken image popped up on the screen."

I didn't need to see it, but there it was. Ellis flashing a soft, brief smile as he pressed a light kiss to the spot above the waistband of my sweats. It tugged at my heart painfully to see it now.

"Ellis told me things have changed," she went on. "He wants a divorce."

Why did I sense a "but" coming? I didn't dare to hope, except I held my breath as if the answer I wanted would make my year. Goddamn, I hoped. I hoped against hope.

"I'm going to be honest with you, Casey." She took a breath and stashed away the camera again. "Those words didn't hurt as much as they should, and maybe he's right. Maybe we're not right for each other. I can't argue when push comes to shove, but—" There it fucking was, and her steely façade was crumbling. Marilyn was uncomfortable. "He doesn't have the whole story. He doesn't know yet that I'm pregnant."

"Jesus." Nausea rose within me, and I rubbed a hand over my mouth. Babies were great news, babies were wonderful news, babies were fucking awesome—right? Yeah. It was purely self-centered of me to hate this moment with every fiber of my being.

He'll never choose me now.

The brick of guilt hit me instantly, and I did everything I could to push away the selfish fears.

"I'm telling him tonight." Marilyn squared her shoulders. "My hope is that he and I will do this together without...distractions, if you will, from other directions." Oh, that bitch. My jaw tensed. "The question is, can you back off and give Ellis and me space—"

"You're not serious," I blurted out. "You wanna see me as a distraction? Be my fucking guest—but you're not gonna speak on Ellis's behalf to me. I'll respect his wishes, all right? And, for the record—" I gestured between us "—I don't think he's gonna be too pleased about you going behind his back to discuss this with me before you breathe a word of it to him—you know, the *father* of your child. If you don't want me to be part of this, then don't fucking include me."

She looked stricken from my vent at first, though her cold mask was soon firmly in place. "I see." Her mouth thinned. "I guess I was foolish, hoping you'd be rational enough to realize he might not see clearly—"

I cut her off again, this time genuinely angry. "Do you hear yourself? It's insulting as fuck. You're basically saying we need to make a decision for him because he might not be able to do it himself." I pointed to her car. "I won't be part of some manipulation game, so you can leave. If or when Ellis reaches out to me, I'll be as honest as I've always been."

Marilyn abruptly gathered her bag, then turned on her heel and got in her car.

I waited for the relief at her leaving to hit me, but it didn't come. The anger simmered below the surface, and my stomach was in knots. The only silver lining I could see was the fact that it was as easy as breathing to redirect my focus to Ellis. It was about him now, not me. Marilyn could go fuck herself for all I cared, but I'd do everything to make this easier for Ellis.

I couldn't pretend to be in a good mood, so I got started on dinner rather than to seek out Keith and the girls. *There might be another girl joining us soon.* How would birthday parties look? Would Ellis and Marilyn show up as a family with their child?

All kinds of shit went through my head, and I'd burn dinner if I tried to do anything complicated. We had leftover barbecue chicken in the freezer that I'd originally packed as work lunches. While I defrosted that, I prepared fries and a spinach dip. Greens—couldn't forget the greens. Opening the fridge, I stared unseeingly at the container holding our vegetables.

Salad, salad, salad...

Ellis had made a good salad that day I made the bourbon chicken. *He's gonna be a dad.* As heavy as the rock was in my gut, I couldn't help but smile a little. He'd make an awesome father, no matter the nature of the relationship he had with Marilyn.

Grabbing a few random vegetables, I put it all on the cutting board on the kitchen island and began chopping. Funny how good I was at chopping shit when I was anxious and upset.

Maybe I needed to divert my attention to anything but the baby news, and what the crap would that be? I hadn't blogged properly since before my trip. If I sat down now and let it all pour out, it would be ugly. Not to mention it would be way more than I was comfortable sharing with complete strangers on the internet.

I glanced at my phone on the counter, thinking perhaps I

should meet up with some friends. Though, the thought held zero appeal, and I had Haley and Lyn another couple days. This weekend, however. I'd need to do *something*.

"Jesus Christ." I sighed and set down the knife. One tiny person could cure my overthinking for the moment; that was a start. "Haley! Come down here and remind Daddy that babies are good news!"

15

I was in the middle of a dream about rock samples when the phone rang. Rubbing sleep out of my eyes, I uttered a "huh," because it was a pretty good idea. There was enough space at work to set up a showroom where clients could see samples of all kinds of things. Types of rock for pathways, photos from my portfolio on the walls, types of wood, soil, grass, and—the phone rang again.

With a grunt, I reached for the offending object and spotted Ellis's name on the display. My stomach flipped as I answered. "Ellis, are you okay?" I didn't see any other reason for him to call at three in the morning.

"I...yeah. Hey."

"Hey." I sat up and rubbed at my face. "How are you?"

"Can...can we talk?" Oh hell, he was drunk. "I'm outside."

Shit. "I'll be right down." Disconnecting the call, I jumped into action and got out of bed. Something was definitely wrong if he was here in the middle of the night. As I stepped into a pair of pajama bottoms, the phone rang again, and I answered on my way down the stairs. "Yeah?"

"I forgot to say—I'm sorry I woke you up."

I snorted and pocketed my phone.

Once I was in the hallway, I unlocked and opened the door, and I'd been right. He wasn't okay at all. If his unkempt hair and the shadows under his eyes didn't speak volumes, his rumpled clothes and growing scruff did. At this point, it was long enough to be a beard, and fuck it all if he still didn't make it look sexy as sin.

He held up a pop and a half-eaten burger. "Mind if we sit out here? I don't—don't want to wake up Haley and Lyn."

Solid idea. The fresh air would do him good, too. I snatched a hoodie from the knobs on the coat closet door, then exited the house quietly. It was a muggy night; the hoodie might not even be necessary.

Ellis stumbled slightly and set the two lawn chairs next to each other. Not much else would fit on the porch.

Wait.

"Hey, what—" I stepped forward, frowning. There was something... I'd caught a glimpse of his knuckles, and did they look bruised? "Ellis, what the fuck?" I inspected his hand. Two of his knuckles had recently been banged up.

"Oh. I think I broke the washer on the yacht when I tried to fix it."

My forehead creased.

He waved a hand. "It didn't work, for whatever reason. I had to go to the house to do my laundry, and..." He stifled a belch. "I was going to fix it today, but the machine and I got into an argument. So I went to a bar instead."

I sighed, as relieved as I was worried. "Before you sit down —" I took his food and drink from him and set it on the chair. "Come here." I hugged him to me, and his breath hitched. The rush of emotions caught me off guard, so I hugged him harder as if I were trying to piece us back together. Maybe I was.

"I miss you." His quiet admission sure as hell pieced *me* back together. "Casey, I miss you more than I can say. I know it hasn't even been a week, but—"

"I've missed you, too." I palmed his face and kissed him firmly. The smell of alcohol wasn't as bad as I thought it would be, though it was clear he'd had more than he should've. "I've been a head case since I stepped off the raft."

Tension left his shoulders, and he smiled carefully, visibly drained, as I combed my fingers through his messy hair. "I've been meaning to tell you... The definition of raft isn't what you think it is."

I grinned, my eyes stinging. "Water castle."

He exhaled and watched me in silence, and I did the same, brushing my thumbs under his eyes. He hadn't slept much lately. His eyes were glassy, full of weariness, and slightly blood-shot. The light was poor, so I couldn't see properly. And despite it all, he was the most beautiful man I'd ever seen.

How quickly could one fall in love? Could it start without someone's knowledge? Had this been building slowly for years, only to get a last, forceful push as our relationship evolved?

It didn't matter.

This wasn't a crush, nor did it resemble anything I'd felt previously.

With Ellis, it felt like I was turning into an all-or-nothing kind of man. There was no off switch to find a balance and slow down.

We hugged again, and I breathed in the traces of his cologne. I stroked his back, gently scratched his hair, and cupped his neck. It was unreal, this need to touch him and make sure he was here. The chemistry was out of this world and was only partly desire. The rest—I didn't know how to explain it, but I was certain I knew the meaning of adoring someone now. Someone who wasn't my daughter.

"You're gonna be a dad," I heard myself whisper. It hit me a second later that I couldn't be sure he knew yet, but it turned out I worried for nothing.

He nodded once, nuzzling my jaw, then rested our foreheads together. "I apologize for Marilyn. I was infuriated when she told me she was here."

"It's okay. We—we had words."

He chuckled under his breath and brought my left hand to his mouth for a kiss. "Oh, she told me." Giving me a light tug, he walked us to the chairs, and I was impressed he remembered his burger and pop. "However you defended me made her call you my guard dog."

"Woof." I smirked lazily and sat down next to him. "So what made you think soul-searching at the bottom of a bottle was a good idea?" I shrugged on the hoodie, after all.

He shot me a narrow-eyed look and took a bite of his burger. "I'll have you know—excuse me." He deduced it was best to chew and swallow before he spoke. "I did all my soul searching sober. Today was just..." He blew out a breath.

"A shitshow?"

"Good word for it." He nodded. "There's the irritating, the painful, the overwhelming, and the embarrassing. Take your pick."

Something told me the overwhelming was related to learning he was going to be a father.

"What was painful?"

He winced and peered down at his food. "She's already four months pregnant, and up until a few weeks ago, she was leaning toward having an abortion." He swallowed. "She wasn't planning on telling me. I wouldn't have known..."

That hit close to home. All I could do was give his arm a squeeze.

"The night before I asked Lincoln if I could borrow the boat...remember?" He flicked me a tired glance, and I nodded.

He and Marilyn had tried to make up or something. Romantic dinner at home. He'd fled afterward. "She'd had second thoughts and decided to tell me about the pregnancy that night. But I wasn't the only one who felt how forced our interaction was, thus she changed her mind again and didn't tell me." He took a breath and rewrapped his burger, obviously no longer hungry. "I fear the embarrassing part and the irritating part are connected, and they involve you."

"I'm flattered." Jesus, could I take this seriously? I felt bad.

He let out a low laugh of surprise. "Don't ever change, Casey."

I smiled a little, a lot relieved.

"There's another reason she didn't think she wanted the baby at first." He got us back on track. "She's been dating and didn't believe it was mine because—well..."

"Holy fuck, are you—You gotta be kidding. *Ouch.*" That would fucking kill me.

"...I wore protection, of course. And we've only been inti-mate once or twice in the past *year*..."

"I mean, honestly," I went on. "That's way more suspense than I'd be able to handle. Although, technically, I guess you didn't—if you didn't learn of the pregnancy until she was sure it's yours, which—" I quirked a brow. "How does she know the baby's yours?"

He stared at me, and I frowned, registering what he'd said while I rambled over him. My bad.

"Ah, right." He cleared his throat and scrubbed his hands over his face. "She had a paternity test in the...sorry, I forget what week. It's been a long night with a colossal amount of information." He grabbed his pop off the floor but didn't drink from it. "It was between this new man she's been seeing and me, and the results ruled him out."

"Good God, it's like a soap opera." I rubbed a hand over my

mouth and jaw, processing everything. "Let me get this straight. She's with two men—you and someone else—around the same time. Since she believed the father was the other guy, she didn't want the baby—presumably because they barely know each other." I didn't mean for it to sound like I was judging her in any way; I just wanted to get the facts right. "Then she had a paternity test done...with the intention of going through with an abortion?" Didn't quite add up to me.

"She went back and forth, she told me," he said. "Or rather, she went from definitely not wanting a baby to hesitating, at which point she contacted the other guy and went through with the test. When the results showed he wasn't a match, she reconsidered further. It's...goddamn, so complicated." He leaned forward, resting his face in his hands. "I told her I want to take a paternity test as well, to be sure, but she has no reason to lie. She's—well, as we all do, she has issues, but she's not devious."

I wouldn't go so far as to call her devious, either. "Okay, so what's the embarrassing part?" 'Cause I could do the math on the irritating bit. Learning about the pregnancy this late, the timing, and all the details, I'd be ticked off, too.

"We should play it safe and get tested, Casey."

The way he said that caused me to recoil. "Wait, what, *we?*"

"I feel awful about this, but if the protection failed with her, it means I haven't been completely..."

Safe. Shit.

"Right." I rubbed the back of my neck. "Yeah, I guess that will make a fun outing. Getting tested for STDs together."

Although we hadn't fucked unprotected, there was still a risk with oral.

"I'd understand if you're mad," he told me.

He was being silly.

"This is literally the least of my concerns," I chuckled. "Let's move on instead. Is there still a second date in our future? Marilyn was pretty vocal about not wanting me around."

His jaw ticked with tension, and he leaned back in his seat. "I almost told her where to go." Knowing him, he'd feel guilty. He didn't have a malicious bone in him. "I can't apologize enough, Casey. This isn't your mess to deal with—"

"I want you to be my mess," I replied bluntly. "I mean, I want your mess to be mine. You know what I mean."

He watched me, a soft smile tugging at his mouth. Then I felt his fingers slipping between mine. "Fuck, I missed you."

Glad I wasn't the only one. Mirroring his stance, I leaned back, my head resting against the house wall. The silence was so comfortable that the night crept back in, and I yawned.

"You haven't blogged much," he noted.

I smirked sleepily and closed my eyes. "Have you been stalking me online? Please say yes."

He chuckled quietly. "I admit I checked a few times and made sure I was still a subscriber."

Life goal: achieved. I'd always wanted an online stalker. "I did post a selfie with the girls the other day."

He hummed. "I saw it. You were wearing your beanie."

Dammit. I didn't want him to read too much into that—or, possibly, see the truth. Opening my eyes once more, I tightened my hold on his hand and pulled off what I hoped was a convincing smile.

"You look hot in a beard."

He wasn't impressed by my change of topic. "Be serious with me, please. Have you been having anxiety?"

Okay, fine, I could fess up, but I refused to make this bigger than it was. "I've been anxious, sure, and I've been fretting like whoa—all of it self-inflicted. I worry too much. I know it's irrational."

"Hm. Well, if my mess is yours, your mess is mine. I want to be there for you."

"*Mi* mess *es su* mess," I mumbled, because I couldn't *not* go there.

I was a dork.

He smirked and shook his head.

"So..." I trailed off. All questions hadn't been answered. "What do we do now?"

"Deal with our messes?" The exhaustion blended with the remnants of humor. "Marilyn and I are meeting with our lawyers next week. On that front, there isn't much to do but wait."

Okay, good, confirmed. The baby news didn't change anything in that respect. They were still getting divorced.

"Is there any bad blood between you?" I wondered.

He weighed his answers. "Not *too* much, I'd say."

"That's good." It was a big relief, actually. "Children pick up on that." It was way better if the parents were on friendly terms.

It was unlikely that they'd already hammered out details on custody, so I figured I'd wait a while before asking. He probably needed more time to digest it all.

"I don't want to look for my own place, Casey."

I furrowed my brow, instantly guarded. So he was going to stay at his house with her? Ex-spouses turned roommates and co-parents? That might be poking a little too hard at my insecurities, not that I'd speak up. Children came first. He had responsibilities bigger than ever now.

"Okay," I replied warily. "Have you discussed this with Marilyn? You living together, I mean."

It was his turn to frown. "What? No. That's not—I spoke to Lincoln, and he told me I could stay on the boat for however long I needed." Straightening in his seat, he shifted his chair to face me more. "I've thought this through more than once, so please bear with me here." He took a breath. "I've kept my personal life as simple as possible for as long as I can remember. Easy marriage, easy roads. And it would be very easy to go back to that. Marilyn and I would be just another married couple raising a child together, and...we'd be completely miserable at home."

Sounded lovely. Sounded exactly how my parents raised *me*. They stayed together because it was convenient.

Ellis wasn't done, and he gathered my hands in his. "Choosing you would complicate everything in my everyday life, yet it's the most uncomplicated choice I've ever made." *Fuck me.* "I don't want anyone else, and though it wouldn't do me any good to rush into anything new, I need it to be clear that it's ultimately what I want."

For some reason, I probably wouldn't reach for my beanie tomorrow. Because he wasn't going to look for his own place, because his place might eventually be here, because he was choosing me.

I'm not gonna get mushy.

In all seriousness, it was good we didn't rush. Taking our time to date and explore this new relationship in our regular life was exactly what I wanted, too. Everything was easy on vacation. Less stress, fewer responsibilities. Here at home, we'd have a shitload of all that. Haley, work, a new baby on the way—adjustments coming in every direction. And I couldn't fucking wait.

"Come here." I fisted his shirt and pulled him close for a kiss, because words failed me. I kissed him hard and deep, excitement brimming over while my mind, for fucking once, was at perfect ease. "You're in a relationship with Complicated now."

He chuckled breathily and pinched my thigh. "You're not as complicated as you seem to think, sunshine."

I grinned. "Let's not make that nickname stick."

"Maybe it'll be as sticky as princess."

That was a tough one. To *unstick* sunshine, I'd have to drop the princess.

"I'll think about it." I went in for another kiss, contemplating asking him to stay what was left of the night. Was it weird that I looked forward to a bit of sneaking around? Our family obviously didn't know about this, and I wasn't going to rush that, either. Not where Haley was concerned, anyway.

"I should get back to the boat," he murmured huskily.

"Worst decision ever." Especially now with the lust evident in his voice. "You're sober enough to be quiet on the stairs now, aren't you?"

"Don't tempt me," he warned under his breath. "I'm not sober enough to fuck you quietly."

"Shit." I shuddered, a bolt of lust shooting through me. "Actually, I didn't say I'd put out."

Who was I trying to fool? Not me, definitely not Ellis. He gave me a heated look, a knowing look, that said...yeah, I'd definitely put out.

"We need some time soon, though." He sighed softly and rested his forehead against mine. "I miss touching you...sharing a bed with you."

"Yeah. So much." Thinking of when we could have a moment together made me think of Sunday. I was dropping off the girls then, and we were back to our regularly scheduled brunch. "I'll see you Sunday for brunch, right?"

He nodded. "Wouldn't miss it."

16

Some news traveled fast. Not all of it, though definitely the part where Ellis and Marilyn were expecting. To everyone's surprise, it was Marilyn who'd called Adeline to break the news, so it was the hot topic at brunch that Sunday once the girls went off to play.

Even Madigan graced us with his presence today. "Talk about a special parting gift. I hope Hallmark makes cards that say 'Happy Divorce Day! Also, You're Gonna Be a Dad.'"

I snickered into my coffee, earning myself a playful glare from Ellis.

"And four months along already? Wow." Adeline was baffled by the whole thing. Who could blame her? "Do you know what you're having yet?"

I shot my gaze to Ellis, curious about that one, too.

He shook his head. "We have an ultrasound next week."

Ultrasounds were fucking terrifying, though that was coming from a guy who hadn't had his life together when he found out he was gonna be a dad. Given my late start, I was still in school when we found out.

Lincoln, who'd been eerily quiet about Marilyn's pregnancy, finally spoke up. "Are you happy?"

"I'm..." Ellis paused, then nodded slowly. I didn't miss the brief glance he sent my way. "I'm getting there. It's a lot to process, and it's difficult to break free of the mind-set where I consider everything as a married man. Once I remind myself that we're getting divorced, it gets easier. I don't want parenthood to be tainted by a toxic marriage."

Adeline settled her hand on his and smiled reassuringly. "We'll be here, too."

The gratitude was visible in Ellis's eyes.

Lincoln wasn't done, evidently. "I assume you'll be sharing custody, and...you'll be raising your kid on the water?"

Oh, shut up, you inquisitive bastard.

I'd done the math. After a year of dating, it was perfectly normal for a couple to move in together—if they had the same goal. The remaining time of the pregnancy plus the first few months where the baby understandably wouldn't leave Marilyn's side much would add up to at least eight or nine months.

"I think I'll find a place before that becomes an issue." Ellis was good. He took a sip of his coffee and kept his expression composed. In a situation like that, I'd fidget and laugh nervously.

Lincoln was satisfied with the response. "In that case, don't we have shit to celebrate? There's your divorce, your baby, Kid's park project, and my boy signing with Vancouver."

I whipped my head in his direction at the head of the table. "He did?" Madigan and I spoke at the same time.

This was fucking awesome. Abel could come home more often if he played for a team just two hours away. It sure as fuck beat having him on the East Coast.

"He didn't want to tell us until his agent knew for sure." Ade was practically vibrating in her seat. I knew it'd been rough for her to have Abel and Jesse far away. Now it was one down and one to go.

"Fucking A." I grinned.

I donned my Mr. Mom hat after brunch. Lincoln wanted to show Madigan something in the studio, Ellis excused himself to go to the bathroom, and that left Adeline and me to discuss some back-to-school crap for Haley and Lyn.

"Haley asked—since she'd finished her first year now—if she was finally going to be in Lyn's class." I shook my head. It hadn't been a fun conversation. "When I explained to her it doesn't work that way and that Lyn's also finished another year, Haley got so fucking angry."

"Aw, sweet girl." Adeline laughed and pouted at the same time. "I'm seriously dreading next year."

I nodded, sharing the sentiment. This would be their second and last year in the same building. If having them in different classes was a struggle, it was nothing in comparison to how it would be when they were at different schools.

"Did you see they raised the tuition again?" she asked.

"They do that every year." I opened the app on my phone where I kept all notes about Haley. "You're in charge, Mrs. Hayes. Where do we go first?"

She flipped open her day planner. "I was thinking Staples. After work on Tuesday?"

This part was easy for me. Adeline didn't throw money around the way her husband sometimes did, and since the girls wanted the same things most of the time, I took the back seat while Ade handled most of the shopping. Then when it was time to pay for everything, I could relax knowing she hadn't thrown too much crap into the cart.

Between her and me, we covered the planning in twenty minutes, and we'd do the same thing we did last year. Even though the girls arrived separately at school, we'd split the lunches on a weekly basis. One week, I'd do the lunches and drop them off with Haley. Then Adeline would do them the next week. That way, we could eliminate the "But she got the better yogurt!" fights that ensued often enough.

I scratched my eyebrow, jotting down a note on adding some boundaries on that subject. A two-year difference between Haley and Lyn didn't seem like much now, though that would change soon. And it was often Haley who ended up cranky because she didn't get the same thing Lyn did.

"Is Ellis still in the bathroom?" Ade checked her watch as I looked up from my phone. "I hope he's okay. He's got so much going on."

"I'll go check." I was out of my seat before I knew it, and then I left the kitchen. As I headed toward the hallway where the guest bath was, I passed the stairs and happened to glance up. "Ellis?" He wasn't hard to find. I took the steps two at a time until I reached the first landing on the way to the second floor. He was studying photos on the wall.

"I take it it's normal to be nervous?"

I assumed he was talking about becoming a dad.

"Very." I gave his pinkie a gentle squeeze. The photo he was looking at was of Lincoln and Lyn Eskimoing and making funny faces. It was a great shot. "It won't go away, either."

"That's reassuring." His mouth twisted up, and he side-eyed me ruefully. "I'm terrified I'm going to screw up."

I nodded. "That's what will make you a great dad."

Releasing a breath, he went back to the photos, this time one of Jesse, Abel, and Lyn together on a couch. It was from last Christmas.

"I ran into Haley on the stairs earlier. She invited me to a

Play-Doh dinner next week. Then we chatted a bit about the economy."

I laughed. "Oh, really?"

"Indeed. She mentioned wanting to break her piggy bank to buy a doll, but apparently, Daddy thinks the doll is too expensive."

"Daddy's a mean bastard." I shook my head. "That poor little girl will just have to play with some of her fourteen other dolls."

Ellis turned to me, pensive. "You're a wonderful dad. If I can be half as good as you..."

That packed a punch—of heat and self-consciousness. "You'll be great, Ellis. And you won't be alone."

He linked our fingers together and leaned in for a soft, way too chaste kiss. "I accepted the dinner invitation, so you know. I want to get to know her better, too."

Fuck, that little kiss wasn't enough. "Come on. Mom and Dad won't notice." I took the lead and ushered him up the second set of stairs.

He laughed huskily. "Dirty boy."

Passing Lyn's room, Abel's room, Jesse's room... There was a bathroom between his room and my old one, and I opened the door—a door that could be locked.

As soon as it was, I was pressed up against the wall, and we were all over each other. Simultaneously, my brain was in the mood to kick-start a new *possible future*. Only, this time it didn't feel as outlandish.

If we kept the peace between Marilyn and us, maybe the home I would share with Ellis one day—hopefully—wouldn't feel very divided. Maybe Haley would become a big sister. Maybe she would find another parent in Ellis. *Maybe, maybe, maybe.* Maybe his son or daughter would like me, too.

"Fuck," I breathed out. Ellis pressed openmouthed kisses to

my neck and rubbed my cock, causing my eyes to roll. "Let me suck you off." I fumbled with his zipper.

"Is—hell—is this really wise? Oh God." He groaned as I sank to my knees and fisted his cock. "How the fuck do you make me *need* you so damn much?"

No clue, but he had the same effect on me. I couldn't describe it.

Two seconds later, his thick cock filled my throat.

Time flies when you have good sex.

The following week had two headliners, in two highly different ways. Ellis and Haley. Thanks to my girl, everything during the day was about school or getting ready for it. Then I had my nights, where Ellis and I either managed to get sneaky and we got to christen my bed—and the entire house—or we talked on the phone when he stayed on the boat.

I dedicated a whole blog post to First Day of School for Cheeky Preschoolers, in which I listed my dos and don'ts that I'd learned the hard way the previous year. It included not making your kid's lunch the same day because emotions were running high. I also couldn't stress the sleeping schedule enough. Summer break needed to end before it actually did; otherwise, you would end up with one cranky spectacle on D-Day who was used to sleeping in and being all chill.

One not-so-anonymous reader left a message that gave me a chuckle.

I'm taking notes. :.

He didn't leave a message on my blog post about the importance of testing for STDs, funnily enough. Poor man was uncomfortable and hilariously formal when we went to a clinic together. In a hushed voice as we met up outside, he said, "My employees think I'm off on an important business lunch."

I laughed so hard.

On Thursday, Ellis and Marilyn went in for their first ultrasound together and found out they were having a boy. They also took another paternity test, and since it would be the weekend soon, the results wouldn't arrive 'til Monday.

Ellis was a bit difficult that weekend. Mainly because he was officially excited about becoming a dad, and on the off chance he wasn't the father... Shit, it would break him. I could admit it made me anxious too, though I kept that to myself. Instead, I distracted him with parenting memes and links to baby socks. It was just one of those things I'd bought too many of when Haley was a baby. Socks for infants were fucking adorable. They were so tiny.

"I used to put them on my fingers and make them dance," I admitted.

Ellis found that amusing.

"Uncle Ellis!" Haley hollered from upstairs. "Come to dinner now!"

"We ask politely!" I reminded her. Next, I shot Ellis a scornful look. "Have fun without me."

"You're only jealous I have a Play-Doh date and you don't." He leaned in for a quick kiss, then ducked out of the kitchen before I could throw the oven mitt at him. "I'm on my way, Miss Haley."

It was shaping up to be a great Saturday, despite Monday's results looming over us. And since I wasn't invited to the dinner in Haley's room—I was only a little peeved about that—I sat down in the living room with a couple blueprints from work.

We were ordering pizza for the actual dinner, and I'd given Haley one hour for her playdate, 'cause I was already starving.

But for now, I could immerse myself in my plans for the park in Camas.

The north side of the park bothered me because it was one industrial spill away from being a fucking brownfield. Cedar Valley, the district in the south, had once been the home of mostly factories, and Camas—being the working-class neighborhood of our town—had been the dumping site. It was the ripple effect in action. One park-sized dumpster had lowered the property value, and everything went to shit from there. The district was a big expense and a thorn in the city council's side. That much was clear from seeing the park budget.

Chewing on the end of my pen, I dug out my digital sketchpad from my messenger bag on the floor. Then I retrieved my phone, because if there was one person who knew Camas, it was Adrian. He lived and worked there.

He answered on the third ring. "Hey, Casey."

"Hi, do you have time?" My sketchpad lit up, and I zoomed in on the north side of the park. Then, looking around me, I searched for my notes while I scratched my forehead. Where did I put the... *There.* The results of the soil tests.

"Yeah, sure. What's up?" A buzzer went off in the background, and I could bet Adrian was cooking dinner. He wasn't the takeout type of guy.

"You've told me you have a strong community, right?" I asked.

"Very much so." It was something he took pride in, not to mention played an active role in. "Are you working on the park?"

I nodded even though he couldn't see me. He'd been stoked to find out I was the one chosen to design it because he knew how passionate I was about sustainable design. "Yeah, and here's the thing. What are my chances on involving the community for maintenance? Because the old dumping site isn't good enough to use for urban agriculture yet, but it is the perfect location for the compost. Which..." I swiped sideways on my pad for the site where I wanted an orchard. "Which would be about a five-minute walk from the garden."

The north plot would thrive with natural fertilizers. Bioremediation was the best sustainable option, where we helped nature take its course with certain fungi and plants, and so...if I could present a solution where the community helped out with park service, the cheap bastards on the council might just expand my budget. Because in the end, it would increase the value of the district as a whole. Plus bring in more money and lower costs of energy.

"Goddamn, you're really going all in," Adrian chuckled after my rant. "This is incredible, Casey. I can talk to the guys down at the Quad." That was the community center he volunteered at. "The kids are always looking for something to do..." He went on, talking about work practice for the teenagers; meanwhile, I spotted Ellis and Haley coming down the stairs.

Had it already been an hour?

Covering my phone, I addressed Ellis in a hushed voice. "Sorry, I didn't know it'd been so long—"

He shook his head and smiled. "I'll order pizza. You take your time. What do you say, Haley? Should we order pizza?"

"Yeah, the Play-Doh isn't yummy," she said frankly.

I grinned and watched them disappear into the kitchen.

This is all I want.

A family working together. A family life with Ellis. It had to be him.

I sighed contentedly and refocused on Adrian, who, at some point, had changed the topic. He wondered why I hadn't called Toby again, and it took me a minute to even remember the guy. Then I cringed, feeling bad. It wasn't Toby's fault. Crappy timing. And then I kind of went and fell in love with someone else.

I didn't tell Adrian that last part.

"Tonight was lovely," Ellis murmured.

"Tonight was perfect." I threw a handful of popcorn into my mouth and stretched out my legs on the couch, crossing them at the ankles on the armrest. Ellis was my pillow, his fingers were doing magical things to my hair, and Vin Diesel was eye candy on the flat screen. "Can we keep you?" I glanced up at Ellis.

The corners of his eyes crinkled, and he lowered his head to kiss me. "Be careful what you ask for. It's already difficult to pace myself."

"Do you really think so?" I had to make sure.

"I do." He stroked my cheek. Vin Diesel didn't stand a chance. "All day at work yesterday...I kept thinking it was the first time in years I looked forward to going home—even if it's yours."

Was it okay to be blunt about it? It was implied already— our goal—but we hadn't said it outright.

"It will be ours, though, right? One day." I forced back the nervousness.

He nodded and kissed me again, lingering. "I want nothing more, sunshine."

"Christ, you—" I snickered into the kiss and bit his bottom lip as revenge for that stupid nickname. At least I was funny when I called him princess. "You know, you could practice. Calling this your home, I mean. Nothing wrong with practice."

"Hmm, you make an excellent point." Unfortunately, he stopped kissing me and then peered toward the stairs. "What're the odds of Haley waking up?"

"The odds are in favor of couch sex."

"Perfect."

While the lust and hunger spiked immediately, everything around me slowed down. We only broke the kiss to get rid of our clothes, and as I crawled over him and watched his unbelievably sexy body, another need made itself known. Possessiveness built up inside me.

"Turn around. I wanna touch you," I said quietly.

He searched my eyes, maybe noticing I was stealing the control. It couldn't be helped. I wouldn't rush him on the matter of bottoming, but I *would* be in charge on occasion. And he clearly didn't mind. With an easy sigh, he turned onto his stomach once I gave him room.

Fetching everything I needed took me about twenty seconds.

"Fuck, you're perfect." I pressed one knee between his thighs, my other foot firmly planted on the floor, and grabbed the bottle of lotion. "It's been too long since I got up close and personal with your back and thighs." And ass, definitely ass.

"Use the oil instead," he murmured.

I wasn't sure... Whatever I massaged him with was eventually gonna rub off on me with the way we touched one another. "If I get oil up my ass and you fuck me, it could break the condom."

He raised himself up enough so his elbows hit the cushions, and he glanced back at me quickly. "We're clean."

God, I'd forgotten. We wouldn't have to use rubbers anymore. "Are you sure?" I was sure he could tell by the sound of my voice what I wanted.

"Screw the condoms, Casey."

I'd rather screw you, my lovely man.

I went for the oil instead, increasingly excited. Nothing beat skin on skin, no barriers between, something I'd experienced way too little of in my life. A high school girlfriend, Haley's mother, and an ex-boyfriend.

This was a dream come true, and I took my time. Leaning over Ellis, I rubbed the oil into his skin in long, firm strokes. In return, I was rewarded with muffled groans and low growls of pleasure. He had some soreness in his lower back, so I went for the deep tissue and slowed down my movements.

The TV was on mute and provided the only light in the living room, each flicker from the screen showing Ellis's glistening skin. Needing more space, I removed a couple cushions so he could spread his legs a bit and I could get my second knee between his thighs, too.

My thumbs dug in on either side of his spine, drawing up and down, up and down, in unhurried strokes. Each downward pass inched closer to his ass, until I cupped both cheeks firmly and pushed them apart.

He hissed and ground his cock against the couch.

I didn't even ask. One second I was massaging him, and the next I was lowering my face to lick him. In my defense, I had to take the opportunity. I hadn't messed him up with oil here yet, and I'd rather use spit.

Ellis cursed as my tongue circled his constricted opening, and I tried not to grin. When I caught him off guard and introduced him to something new, he would curse, inhale sharply, and then do a full-body shudder. It was sexy as hell.

"Oh hell, Casey," he groaned into the pillow. "Goddamn— oh, that's so...so fucking..."

Amazing, I knew. With two fistfuls of his ass, I got greedy and fucked him with my tongue. I got comfortable against the cushions too, because I had a lot of payback to give. For every time he'd teased me...

I hummed, noticing the second he relaxed for me. He exhaled a long moan and rolled his hips slightly to meet me, and I failed to be evil. The whole idea of payback failed. Instead, I twisted my tongue to give him more pleasure. I licked, fucked, rubbed, and sucked until we were both struggling to control ourselves. His breathing turned heavy, his rocking constant, and my cock needed some goddamn friction.

"Give me more," he demanded in a shallow grunt.

In a minute. He'd get to fuck me soon. First, I wanted to get off right between his cheeks. So I dropped a last kiss to his ass, then reached for the oil again.

He mistook my intentions. "Finally," he sighed.

I quirked a brow, even though he wasn't facing me, and coated my cock with oil. Did he think I was gonna finger-fuck him? I wasn't. This was about me.

I worked my cock in between his cheeks and pressed them together, groaning at the feel. He was warm and wet and impossibly beautiful. Wedged in as tightly as I could be, I fucked the crease in measured movements and lowered myself so my chest touched his back.

"Are you purposely trying to make me suffer, Casey?"

"No," I breathed out, speeding up. "I'm trying to get *off*." I moaned as the head of my cock pressed against his tight hole, and I buried my face in his neck. "I wanna fuck you so goddamn much, Ellis." I was too turned on to feel guilty about my admission. "Please don't feel pressured. I just had to say it."

"I don't know what the hell you're waiting for." There was a generous dose of sexual frustration in his voice, enough to pierce through my lust-filled fog and for me to go, what? Did this mean he wanted...?

"I've been waiting for you to say you're ready, of course!" I eased off of him and sat back on my heels. "*Are* you?"

"Christ, yes." He rolled over, displaying his large, thick cock pointing toward his face. My mouth pooled with saliva at the sight. "How could you not know? I've had four fingers up there—"

"Three, actually," I said absently. Fuck, his cock was a work of art.

He sighed. "Casey. I should have been clearer. I admit that. I suppose asking to get fucked for the first time isn't very easy, but—Casey?"

My gaze snapped up, and I looked him in the eye. Narrowing my own eyes, I replayed what he'd said and then shivered. So he was ready. Excitement and affection washed over me, and I crawled over him again, preferring him on his back. Now, I could kiss him easier, and I didn't stop until my lungs were burning and he was relaxed once more.

"Four," he whispered against my lips. Four? Oh... "The nights on the boat got lonely. I had an affair with my hand."

I chuckled through a groan and loved his silliness. "I'll see if I can forgive you...for not letting me be there to watch." Stealing another kiss, I blindly sought the oil to slick him up extra.

Desire and amusement sparked up in his eyes, and before he could return with a witty comeback, I pushed two fingers inside him. It set his gaze on fire, and he clenched his jaw.

"What was that?" I spoke in a hushed voice and kissed him lightly. "I couldn't quite hear you."

"Ah—fuck." He didn't even try. He sank into me and shifted around my fingers, focused on the pleasure. The funny times were over, and I fucked him gently, adding a third digit. "So good..."

Ellis decided when he was ready for more, and I instructed him to keep his cock hard for me. I kissed him passionately and positioned the head of my cock as he stroked himself tightly but slowly. Then it was a slow, torturous test on my self-control that followed. Forehead to forehead, I breached the first ring of muscle, and I grabbed his jaw and kissed him hard before I lost it. *Fuck, fuck, fuck.* He felt too good.

It didn't help that he spurred me on. By palming my ass, he

forced me deeper, and I buried myself all in with a strained moan. The discomfort in his features was evident, and he didn't seem to care. For that moment, he was in charge again, not satisfied until I was fucking him properly.

"You're killing me," I growled—or possibly complained in a much less primal voice. "Are you sure you're not in—"

"Don't fucking stop." He took my mouth with his. "I've thought about this for too long. Don't stop."

I thought back on how much he'd loved fingers the first time —hell, anything with at least one ass involved. The man had found his playground, and I had won the motherfucking lottery.

The tension built up. Knowing he was taking as much pleasure from this as I was when I bottomed opened up all kinds of doors for future fun. I pictured long nights of driving each other wild, weekends of hard, sweaty flip-fucks, and a lifetime of being myself and playing across the entire spectrum.

"So hot," I panted, peering down between us. "Are you seeing this, love?"

"Yeah." He swallowed and stroked his cock a little faster, clear fluids seeping out of the slit. I licked my lips, fucking thirsting for him. "God, you feel amazing, Casey..." He let out a groan as I pushed in, and then he was back to kissing me—a bruising grip on my jaw that only ignited me further. "You're mine, aren't you?"

I nodded once, and a traitorous whimper slipped out. "I'm close."

He hissed, and for the last leg of the race, we grabbed at each other to leave marks. The frenzy caged us in, the air around us thick with sex. Between the moans of pleasure, the groans of exertion and aching muscles made us chase faster. And then we were gone, me slightly before him because I couldn't fucking hold back. He clenched down hard around my cock and elicited a gasp from me.

My chest rubbed against his, the wet sounds of come and oil driving me crazy. I rocked into him a few more times, and I was beyond spent, yet the feeling of pushing my cock through my release inside of him was its own high I couldn't get enough of.

Messy sex was the best sex, and I collapsed on top of him when I couldn't hold myself up any longer.

"We're gonna need to keep towels down here." I swallowed dryly, my heart going a mile a minute. "Maybe a box with stuff. Lube, a couple toys..."

His cock gave a small twitch from where it was trapped between us, though it could have been from his orgasm. Either way, it made me snicker tiredly.

"Why stop there?" he chuckled lazily, out of breath, and drew his hands softly up and down my arms. Goose-flesh warning. "While we're at it, why not a video camera and a sex swing?"

I grinned and pinched his side. "Looks like you've gotten a load of funny in you."

He rumbled a laugh.

"Why are you *smiling?*" Ellis asked irritably, lowering the heat on the stove. "You think it's funny we're arguing?"

I smiled wider and took a sip of my coffee. He was genuinely ticked off with me, and it was okay. I had logic on my side. He didn't.

"You gotta admit, we're cute when we fight," I told him. Pajama bottoms and graphic tees made everyone cuter. "Plus, this is a milestone in our relationship."

He wasn't amused one bit. "This is serious, Casey. Silly milestone or not, I loathe fighting—particularly with you."

That was sweet, although it wasn't fucking silly.

"I don't disagree. It *is* a serious matter." Setting the mug down on the kitchen island, I smoothed down my bed head as I heard Haley coming down the stairs. "Little ears approaching. Also, I'm right and you're wrong."

He threw me a frustrated look, then continued flipping pancakes.

Haley scowled sleepily and rubbed her eyes as she stopped in the doorway. "Hi."

"Good morning, sweetheart." Ellis had a smile for her.

"Morning, baby." I patted the stool next to mine. "Did you sleep well?"

She nodded, and I helped her up, which wasn't enough. She merely used the stool as a footrest and sat her butt down on the countertop. "Did you and Uncle Ellis have another sleepover?"

"We did." Best part of being family, spending a lot of time together was normal. "We ate all your leftover candy and broke in to your piggy bank." I waited for the shriek.

First, she dropped her jaw. And *then*... "*Daddy!*" The sound was shrill as fuck.

"I'm kidding. Come on, would I do that to you?" I leaned in and peppered her with kisses.

"Not funny!" she huffed and pushed me away.

"You truly are a menace this morning, Casey," Ellis muttered.

"Yeah," Haley laughed.

I raised a brow at her. "Do you know what menace means?"

She shrugged and shook her head.

Then she couldn't know I was one. End of.

"We're not going to Lincoln and Adeline's for brunch," I told her. "You know what we're gonna do instead?" I leaned in, as if to say something exciting. To her, it wasn't. "We're gonna buy a hot tub for the backyard." 'Cause Daddy got a huge discount.

"Um, okay..." She wrinkled her nose.

Bored with the adults, she declared she was going to watch

cartoons until breakfast was ready. Her little feet ran away, and Ellis and I faced each other at the same time, both ready to speak. So I nodded for him to start, and for some reason, that earned me a strange look.

"What? I thought you were going to say something." Maybe I got it wrong.

He frowned. "I was. I am. I just wasn't prepared to be allowed to go first."

What the crap was he talking about? "I don't understand. Allowed?"

"Well, yes." His shoulders stiffened. "See, this is the whole thing with Marilyn. I won't bad-mouth her and say my word never matters, but the floor is hers first, and if she's certain about something, she won't listen. This is why I detest arguing. I only end up shutting down to make it stop."

I had a feeling his marriage wasn't unique in that regard...

"Ellis." I left my seat, brow furrowed, and wondered how I could put this. I didn't have any eleven-year-old relationships behind me. In other words, he would know this better than me. "I get it, and I can only draw on the experience of watching my folks. They fought wrong and turned to passive aggressiveness, then gave up. It wasn't worth it. And, I guess what I'm saying is, a fight is worth it to me if we're on equal ground and no one is trying to put the other down." I paused and rubbed my neck. Was I getting this right? "Look, I'll always be honest. If something's wrong, I'll bring it up. I can't guarantee I'll always fight fair or be rational, 'cause emotions can twist shit up, but the enemy is never you. I mean, problems are meant to be solved, yeah? And sometimes we can't get there without fighting, but then at least the solution is the goal. Does that make sense? It's not like picking a fight because you have a problem with a person."

Ellis cleared his throat and turned off the stove, and he

appeared to have a shitload on his mind. "I think I understand. Of course, I wouldn't expect anyone to stay rational at all times. I'm hardly a saint." Leaning back against the counter, he sighed and folded his arms over his chest. "I apologize for thinking a fight with you would be the same as it is with Marilyn."

I lifted a shoulder. "You were with her for a long time. It'd be weird if you didn't have some patterns to break."

"God," he muttered, scrubbing his hands over his face. "You have no idea how refreshing open communication is."

I snorted softly and stepped closer, one of my hands landing on his hip. "I'm sure we'll get stuck in plenty of ruts."

"I have no doubt." He smiled faintly and touched my cheek. "New relationships are easier too, but I have my priorities in order this time. For you, I'd fight."

I stole a smooch, then a pancake. "This includes sometimes fighting *with* me." I chuckled and dodged him when he tried to poke me in the ribs. "None of that. Back to the issue with Marilyn. I think you misunderstood me earlier." Chewing half the pancake, I phrased myself better so he'd get it. "I understand. You're not her biggest fan—"

It was his turn to snort.

"I understand, Ellis," I repeated. "And I'm not asking you to spend more time with your ex-wife-to-be. I'm asking you to be on better terms with the woman who's carrying your son. There's a huge difference." Knowing Haley would soon announce she was starving like a kid in Africa, I opened the fridge to pull out the rest of the food. "This applies to Marilyn, too. Whatever grudges you guys have, you gotta bury them ASAP. She can't treat you like an ex, either. Draw boundaries if you need—just...dammit, you gotta get along with your baby's mother."

It was important on so many levels, most of all for the child.

"This is personal to you." He said it like it was a revelation.

"Maybe." I concentrated on the bowl of strawberries, seeing if there were any bad ones. It was a job that couldn't be half-assed and required my full attention.

"Casey? Tell me, please."

Knew this honesty bullshit was gonna come back and bite me in the balls. I'd say ass, but that was actually enjoyable. Something I'd discovered on the yacht.

"You don't want to be in my position, that's all." I planted my hands on the kitchen island and mustered a firm expression. "In your case, it would be good for everyone involved if there was no bad blood. Even for me, if you want me to be a part of your son's life—"

"Of course I do." He tilted his head, concerned.

I nodded once and swallowed. "Good. Me too. And it will be easier for me to try to smooth things over with Marilyn if you do it, too."

"Ah." He took a seat by me and covered my hand with his. "You're right—I know. You're right. I'm only seeing this from the bitter ex-husband's point of view."

"Are you bitter?" I hadn't gotten that impression.

"Perhaps not," he conceded. "However, I have no desire to be friends with her. But again, you make a good point. I have to leave the past behind me in order to start fresh with her in another way—as the baby's mother." He coughed lightly. "It's possible I'll need your help with that."

I could do that. He knew it, too.

"You know I'll be here," I told him. "Talk shit over with her, though. You don't wanna get off on the wrong foot and make it worse because you have different approaches."

He pressed his lips together and inclined his head. "Consider me schooled. Now, you weren't done telling me how this is personal for you. I suspect Haley's mother is the reason, as well as your parents."

"Incubator," I corrected him. Kendra was no mother of Haley's. Over my dead fucking body. She gave up that right when she split, and her suddenly changing her mind and trying to come back didn't mean anything. "But, yeah. Not being on good terms with the person you created another life with can get ugly."

Someday, the one who had to suffer from that was Haley.

Speaking of... "Daddy, I'm super hungry!"

I blew out a breath, and Ellis squeezed my hand.

"We'll take care of it together, okay?" He waited until I surrendered with a nod. "It's our mess, right?"

"Our mess," I huffed a tired chuckle. "Yeah."

17

In October, I felt like I was on the top of the world. Ellis and Marilyn made a breakthrough and agreed to be civil; if I remembered correctly, the words *tentative friends* were used. And it seemed to work as long as they focused on the baby—or anything that wasn't their failed marriage.

Another triumph came the day before yesterday when I got an extra $70,000 for my green park project. The numbers spoke for themselves during my presentation, and it was money they'd be getting back, and then some.

Ellis and I sucked at taking things slowly, and he spent most nights at the place we both called home. Although we went on dates like any other new couple, I was pretty sure we enjoyed the lazy mornings in bed and late-night coffee dates on the porch more than going to a restaurant.

It messed with our heads to find this transition so easy, something we chalked up to us having known each other for years. While a crapload of things had changed, we were the same people in the sense that we could predict certain things. If he told me he was into something, I had six years' worth of knowing him to determine if it was out of character or *very him*.

Pulling in at the parking lot outside the school where I was picking up the girls, I pretended to be a drummer and used the wheel to tap out some of my jitters.

I didn't know why I had jitters. Ellis and I had agreed to tell Ade and Lincoln we were dating this Sunday, and I didn't think that was gonna be a problem.

As I checked the time on my phone, I thought I could text Ellis, but a message from Marilyn popped up right then and there.

Hello, Casey. I have some pressing matters I'd like to discuss with you in regards to Ellis and my son. Rather, your involvement. Do you mind if I come over after work?

I rubbed my forehead, the unease spreading through me like wildfire. This is it. Things were going too fucking smoothly, and now...now, *fuck.*

Swallowing the rising anxiety, I fired off a quick reply.

Yeah, sure. I'll be at home.

And Ellis wouldn't be. He was in and out of meetings all day and would be home late. I should call him, though. Unless he already knew she was coming? No, he would've given me a heads-up.

Drumming out the jitters was an impossible feat now, so I turned to Beyoncé. When life gave you lemons, she knew a thing or two about lemonade.

I was going to need vodka with mine.

"Fuck. Fuck, fuck, fuck." I tossed the phone on the seat next to me and rested my forearms on the wheel. Was my face draining of color? It felt clammy all of a sudden, and my stomach twisted painfully.

What *about* my involvement? My involvement so far

included sending links to reading material to Ellis, and whenever he had questions, I did my best to answer them. Was that so goddamn horrible? She couldn't stop me from being around, could she? Shit.

I forced myself to function. The clock hit three, and I left the truck.

Ellis would never agree to it. I was pretty sure.

He wanted me to play an active role in his son's life.

I wanted me to play an active role in his son's life. Didn't people realize I got attached? Sharing pictures of baby furniture for a nursery while we were at work wasn't for shits and giggles. Granted, I was the one who initiated most of that talk. Ellis appeared cautious, once admitting he worried he was imposing on my life, or the house I'd recently bought. I didn't function that way—evidently. Thanks to that motherfucker, I was now all in.

I clenched my jaw and accidentally glared at a fellow parent who was here to pick up their kid. Yeah, I seriously wasn't fit for public consumption anymore—not after that text. I was gonna worry myself halfway into a panic attack until I'd seen Marilyn.

Within seconds, I was surrounded by preschoolers and their teachers signing off kids to their folks.

Haley darted out with a carefree smile and gave me a quick hug. "I thought Auntie Ade was picking us up. It's 'sghetti night!"

"She got held up at work, but I'm taking you there." I nodded to her teacher and grasped Haley's hand. "Let's go get Lyn."

Lyn was waiting for us across the playground when we got there.

"Hi, Uncle Casey."

"Hey, hon. We ready to go?" I grabbed her backpack for her.

The girls chatted among themselves, making my job easy. At this point, I wasn't sure I could fake interest in whatever they said. Bags thrown in the back, seat belts attached, the right music playing, we were off.

I drove farther up the hillside to where Ade ran her organization. At the end of the road in the northern part of the district, the gated property couldn't be more remote before it was all woods and cliffs that shot straight up from the ocean. I idled outside the gate and dug out my ID, and I showed it to Hernando, despite the fact that he knew me by now.

He let us through, and the gates opened.

"You remember how to act in here, ladies?" I eyed Lyn and Haley in the rearview. *Ladies* was the keyword.

"Yeah, no yelling or running," Haley answered. "No scary stuff."

"We'll behave," Lyn promised.

"Good." Because some of the women and children—and a few men—who stayed here could get triggered by anything from the lightest touch to the faintest sound. Ade and her staff worked hard to keep this a safe environment to recover from whatever abuse the residents had escaped.

After parking next to Adeline's car, I ushered the girls inside where I nodded politely at the receptionist.

"Is Ade in her office?" I asked.

I learned she wasn't, but the lady was gonna call her for me, and we could wait in the office. So we crossed the little lobby, passed the corridor where the first floor's rooms and studio apartments were, then got to the hallway with three offices, the last one being Ade's.

Haley and Lyn weren't strangers to this place, and they bounced over to the couch they called theirs. Other than a corner decorated for children, the office was fairly empty, not counting Ade's desk. Or the walls filling up with drawings and pictures.

Restless and antsy, I stood in the middle of the floor and checked my watch every fifteen seconds.

"Hi, Mommy." Lyn waved, and I looked over my shoulder.

"Hi, guys." Ade walked in with a smile, though she faltered when she saw me. "Are you okay, sweetie?"

I was that transparent, huh?

I nodded once and rubbed a hand over my jaw. I was so tense I barely noticed. "Yeah, sorry. Long day at work."

"Oh, I'm sorry to hear that. Why don't you come over for spaghetti night, too?" She closed the door behind her and walked over to give the girls kisses.

"I have some design proposals to go over," I lied. "Is Haley staying the night or do I pick her up later?"

"She's more than welcome to stay. You get some rest." Ade headed to her desk next and opened a drawer. "How's Ellis doing? Haley told me he's over at the house often. I think that's great, by the way. It's about time he spends more time with family."

I scratched the side of my head and glanced over at an oblivious Haley. She and Lyn were whispering and giggling.

"Isn't she a little young to be a gossip?" I asked.

Adeline snorted a chuckle and lifted a brow. "You think she wouldn't tell us that Uncle Ellis has lots of sleepovers with Daddy?"

What did that mean, exactly? Ade wasn't reacting the way I thought she would if she were to learn what those sleepovers entailed. There was no surprise or disbelief—or her trademark demand for details.

"When he finds his own place, I hope that doesn't change," she went on. "Either way, I'm glad he's with you rather than spending all his time on the boat."

Oh. *Oh.* Right, I was only the friend who lived five minutes away from the marina, and spending time with me helped him get over his divorce. Was I getting that right?

"Huh," I muttered. "Being family really is a good cover." It made me wonder what it would take for people to suspect it was more than friendship. A slap on the ass would be interpreted as a joke, I assumed. What if they saw us having dinner together?

"What?" Ade gave me a strange look.

I lifted a shoulder and pulled out my car key. "I guess I thought people would raise brows, that's all." Eh. I had to get home and come up with a strategy for handling Marilyn. I could chitchat with Adeline another day. "Anyway, I should get going."

As soon as I got home, I broke out the rum—that was my strategy—and sat down in the kitchen to text Ellis.

Having a crap day. Hope yours is better. Miss you. Oh, and Marilyn is on her way over.

I wanted some fresh air, and the backyard looked like shit. That left the porch on the front, and I brought my good friend, the rum. It started raining when I stepped out, kind of fitting to the mood I was in, and I sat down in the corner and kicked up my feet on the railing. My head hit the house wall, a heavy sigh escaping me.

No matter what, I was going to do everything in my power to convince Marilyn I could be a good side dish in their dynamic. I'd do whatever it took, basically, because I wanted this house to be the home of a family, not a handful of people who were divided by restrictions and custody agreements.

The sound of a car pulling in drew my attention, and I peered over the railing to see what neighbor was coming home—

oh, she was already here. I slapped a hand over my face to look alive.

She was out of her car and about to open the gate, her stride purposeful.

"Hi, Casey... I, um—" She jerked a thumb over her shoulder for some reason. "I was in the neighborhood. Is now a good time?"

Well, she did say after work. This was after work.

"Yeah, it's fine." I cleared my throat and sat up straighter. "How are you?"

The confidence in her step faltered. She closed the gate after her and approached almost cautiously. "Before I forget, I wanted to return this to you." She opened her bag, and it was the damn camera again. "Ellis forgot it... It's his—it should be here."

Was she moving him out of their house? Surely, he had a lot of crap there. Most of his clothes were on the boat by now, if not in the closet upstairs. Some work-related items had found their way into my house too, something I admittedly got a kick out of. Nevertheless, there was still other stuff. They'd shared a home for eleven years. There had to be more than a camera.

I accepted the camera, feeling awkward and on edge.

Marilyn fidgeted with the strap of her bag. "I...I haven't seen him that way before. That happy and...so peaceful."

I looked at the camera in my hand and turned it on. The photo was still there, the one where he kissed the spot above my sweats.

"Not that one." She cleared her throat. "The, uh—the other one. I think you took it."

Clicking to the previous one, I saw the goofy selfie I'd taken. This time, he was kissing my shoulder while I was smirking into the camera. The sun was shining down on us. He did look happy. Serene, almost. Even with his eyes closed, his expression was telling.

"He told me you were serious about each other a while back," she mentioned. "To be honest, I can't say it wasn't shocking to find out about you two. If there hadn't been a picture to go with the story, I wouldn't have believed him."

She wanted to chitchat before she laid into me? I drained my drink and made a vague gesture to the available seat next to me. In the corner of my eye, I caught the sight of when her thick cardigan parted, displaying a baby bump.

Oh God. It was real. The baby was really fucking in there. A few months to go, and then a little baby boy who hopefully looked like Ellis would be here.

I thought of last night, Ellis with his head on my lap, browsing through an online catalogue of bedding for babies. Haley had been there too, sitting snugly in the little space between him and the back of the couch. She'd gotten so used to his presence now, and she was excited about the baby. Although, upon learning it was a boy, her initial response had been, "Um, Daddy, what do I do with a *boy*?"

My chest tightened. Everything I wanted was suddenly in the hands of Marilyn.

"I have a question I'd like to ask you," she said. "It's not my place, so I understand if you wish to keep it to yourself." She waited for my response; I merely dipped my chin. "It's about Kendra." That threw me. "May I ask what pushed you to seek sole custody of Haley?"

Wasn't that obvious? "Well, Kendra left," I said slowly. "We agreed to do the right thing and raise Haley together, and a month after she was born, Kendra went back home."

I wasn't going to pretend everything had been perfect. Hell, I'd still been on parole; I was busy with school and getting my life back in order. Kendra became the breath of fresh air, and we were friends for a long-ass time before anything happened. Because it was always her plan to return to Pittsburgh. She was only here for school. Then one thing led to another one night, and we started dating.

It'd been an awesome month. Then she got knocked up because we'd been careless.

"But she came back," Marilyn pointed out.

I frowned. "Hasn't Ellis told you this?" It wasn't exactly news, nor was it a secret.

Marilyn shifted uncomfortably in her seat. "I fear I wasn't particularly interested when it happened."

A snort escaped me.

Having no clue where this was going, I offered her the CliffsNotes so we could get on with things. "All right, yeah, she came back after a few months because Lincoln hired lawyers for me. I was gonna take her to court. For no other reason than the papers arriving at her house—she lived with her parents—she flew back here." And it turned out she'd never told them squat. Her parents were, to this day, oblivious to the fact that they had a granddaughter. "She claimed she'd panicked because her folks are strict." Frankly, I didn't give a shit. Either she was a mother to Haley, or she wasn't. There was no in-between. "I think she stuck around a couple months, going back and forth before coming up with the *stupid* idea that she could be a temporary mom who *visited whenever she could*. That way, she wouldn't have to tell her parents anything."

By then, Lincoln and Ade were ready to send a pack of dogs after her.

The legal option was sharks in the shape of lawyers, and with Haley as my only focus, I didn't hold anything back. I told Kendra to choose.

"And she left permanently," Marilyn concluded.

"That was her choice," I replied and refilled my drink. "My goal was to get full custody. She could fight me for visitation rights, but that sort of thing would've eventually gotten back to her parents." I didn't have the right to forbid Kendra from ever seeing Haley, and there were plenty of distant parents who only had their kids on holidays and whatnot. The problem was her refusal to be honest with her parents.

That spoke volumes to me, and my daughter wasn't gonna be anybody's goddamn secret.

In the end, Kendra signed all the papers and headed home. I hadn't heard from her since, though I knew Lincoln kept tabs. As long as she wasn't on her way here, I didn't wanna know.

"I'll never understand it," I muttered into my glass. "Useless pieces of shit—dare call themselves parents, only to split." To the men and women who completely skirted their responsibilities, I had nothing good to say.

What sounded suspiciously like the ragged breath one took before falling into tears made me whip my head in Marilyn's direction. What the—She fucking *was* falling into tears, and I didn't know how this was happening, or what I was supposed to do, or why. Oh God, *why* was she sitting on my porch crying?

"I'm sorry." She whimpered and eyed my no doubt bewildered—slightly drunk—expression and wiped at her cheeks. "I'm so sorry. I didn't mean to—I'm sorry."

Get your shit together, man.

I shook my head in a daze, and I *tried* to get my shit together. A pregnant woman was crying on my porch; I had to make myself useful. "Will, um, I mean...what's wrong? Do you want me to call Ellis?"

"God, no." She definitely didn't want that, given how quickly she shook her head. "I'm sorry. I'm...so exhausted, and, and, and—" She let out a sob and covered her face with her hands, and I acted out of instinct and left my chair. "I'm horrible. I came here to see... I want you and Ellis," she hiccupped, "to have this whole family thing, because then I'd feel less guilty..."

She crumpled once more, and I got down on one knee in front of her, tentatively placing a hand on her knee.

"Less guilty?"

She sniveled and exhaled shakily. "Wh-what if I'm like Kendra?"

I furrowed my brow, immediately rejecting what she said. I could list dozens of things that made Marilyn and Kendra different.

"I highly doubt that," I responded mildly. My ass hit the floor, and I brought my drink with me, leaning back against the railing.

She sniffled some more and hiccupped again as she fruitlessly wiped away her tears. "Mind you, I would never abandon my son, but things aren't so black and white, either."

"What do you mean?"

"Ellis left me a message the other day and said we needed to sit down soon and discuss custody." She closed her eyes, and she took a couple deep breaths to calm down. "He presumes we're going with shared custody, and I'm wondering if-if there are other options." She drew a shaky breath, seemingly scared to look me in the eye. She was literally the opposite of how she'd come across in her text today about coming here. I didn't know what to make of it. "My mother suggested it, actually. She knows I'm struggling and how...how *liberating* this new sense of freedom has been for me. Without the guilt and the fighting with Ellis hanging over me— all of that gone—I've finally been able to focus on things that make me *happy*."

Wait, what...? I didn't want to be right here, if my suspicions were correct, and they couldn't be. She'd already mentioned never wanting to abandon her son.

That she treasured her newfound freedom wasn't weird. Ellis was doing the same, only in his own way. Their marriage wasn't one I was going to waste time playing the blame game with. As far as I knew, they'd both fucked up and were now more than ready to move on.

"What is it you want, Marilyn?" I had to ask.

I understood the baby's arrival was...inconvenient, for lack of a better word. Rather than divorcing and going separate ways, she and Ellis would be tied together in some way for as long as they lived. Lastly—and I prayed this wasn't wishful thinking—it was entirely possible she didn't know what she ultimately wanted. There was a time I didn't know a baby would be good for my life. Learning Kendra was pregnant had turned my life inside out, and it'd taken some time to adjust and grow into the person who couldn't fucking wait to see those ten little toes and ten little fingers.

Marilyn looked downright ashamed. "I would like to propose to Ellis that this..." She faltered, swallowing heavily and closing her eyes for a moment. "That this becomes our son's primary home."

I blew out a breath, stunned, and felt the need to look over my shoulder to make sure she was actually talking to me. Where was the hatred? Where was the speech on how she didn't want me in her kid's life?

She went on, her posture screaming of defeat. "I wanted to discuss it with you first because—because I won't bring it up with Ellis if you think there is the slightest chance this will end up with me losing my baby boy. I don't want there to be any misunderstandings. I love my son dearly already. I will always be here for him. It's the matter of a primary home I want him to have here, not his only home."

Okay...it was getting slightly clearer. "What you're saying is, you want him on weekends and stuff?" Was this happening? "How the hell would this make you even remotely similar to Kendra?"

"No, I mean," she stammered, "about the whole selfish thing.

This would be my way of having the cake and eating it, too. I have this vision." She sighed softly and leaned back, closing her cardigan as a wind swept through the porch. "I was thinking Ellis's home—" she flicked me an uncertain look "—*your* home... would be the place he calls home. And then there's me. 'Going to Mom's place.'" My mouth twitched at her use of air quotes. It was almost sweet. "I want to be there, Casey. Always a call away. I could picture myself coming over for dinner and holidays..." The discomfort made a swift return. "If I'm welcome, that is, of course. I would also want certain weekends, school nights here and there—a schedule that's more flexible. Like how you and Adeline and Lincoln do for your girls."

With each word she spoke, I relaxed more and more.

Marilyn wasn't like Kendra at all.

I wasn't entirely certain Marilyn was like Marilyn, either. The Marilyn I used to know, anyway. Thinking back on holidays and dinners, the words forced politeness came to mind. She was formal, rigid, and cold. Yet what I'd witnessed today... Fuck, I'd been introduced to a person who was more...human.

"I know it's selfish of me," she said and looked down. "I'm supposed to want everything, right? This last week...I've been up all night reading mommy blogs and magazines, and it's all so..." She released a heavy breath and looked up for a moment. "These amazing women identify so strongly with their motherhood. It's everything to them, and here I am, dreaming of taking a higher position at my father's company."

Yeah, so?

"Are you turning this into a gender issue?" My forehead creased, and I had to admit I was confused. I mean, in this day and age... "I'm not gonna deny biology, but there's more to a woman than having kids. Some will burn passionately for it, some won't. Just look at me." I widened my arms. "Dads are either these stereotypical providers or distant deadbeats, right?

Yet here I am, proudly getting my nails painted and braiding hair. Likewise, there are gonna be women who *don't* want that as much."

The lines in her forehead smoothed out slightly, her teary gaze softening. "I suppose I haven't thought of it that way before." As she looked away, a pensive expression on her face, she touched her belly gently. "I do believe I'm being selfish, though. I'm not certain I like this vision of mine because it seems like a healthy upbringing for a child, or because it's self-serving."

"That word," I said, shaking my head. "Fuck it, Marilyn. We're all allowed to be selfish at times. In fact, I'm selfish every damn opportunity I get. As long as Haley doesn't suffer, I will continue to take time for myself. In my opinion, there's nothing wrong with that."

"But I wouldn't be taking half the responsibility," she argued.

"And you wouldn't reap all the rewards," I answered. "You do realize your kid will view me as a parent at least as much as he does with you, yeah?"

Her delicate brows knitted together. "Is this an issue for you? I apologize, Ellis made it sound like that was what you want—"

"It is," I was quick to say. "Jesus, you have no idea. But before you came here today, I was under the impression your pressing matters was about telling me to take a hike." That seemed to genuinely surprise her, so I pointed something out for her. "Last time you visited me here, you called me a distraction and hoped I wouldn't be around Ellis too much."

Guilt clouded her features once more. "I owe you an apology for that. So far, this pregnancy has been a roller coaster from hell. I'm sorry. I've been so overwhelmed, and I have all these emotions that freak me out."

I cut her off gently because she could set herself off. She looked damn close to tears again.

"It's okay, Marilyn." In fact, I could barely describe the relief. She wasn't going to ask that I remove myself from their family dynamic. I was gonna be a part of it. "For the record, I don't think you should feel like you're selfish. Will you be here for your son whenever he needs you? Actually needs you, not when he whines. Kids whine a lot."

"Of course I will!" She was affronted I'd suggest otherwise.

I lifted a shoulder. "Then you're not much different from the parent who works a lot while the other stays at home." She'd brought up coming over for dinner and holidays, which I honestly thought was a brilliant idea. Their son would see us as a united front, and there would be less shuffling between different places. Whether we hosted birthday parties here or at her house didn't matter, as long as we got along well enough to spend them together.

Marilyn relaxed further, despite some lingering skepticism. "You and Ellis work full time and run your own businesses, as well."

I nodded. "And since I had Haley, this is sort of all I've dreamed about. I may love my career, but I'm a family man. I love coming home to a full house." The fact that I'd get the chance to share that with Ellis was nothing short of mind-blowing. For once in my life, everything was falling into place. It wasn't the time to be shy about what I wanted. It was the time to jump in headfirst and live the dream.

This could be one of those lucky breaks Marilyn should accept and not question. Because there were three of us, no one would be neglected, Ellis and I would get our madhouse, and Marilyn could be a career woman and still be a great mother. If she'd hired a nanny so she could work more, people wouldn't bat an eyelash. It was those fucking stereotypes again. They needed to die.

After a moment of silence, I glanced up at Marilyn, my

opinion on her beginning to change. "This is a new side of you." I kept it honest, as it was what I did best. "We've never talked like this before."

"Yes, well." And because of that, she went back to stiff and formal. It was comical, and I grinned at her. "Ellis has always spoken so fondly of you. I think you've been special to him for quite some time, platonically or not, and I suppose I'm understanding why now. I see why he looks up to you."

"Thank you, Marilyn." It meant more than I could say. "Does this mean you'll be coming over to Ade and Lincoln's more often?"

Welp, that was a firm no. She literally squeaked at the notion.

I chuckled.

I guessed Ellis hadn't been lying. "Ellis told me you find us loud and meddling."

"Why would he blab on me?" She sounded endearingly miffed. "I'm just...*private*."

I nodded, understanding that. "I'd like to get to know you better, though. You seem very accepting of everything—with Ellis and me, I mean. With my becoming a part of your son's life."

That earned me a playfully superior smirk. "Dear, when the lipstick comes off, the truth comes out. You weren't around for my meltdowns—in private, thank you very much—where I paced around my house chanting, 'oh God, he's gay now, oh God, he's gay now' for hours on end."

I exhaled a laugh, picturing it. "Could've been worse."

She shrugged slightly. "Thank goodness there's one issue I don't have."

Definitely seeing this woman in a new light. It lifted a weight off my shoulders I hadn't even known was there.

"You do have one issue," I was kind to point out. "You're

gonna have to tell Ellis all this—and once again, you let me in on the news before him."

She winced. "It would help if you put in a good word for me."

"I'll do my best." I winked.

18

"Casey."

I rolled over—or tried—and smashed my face against the back of the couch. "Balls..." Why wasn't I in bed?

A quiet chuckle coming from behind me stole my attention, and I blinked sleepily and looked over my shoulder. Ellis was home. Shit, at what time?

"What time is it?" I yawned and forced myself to sit up.

"Almost eleven." He slid in next to me, still dressed sharply while my sweats and tee had seen better days. "I came home as soon as I saw your text, but by then, you were already asleep on the couch."

I hummed and glanced around us. The living room was dark, and I remembered Haley was at Lincoln's. Then the memories from my talk with Marilyn rushed back, at which I whipped my head to find the nearest clock. It was *how* late? Holy crap, eleven. Ellis's words had barely registered.

I'd slept away the evening.

I scratched my head and squinted.

Ellis smiled. "You're too cute sometimes."

Another yawn escaped me, and I leaned against him as I let

the relief from earlier sink in. "Why didn't you wake me up sooner?"

"I was going to." He loosened his tie. "Then Marilyn called, so I drove over to her, and we talked. We—" He laughed softly. "We talked for a long time. It was almost pleasant."

"Almost," I snorted, half amused.

"Mm." He gathered me close and dropped a kiss to my temple. "It's been difficult for both of us, I think, which is ironic. It's easy to walk away from something you haven't put much effort into—at least for several years. Much harder to reconcile the fact that we have none other to blame than ourselves for all the time we wasted."

I tilted my face up to look him in the eye.

He searched my eyes, one hand coming up to stroke my cheek. "What Marilyn suggested today about our son's living arrangements is everything I want, but you have a choice to make. We haven't been together very long, and it's understandable if you believe I'm rushing into this for the wrong reasons."

Hadn't I already made that crap abundantly clear? I was done giving a fuck about how long we'd been together. A few months or a few years—I knew Ellis. I trusted him. I loved him. This was something I refused to complicate.

"I want you to quit holding back, Ellis. You know me. I wouldn't play house with you if I didn't want it to be real."

He exhaled and pressed his forehead to mine, his eyes closing.

"I'm serious." I covered his mouth with mine and kissed him slowly. "I should have known I was toast from the first night we spent together." I'd been a fool for thinking it could ever be a silly infatuation. The chemistry and sense of rightness had been there from the start.

"I think I did know," he murmured. "You woke me up."

"And you anchored me, okay?" Heat and need rose within,

and I scrambled up to straddle him. The kiss grew hungry as he whispered a curse and palmed my ass. "We're doing this. We'll learn together."

He nodded and angled my head to go deeper, and when he spoke again, there was no surprise. It just fit. "I love you, Casey."

The words didn't rock me. They stabilized me.

"I love you, too." I pushed his suit jacket down his shoulders and swept my tongue across his, reveling in the perfection of the moment. We fucking clicked. Maybe the notion of soul mates was completely bogus, but damn it if I didn't feel our connection on every goddamn level.

The following Sunday, brunch became lunch because Ellis and I had errands to run before we headed over to Adeline and Lincoln's. Basically, Ellis agreed to get past his hang-ups—or fears that he was imposing—if I picked something out for what was going to be a boy's room.

I'd never picked shit out for boys before, so I owned up to my cop-out. Rather than driving to the nearest toy store, we went shopping for paint. Haley was a solid excuse; she was with us, and she never would've wanted to leave the toy store. She didn't have the same attachment to checking paint samples.

"Have you narrowed it down any?" Ellis wondered.

I pursed my lips, eyeing the wall of swatches. "Green. Some lighter shade." It was easier to match with other colors than blue, in my opinion.

While he grabbed a handful of samples, my phone vibrated, and I checked it to see Marilyn's reply.

Wednesday is perfect. Around one?

I nodded to myself, keeping Haley in my periphery, and answered the text.

"Is Adeline telling us we're late?" Ellis asked. "She sent me a message earlier."

I grinned, pocketing my phone. "No, I'm having lunch with Marilyn on Wednesday." Haley picked that moment to reach for a paint roller, so I let out a sharp whistle. "Hey! Baby, be careful. It almost fell on top of you."

She let out a disgruntled noise and put it back. "It's boring here, Daddy."

Luckily for her, I wasn't gonna be long. There was one called mint green that was cute.

"You're having lunch with Marilyn?" Ellis was giving me an odd look.

"This one. Yeah." I handed over the sample. "Is that not okay?" It hadn't occurred to me he might have a problem with my getting to know her better.

"Of course it is." He killed my concern and held out a hand for Haley. "Let's go, sweetheart. We're done." She ran over and took his hand as if she'd done it a million times before. It made me happy. Then we walked toward the counter to order the paint, and Ellis leaned in slightly. "Am I focusing too much on the baby? It's all I can think of, it seems. Meanwhile, you're bridging gaps with Marilyn and—"

"I think it'd be pretty weird if you focused more on her than your son," I whispered back. When he met my gaze, I smirked. "Relax, princess."

He sighed whereas Haley giggled madly.

"He can't be a princess, Daddy. You're silly."

"Didn't you have us call you Prince Haley before Disney?" I retorted.

That gave her a thinker.

"Whose truck is that?" Ellis asked.

"No clue." I stepped out of the passenger's seat and helped Haley, noting that Madigan's car was here. Maybe the other guest was a friend of Ade's or coworker of Lincoln's. "You ready for lunch, baby?"

Haley nodded and held up her arms.

It wasn't often she wanted me to carry her anymore, so I was all for it. I picked her up with a smile and shut the door.

She played with my hair. "Can you tell Lyn that the new baby will be a little more mine?"

I furrowed my brow at her. "He'll be what, now?"

She rolled her eyes, making me narrow mine. The girl was picking up some attitude from Lyn; only, Lyn did it playfully, and she was older.

"Because he will live in my house, Daddy," she explained exasperatedly. "I will see him more. Lyn has two brothers! I want one."

"Oh." I didn't know what to say, although it made sense...

Thankfully, Ellis had this one covered. He passed us and kissed her cheek. "He'll be your baby brother."

She beamed at him. "I can help with his homework."

"Aw, my adorable little shit." I laughed and blew raspberries on her cheeks. This from the girl who hadn't reached the age where she got any homework herself. But God, she was excited to become a big sister. Even if it was to a boy.

The three of us headed up to the house, and Ellis and I decided to be quiet about our poorly kept secret until the surprise guest had left. At this point, it was a miracle no one suspected there was more going on between him and me. For fuck's sake, if Haley and Lyn argued over where the baby would live, it felt like Adeline would've picked up on that by now.

"Auntie Ade, Uncle Lincoln!" Haley shouted as we entered the estate. "I'm here!"

There was laughter coming from the kitchen.

The moment she was on her feet, Haley ripped off her jacket and shoes, then bolted into the kitchen where I heard Adeline was quick to greet her. Questions about what we'd done today and how Haley's weekend had been followed, but I tuned into the other voices. Was that Jameson I heard?

I arrived in the doorway approximately two seconds before Ellis did, long enough to confirm everyone was already seated, and yeah, Jameson was here.

We got through the rambunctious greetings, and Ellis leaned in and murmured, "That's Jameson, correct?" as I directed Haley to her seat next to Lyn. And I nodded once in response, okay with the whole thing, albeit unsure of whether or not he was.

To be honest, I didn't believe Jameson would mention anything.

I bumped fists with Madigan and gave Jameson's shoulder a squeeze. "Who are you hiding from by being here?"

More laughter erupted, and my eyebrows shot up. Lincoln, in particular, was having fun.

"Did I actually guess it right?" I asked incredulously.

"I'm not hiding," Jameson bitched.

Madigan snorted. "No, it's just a coincidence that his step-daughter is over at his house."

That was funny. Ellis had already sat down between Haley and Adeline, which left me with the only option of becoming the meat in a Madigan and Jameson sandwich.

"Don't worry, man." Lincoln clapped Jameson on the shoulder. "We've all been there."

"Excuse me?" Adeline raised a brow. "I may have been young, but I was by no means your daughter."

"I am!" Lyn raised her hand.

"Damn fucking right." Lincoln winked at her, then turned to

Adeline. "Can't you see I'm trying to offer the man some comfort? Lord, woman."

I tuned them all out for a few seconds while I got comfortable. There were a tad too many loud voices and too much gesturing. Pushing up the sleeves of my pullover, I eye-fucked the food instead and dug in. Trust Adeline to be the one who went overboard with food. I filled my plate with mac and cheese, a couple sliders, a few wings, and cheesy rolls with bacon.

Out of the corner of my eye, I caught Ellis helping Haley with her food, the two of them grinning and whispering about something. It was a sight that never got old.

A hand on my leg not only startled me but stole my attention, and I snapped my head sideways to see Jameson inching closer.

"Are you still single?" he asked under his breath.

I smirked, thankful the others were as loud as ever.

"I'm not, no," I chuckled and removed his hand. "Shit's that bad, huh?"

"Ah—sorry. Yeah, you can say that." He sighed and ran a hand through his hair. "I'm going to hell."

I grinned lazily and forked some mac and cheese into my mouth. "So enjoy the ride."

He scowled. "That ain't helping."

I laughed.

After lunch, we decided to take advantage of the weather. Coffee and pastries were brought up on the roof, and Lincoln and Ellis arranged the heaters and the canvas cover over the lounge area.

I was looking forward to sinking into one of those luxurious loveseats when Ellis asked for "a word, please."

"Why does that make me feel like I'm in trouble?" I Eskimoed Haley and tossed her into one of the seats. "Keep that one for Daddy and Uncle Ellis, okay?"

"Okay," she laughed.

On my way back inside, I winced when I heard Madigan ask, "Why's he calling dibs on Ellis?"

How were people *not* suspecting us?

Trailing after Ellis, I added up all the little things that'd changed, and I honestly couldn't comprehend how blind people could be. We were kinda obvious by now. We arrived together, left together, Ellis and Haley had grown a lot closer, we practically lived together—even as far as the others knew... The only thing missing was Haley chirping about Daddy making kissy faces with Uncle Ellis, something we'd started introducing her to be around, however PG we kept it. Or possibly that my spare room was turning into a nursery.

When Ellis reached the second floor, he veered right instead of left where the stairs continued down, and I followed him to the hallway where the "kids'" rooms were. *Are we heading to the bathroom?* Sadly not; Ellis stopped outside of Abel's room and pulled me in for a hard hug.

It wasn't the hot rendezvous I had in mind, but this always worked.

He backed me up against a wall, cupped the back of my neck, and kissed me deeply.

This definitely works.

"My first experience with jealousy was highly unpleasant." He spoke into the kiss and didn't allow me to speak until—shit, I sucked in a quick breath, and then he was back. His tongue invaded my mouth in sensual strokes, his body pressing firmly along mine, and he got deliciously handsy. "What did he say? Jameson got close."

I chuckled, all but breathless, only to groan as he left a trail of openmouthed kisses down my neck. "Fuck," I exhaled and exposed my neck some more. "I, uh—God, that feels good. He only asked if I was single. I said no. He backed off. He's a good guy—no one you need to worry about."

"Good. That's good." His mouth returned to mine, and to my disappointment, he slowed things down. I was ready for a quick getaway to the bathroom. "Do you know how terrifying it is to go from not giving a rat's ass to suddenly have so much to lose?"

Of course I knew. I kissed him back, and it was impossible to wipe the smile off my face. "I love you, Ellis."

"Right," he chuckled huskily. "I love you, too. I'll work on unclenching."

"You don't have to do that for my sake." Because there really was nothing hotter than having your man walk up to you and claim you. "Just wait 'til it's my turn to get insecure about all the models you have around you at work."

He shook his head, amused, and rested his forehead to mine. "You honestly seem to believe I have a catwalk outside of my office, as opposed to a standard cubicle area with too much noise."

I laughed under my breath and—

"You two got news to share?" The unmistakable drawl of Lincoln's voice was a complete mood killer.

With a wrinkle of my nose, I turned to the intruder and found both him and Madigan standing by the stairs.

Madigan *knew*. He didn't seem too surprised. Maybe 'cause he was there when I professed my undying crush for Ellis.

"Maybe," I replied slowly. "To be fair, I thought we were being obvious."

Ellis hadn't moved an inch, so at least he wasn't backing out, though his discomfort was evident. I moved my hand from his hip to his hand and gave his fingers a gentle squeeze that seemed to work a little. His shoulders looked less stiff.

"Not gonna lie, I've had questions for a while..." Lincoln cleared his throat and stepped a bit closer. "Haley called Ellis *hers*...because he and Kid live together now."

Ellis and I exchanged a brief look, and if he was half as happy about Haley's statement, we were good.

"I am sort of hers," Ellis murmured, shifting his gaze from me to Lincoln. "I suppose it's safe to say a lot happened while you were in France."

"No shit?" Lincoln gave us an incredulous look while Madigan snorted. "Okay, since I know both of you, I can assume this is serious. I fucking hope you wouldn't involve Haley for anything less. So..." He sighed and scratched his bicep, then started with Ellis. "If you hurt Kid, I'll hunt your ass down. There isn't anything he won't do for the people he loves, even if it ends up hurting him. We clear?"

I was taken aback by that, not to mention humbled.

"You have my word, Lincoln." Ellis took his cousin seriously.

"Good." Then Lincoln figured it was my turn. "And *you*, you better keep your drama queen on a leash. Ellis lives in his head and just got out of his marriage. Practice patience, yeah? He's a good man."

Now he was only cute.

I saluted him. "Copy that, Daddy-o."

He shot me a look, and then he was done. He muttered about the imminent reaction of Adeline on his way up the stairs again.

I scratched my nose.

"Right. Congrats, guys." Madigan walked forward and shook our hands. "Glad I was right. Be happy and all that."

"How *did* you know?" I had to ask, 'cause he wasn't around as much. My drunken declaration a few months ago couldn't be enough.

He shrugged. "I pick up on these things, I guess."

It hit me instantly *why*. If you didn't go looking for something, chances were you weren't gonna see certain things that were clear to others.

"Maybe I'm starting to do the same." I wasn't gonna say more on the topic, and he knew I was here if he needed anything. But, yeah, now when I thought about it... The tension, the avoiding one another after being so fucking close, the vague replies. Something was up between him and Abel.

Given their differences and rather huge age gap, I kinda-but-not-really ruled out anything of an intimate nature, but who knew.

He smiled stiffly and nodded with a dip of his chin, and that was that.

Madigan went up to the roof again, leaving Ellis and me alone, though we didn't linger. It was time to fess up to Adeline too, and then everything would be out in the open.

Haley was a comical sight. Her little form was sprawled out across a loveseat, and she owned it like a boss. She was the one who spotted us first.

"No one took the seat!"

I grinned and walked around the coffee table. "Good job, baby. High five." I held out my hand as I reached her, and she smacked it with her first. "That's a fist bump." With a grunt, I picked her up and nibbled on her stomach, which earned us all her lovely shrieks. "Whoa, you can shatter glass with those pipes."

Ellis and I took our seats, and Haley wanted to keep on sprawlin'. I got the lower end of her, her feet tempting me to—

wow, okay, shit, Ellis knew me well by now. His look told me I shouldn't tickle her feet.

"You're a shit-stirrer."

"Who, me?" I put on my innocent face.

"Yeah, all right, I can see it now." Lincoln was apparently watching us, a smirk tugging at his mouth.

Lyn climbed on up his lap and grabbed his face. "What can you see, Daddy?"

"*You.*" He smiled and poked her tummy.

"Case and Ellis have news," Madigan, the impatient prick, declared. Out of the four loveseats around the table, I kind of wanted his to magically appear in the pool right now.

We sure as shit had Adeline's attention now. She studied us expectantly and set down her coffee. "What news?"

"Ellis gave me his class ring," I said. "We're going steady." I grasped his hand to make a point, and we rested them on Haley's stomach. "See? Very steady."

Thing was, she didn't laugh. It meant there must've been *some* suspicion. Instead, she straightened in her seat and, funnily enough, looked to Ellis for proof. It was as if the jokester in the family couldn't be trusted.

Ellis cleared his throat into his hand. "Well, he kidnapped *me.*"

"What the—" I faced him so fast I thought my neck was gonna snap. "That's my line, you bastard. You kidnapped me."

His eyes danced with laughter, and he was having way too much fun for being a thief. It left me no choice. I had to twist his nipple.

"Are you *serious?*" He hissed through a chuckle and rubbed his sore spot. "Sometimes you're twelve, Casey."

"Sometimes, you're a thief—"

"Hey!" Adeline wanted us to focus on her. "How about you two stop the foreplay and tell me all the details? This is...holy crap. Are you actually together? Ellis, I didn't even know you were into men, too. How come I didn't know? Tell me everything, boys—right now."

"It's like she forgets you're older than her," I muttered under my breath to Ellis.

He was politer and far more accommodating than I was, meaning the end of our banter and the beginning of *all the details*.

"It's probably best you ask specific questions, baby," Lincoln told Ade. "Otherwise, they'll gloss over everything."

"You're not helping," I accused.

"I'm helping *me*," he argued. "If my wife doesn't get to know everything, I still gotta live with the crazy—ah, ah—" Adeline had a grasp of his neck hair, and Lincoln winced. "With the amazing, beautiful, brilliant mother of my children."

"Nice." Madigan smirked.

This was spinning out of control, and I felt the need to address the girls because someone had to be the responsible adult around here. "Remember, violence is bad."

"Good one, nipple-twister," Ade retorted. "Now. Speak. How did this start?"

Well, I was kidnapped...

EPILOGUE

"**H**on, we ditched you at the hotel for a reason. You need your sleep." I trapped the phone between my cheek and shoulder so I could adjust Theo in my arms. Sitting on a nice beach made it easier. I pulled up my legs a bit, and he made some weird baby noises as I laid him down along my thighs. I could kiss his tiny feet forever.

I'd bought the socks, obviously.

"I know..." Marilyn yawned in the background. "Are you sure he's okay?"

I smiled and tapped his nose gently. "We're fine. He's not crying." In fact, his blinks were getting heavier and heavier.

We could add the sound of the ocean as a way to put him down. Maybe we should spend more time on the water castle...

Boy, was he a fussy little monkey. From the minute we left the hospital, it felt like he screamed for three weeks straight. Then it got easier once he'd adjusted to the breast milk, though he still kept us up most nights.

"That's a miracle," Marilyn laughed softly. "Okay, I'll get some sleep. Wake me up when you're back at the hotel."

"Will do." I ended the call and pocketed my phone. "You are

one adorable little terror, though." Dipping down, I nuzzled his nose with mine and grinned when he sleepily grabbed my ear. "Okay, I think we need to have an important discussion," I told him. "You're eight weeks old. It's time to decide what you want to do with your life. And given the recent developments, I suggest race car driver."

Being in the car was the only other sure way to get him to sleep without much fuss. Poor Marilyn, she'd been near a meltdown a few weeks ago. She'd needed to leave the house and get some fresh air, but with Theo screaming at the top of his lungs, she dreaded taking him someplace public. However, the minute the engine rumbled to life, he was dead to the world.

So Marilyn kept driving.

Hours later, she'd called us all euphoric, albeit freaked out, 'cause she'd ended up in Oregon.

It was how we'd ended up in LA now, too. Everyone needed a quick break, it seemed, and I wanted to check in with Jesse. I was gonna report back to Lincoln later, and then we'd have a few days of chillin' before road-trippin' back home.

Theo suckled on his pacifier—some fancy type for colicky babies—and let his eyes fall close. He was so cute it almost hurt. I remembered thinking the same when Haley was a newborn.

Lifting my gaze, I spotted her and Ellis by the water as he lifted her up to sit on his shoulders. The sun was about to set, and the moment was too beautiful to not capture. I retrieved my phone again and snapped off a handful of photos.

I'd blog a photo tomorrow or something. While a big portion of my single followers had dumped me, a new demographic had found me. They loved it when I blogged funny stuff about parenthood, mishaps, and pictures of my family.

The topic of the post tomorrow would require some sensitivity, though. I'd tone down the humor and hopefully have a sweet story to share about Ellis telling my daughter she could call him Dad or Daddy, too.

Our daughter.

Our son.

I tugged down Theo's cap a little. "I love you, baby." I pressed a gentle kiss to his forehead, and he stirred, which made me go rigid. "Oh fuck, forgive me—don't wake up, please. I don't know what I was thinking—" *Shut up!*

I shut my mouth.

He didn't wake up.

Phew.

A while later, Ellis and Haley returned, and I was quick to hold a finger over my mouth.

Haley nodded in understanding and snuck closer until she was behind me and could hug my neck.

"Let me look at you." I tried to face her, a bit nervous, and she poked her head forward. "You okay?"

She nodded again and appeared oddly shy. Then she whispered in my ear. "I have two daddies now."

"You do?" The relief hit me squarely in the chest. *Don't get mushy.* "That's so awesome."

She grinned.

Ellis sat down next to me and kissed my shoulder, his gaze landing on Theo.

"Are *you* okay?" I asked him quietly.

He was on the same train. They were silent nodders.

"Very," he managed after a while.

It dawned on me a minute too late that it could've been an emotional roller coaster of a conversation to go through.

I decided not to ask. It was between them. It only made me happy to see them strengthen their own relationship.

"Guys, we have a very difficult decision to make." I kept my voice down, because this was serious business. "We need to figure out how to get Theo to the car without waking him. Who's gonna—"

"Not it," Ellis and Haley said at the same time.

My head went from side to side, and I stared at them in disbelief. "When did I become the grown-up in our family?"

"I'm joking," Ellis chuckled. "I'll take him on one condition. Have dinner with me tomorrow night."

That answer was simple, although I didn't understand why Haley suddenly giggled behind her hand and looked all secretive. She exchanged a glance with Ellis, to which she nodded and mimicked me from earlier by pressing a finger to her mouth. She was going to keep a secret.

"What the crap was that?" I asked. "Are you conspiring against me?"

"Yeah," Haley giggled. Having no clue what the word meant.

"Never you mind, sunshine." Ellis gently took Theo into his arms, and the sweetheart didn't even move. "Dinner tomorrow, you and me. Deal?"

Well, yeah, sure. It was just dinner...

MORE FROM CARA DEE

In Camassia Cove, everyone has a story to share

Lincoln & Adeline
Abel & Madigan
Jesse
Adrian
Jameson

Though each Camassia Cove novel is a standalone within the series, the characters tend to make appearances in other titles. Cara freely admits she's addicted to revisiting the men and women who yammer in her head. If you enjoyed *Uncomplicated Choices*, you might like the following.

Path of Destruction
Home
Out

Check out Cara Dee's entire collection at www.ca-radeewrites.com, and don't forget to sign up for her newsletter so you don't miss any new releases, updates on book signings, giveaways, and much more.

ABOUT CARA

I'm often stoically silent or, if the topic interests me, a chronic rambler. In other words, I can discuss writing forever and ever. Fiction, in particular. The love story—while a huge draw and constantly present—is secondary for me, because there's so much more to writing romance fiction than just making two (or more) people fall in love and have hot sex. There's a world to build, characters to develop, interests to create, and a topic or two to research thoroughly. Every book is a challenge for me, an opportunity to learn something new, and a puzzle to piece together. I want my characters to come to life, and the only way I know to do that is to give them substance—passions, history, goals, quirks, and strong opinions—and to let them evolve. Additionally, I want my men and women to be relatable. That means allowing room for everyday problems and, for lack of a better word, flaws. My characters will never be perfect.

Wait...this was supposed to be about me, not my writing.

I'm a writey person who loves to write. Always wanderlusting, twitterpating, kinking, and geeking. There's time for hockey and cupcakes, too. But mostly, I just love to write.

~CARA.

CPSIA information can be obtained
at www.ICGtesting.com
Printed in the USA
LVOW13s0241120818
586683LV00029B/872/P

9 781548 715199